SIREN
QUEEN

SIREN
QUEEN

NGHI VO

A TOM DOHERTY ASSOCIATES BOOK

NEW YORK

SIREN QUEEN

Edited by Ruoxi Chen

A Tordotcom Book
Published by Tom Doherty Associates
120 Broadway
New York, NY 10271

www.tor.com

Tor® is a registered trademark of Macmillan Publishing Group, LLC.

Library of Congress Cataloging-in-Publication Data

Names: Vo, Nghi, author.
Title: Siren queen / Nghi Vo.
Description: First edition. | New York : Tordotcom, 2022. |
"A Tom Doherty Associates book."
Identifiers: LCCN 2022000503 (print) | LCCN 2022000504 (ebook) |
ISBN 9781250788832 (hardcover) | ISBN 9781250788856 (ebook)
Subjects: LCGFT: Novels.
Classification: LCC PS3622.O23 S57 2022 (print) |
LCC PS3622.O23 (ebook) | DDC 813/.6—dc23/eng/20220107
LC record available at https://lccn.loc.gov/2022000503
LC ebook record available at https://lccn.loc.gov/2022000504

Our books may be purchased in bulk for promotional,
educational, or business use. Please contact your local bookseller or
the Macmillan Corporate and Premium Sales Department
at 1-800-221-7945, extension 5442, or by email at
MacmillanSpecialMarkets@macmillan.com.

First Edition: 2022

Printed in the United States of America

0 9 8 7 6 5 4 3 2 1

for Grace

ACT
ONE

❧

Wolfe Studios released a tarot deck's worth of stories about me over the years. One of the very first still has legs in the archivist's halls, or at least people tell me they see it there, scuttling between the yellowing stacks of tabloids and the ancient silver film that has been enchanted not to burn.

In that first story, I'm a leggy fourteen, sitting on the curb in front of my father's laundry on Hungarian Hill. I'm wearing waxy white flowers in my hair, and the legendary Harry Long himself, coming to pick up a suit for his cousin's wedding, pauses to admire me.

"Hola, China doll," he says, a bright red apple in his hand. "Do you want to be a movie star?"

"Oh sir," I'm meant to have replied, "I do not know what a movie star is, but would you give me that apple? I am so very hungry."

Harry Long, who made a sacrifice of himself to himself during the Santa Ana fires when I turned twenty-one, laughed and laughed, promising me a boatload of apples if I would come to the studio to audition for Oberlin Wolfe himself.

That's bullshit, of course.

What halfway pretty girl didn't know what the movies were? I knew the names of the summer queens and the harvest kings as well as I knew the words "chink" and "monkey face," hurled at me and my little sister as we walked hand in hand to the Chinese school two miles from our house. I knew them as well as I knew the lines in my mother's face, deeper every year, and the warring heats of the Los Angeles summer and the steam of the pressing room.

The year I was seven, my father returned from Guangzhou to stay with us in America, and they built the nickelodeon between our laundry and the Chinese school. The arcade was far better than any old apple, and from the first, I was possessed, poisoned to the core by ambition and desire. The nickelodeon took over a space that had once sold coffins, terrible luck whether you were Chinese, Mexican, or German, but the moment they opened their doors and lit up the orangey-pink neon sign overhead, COMIQUE in the cursive I was having such trouble with, they were a modest success.

Luli and I were walking home one hot day, and we would have kept walking if the tall woman lounging in her ticket booth hadn't tipped an extravagant wink at me. Her skin was a rich black, and her hair was piled up on her head in knots so intricate it hurt my eyes. It wasn't until we got a little closer that I could see her eyes gleamed with the same orangey-pink of the sign overhead, and even then, I might have decided it was too late.

"We're showing *Romeo and Juliet* today," she said with a wide smile. "If you hurry, you can still get seats."

"I don't have anything to pay with," I muttered, ashamed to even be caught wanting, but the woman only smiled wider.

"Well, it's a nickel if you're ordinary, but you girls aren't, are you?"

Up until that very moment, Luli and I would have given absolutely anything to be ordinary, to live in one of the pastel boxes off of Hungarian Hill, to have curly blond or brown hair instead of straight black, and to have pop eyes instead of ones that looked like slits carved into the smooth skin of a melon.

The way the beautiful Black woman spoke, however, I started

to wonder. If I couldn't be ordinary, maybe I could be something better instead.

Maybe I could get into the nickelodeon.

Luli tugged at my hand fretfully, but I squeezed tighter, comforting and bullying at once.

"We're not ordinary at all," I declared. "And we don't have any nickels."

The woman touched a neatly manicured nail to her full lower lip, and then she smiled.

"An inch of your hair," she said at last. "Just one inch for two of you."

"Sissy, let's go home," my sister begged in Cantonese, but I scowled at her and she subsided.

"Just one inch," I said, as if I had any control over it. "And why do you want it, anyway?"

She helped me climb onto the spinning chrome stool with its red vinyl cushion; I remember the way the heat stuck it to my thighs where my thin dress rode up. I was already tall for my age. She swept a neat white cape around me, and as she snipped at my waist-length hair with a flashing pair of shears, she explained.

"An inch of hair is two months of your life," she said. "Give or take. An inch . . . that's your father coming home, your mother making chicken and sausage stew, skinning your knee running from the rough boys . . ."

It made sense, or at least I didn't want her to think that I didn't understand. She wrapped an inch of my hair into a little packet of silk, tucking it into the antique cash register, and then she handed my sister and me two grubby olive-green tickets. I still have my ticket in a small box with some other mementos, next to a smooth lock of butter-gold hair and a withered white flower with a rust-red center. My sweat made the cheap ink go blurry, but you can still see the COMIQUE stamp as well as its sigil, the sign of the wheel of fortune.

The nickelodeon was full of muttering patrons, the darkness waiting and full of potential. We were small enough that no one cared if we squeezed onto the edges of the front-row seats, and in a moment, the flicker started.

It was magic. In every world, it is a kind of magic.

Silver light painted words on the flat, dark screen in front of us, and I didn't have to read for Luli because the immigrants around us were sounding out the words quietly.

It was *Romeo and Juliet* as performed by Josephine Beaufort and George Crenshaw, two of the last silent greats. She looked like a child compared to the man who had loved the Great Lady of Anaheim, but it didn't matter, not when she filled up the screen with her aching black eyes, when his lip trembled with passion for the girl of a rival family.

Their story was splattered over the screen in pure silver and gouts of black blood. First Romeo's friend was killed, and then Juliet's cousin, and then Romeo himself, taking a poison draught that left him elegantly sprawled at the foot of her glass coffin.

When Juliet came out, she gasped silently with horror at her fallen lover, reaching for his empty vial of poison. She tried to tongue the last bit out, but when no drop remained, she reached for his dagger.

It wasn't Juliet any longer, but instead it was Josephine Beaufort, who was born Frances Steinmetz in Milwaukee, Wisconsin. She might have been born to a janitor and a seamstress, but in that moment, she was Josephine Beaufort, bastard daughter of an Austrian count and a French opera singer, just as much as she was Juliet Capulet.

The entire nickelodeon held its breath as her thin arms tensed, the point of the dagger pressed not to her chest where a rib or her sternum might deflect it, but against the softest part of her throat.

Her mouth opened, and a dark runnel of blood streamed down her unmarked white throat. She paused, long enough to build empires, long enough for a dead lover to marvelously revive. Then her arms tensed, her fingers tightened, and the dagger disappeared into her flesh, all that white destroyed with a river of black blood. It covered her breast and her white lace gown, speckling her round cheeks and marring her dulling eyes.

She slumped over the body of George Crenshaw and the camera pulled back, back, back, showing us the spread of black blood over the chapel floor before finally going dark itself.

My sister set up a wail that was lost in the chatter of the other patrons.

"She died, the lady died," Luli sobbed.

I took her hand, squeezing it like I did when I was trying to nerve us both up for another day beyond the safety of our bedroom, but my mind was a thousand miles away.

"No, she didn't," I said with absolute certainty.

You might say my family is in the business of immortality.

My father came from a long line of apothecaries and sorcerers. There were no imperial appointments, nothing as grand as a jade seal or a French house in Beijing, but they did well for themselves, ensuring a kind of small immortality for magistrates and county governors.

Even after he came to the United States, he kept with him a tortoiseshell cabinet that was second in reverence only to the family altar. It gleamed black and calico with thirty small drawers on the front and at least fifteen secret ones hidden throughout. It contained a continent's wealth of dinosaur bones, mercury captive in small vials, powders and tinctures of all kinds.

Once in a while, an old man would come from Chinatown, bent and with all of his weight carried by the two hands clasped at the small of his back. There would be a hurried conversation with my father in the alley in back, which we shared with a Polish tailor.

These old men sat stoically on the rickety wooden chair we kept in the back while my father reached for his cabinet. He would grind and pour, slice and drown, and at the end, there would be a little green paper packet of immortality for the old men, cunningly folded to be tucked into a sleeve or a jacket.

My father spoke often of our ancestor Wu Li Huan, who had given the governor of Wu eight hundred years.

"Not a speck of gray in his hair, not a tremor in his writing hand," my father said.

The old men came for my father's potion two times, three or even four, but they never came after that. My father was no Wu Li Huan, and instead of centuries, he sold months and weeks.

My mother was the second generation to be born to the golden mountain, her English perfect, her Cantonese stilted. Her people hadn't even hoped to serve regional officials while they were in Guangzhou, which my father called home and she never did.

Her immortality, what tiny scraps of it she could claim, was in the trains that raced from coast to coast. Her father worked on the Chinese crews that broke ground for the iron tracks, sometimes only six inches a day through the frozen mountains. She told us he was an enormous man, bearded and broad with a face that was turned red by the cold of Montana.

He bellowed and bullied and coaxed so well that he sent money home, and in return was sent the ambitious village beauty.

To everyone's surprise, they loved each other and would have kept going on together forever if a premature blast had not dropped a mountain on his head, his and his crewmen's.

Forty men, and by then the exclusion acts had barred the way, so she was the only widow.

With her little daughter in tow, she went to live in Los Angeles where there were other Chinese, but she had had enough. When my mother could take a job at the Grandee Hotel at fourteen, her mother left for China, ready to be home.

Sometimes, when the wind blew just the right way, we could hear the trains whistling to each other from the yards, shrill cries of *I am here*, and *do not stop me*. When my mother heard them, her hair blackened slightly from ash to soot and the lines on her face grew just a little less deep.

Like we understood to make wide circles around the drunks on the streets and how calico cats were the luckiest of all, we understood immortality as a thing for men. Men lived forever in their bodies, in their statues, in the words they guarded jealously and the countries they would never let you claim. The immortality of women was a sideways thing, haphazard and contained in footnotes, as muses or silent helpers.

"But things are different here," my mother always said.

She had never set foot in China, would pass all her life on American soil, but she knew how different things could be. She clung to that, and so did we.

|||

I ran back to the Comique as often as I could. When my mother gave me a nickel for my lunch, I would go hungry, feeding myself on dreams in black and silver, and then much, much later, miraculously and magnificently, in color. I ran errands for the neighbors when I could get away from the laundry, and when it had been too long since I had last sat on the painfully hard pine benches, I sold another inch of my hair.

The movies on the marquee changed every week, but the ticket taker, gorgeous, smiling, and sly, never did at all. I grew like a weed, but she remained a fixed twenty, which she told me once was just the perfect age for her.

"What about being twenty-five or thirty?" I asked once, while she clipped my hair. There were probably ages beyond that, but at the age of ten, I couldn't quite imagine it.

"Fine for some people, but not right for me. Forever's a long time, you know, and it's no good if you can't have it like you like best."

What I liked best was the movies, and for the day the actors opened their mouths and spoke, I gave her a shade of darkness off of my eyes. It was worth it to hear the first tinny voices spilling to the enraptured crowd. It was a revolution, new stars in and old stars out, but in a year, we took it for granted. Movies were a cheap magic, after all, never meant to be beyond our grasp.

I started pinning my hair up to hide how short it was getting, and my father and mother, exhausted by the steam and the weight of so much silk and wool and rayon and polyester on top of us, never even noticed.

Luli noticed. She went with me sometimes into the Comique, wrinkling her nose as if she had smelled something bad, holding her breath as if the vapors would somehow contaminate her.

She liked some of it. She liked the romances, the ones that ended happily with a kiss. There was even a Chinese actress, Su Tong Lin. She always played the daughter of a white man with a painted yellow face, and she always fell in love with a handsome chisel-faced hero who loved another. Luli loved Su Tong Lin, and I think I did too, but I couldn't love her without a twisting in my stomach of mingled embarrassment and confused anger. I went home angry every time she threw herself into the ocean, stabbed herself, threw herself in front of a firing gun for her unworthy love.

It was different from Josephine Beaufort's turn as Juliet, as different as wearing wet silk is from dry. It was Juliet that earned Josephine Beaufort her star, set up high in the Los Angeles firmament. The darkness of the Los Angeles night receded year by year from a city fed on electric lights, but no matter how orange the sky paled, those stars never dimmed. You can still see hers up there, enshrined for her Juliet, her Madame Bovary, and her taste in fast men and even faster cars.

I wasn't thinking of Josephine Beaufort or stars or immortality the day I accidentally wandered into fairyland. One moment I was crossing the invisible border that separates Hungarian Hill and Baker Road, and the next, it was as if the very air turned sharp and chemical. I dodged around a group of people who were standing stock-still on the sidewalk, wondering as I did what was going on, and the next I was nearly rushed off my feet by a man carrying an enormous box over his shoulder.

"Outta the way, asshole," he growled, not stopping to look.

I was twelve, and my startled eyes took it all in at once, the tangle of cords that connected the cameras to their generators, the shades that blocked out the harsh sun, and the lights that gave them a new one. Everyone rushed around so quickly that I thought for certain that there would be some terrible crash, but instead it was as if all of them, cameramen, grips, script girls, and costumers, were on rails. They ruled over their own thin threads, weaving in and out to create a setting fit for . . . Maya Vos Santé was what they called an exotic beauty, not quite white but not dark enough to frighten an easily spooked investor. There were rumors of rituals performed in the basements of Everest Studios, peeling away her Mexican features, slivers of her soul and the lightning that danced at her fingertips, leaving behind a face they could call Spanish alone. Rumor had it she held a knife to John Everest's balls until he signed off on passing her contract to Wolfe. She was so powerful, just beginning to understand how to wield her new glamour, and they would never have let her go otherwise.

She has no star, so you will have to settle for what I saw that late afternoon in 1932.

She was born short but lofted herself high in perilous heels, and her dark hair, piled with artful abandon on her head, made her taller still. She was all hearts: heart-shaped face, pouting lips, round breasts pushed high, and round hips pushed low.

The red dress she wore—which ironically became something of an immortal thing itself after Jane Carter wore it in *High Over the Chasm*—gave her eyes a peculiar cold maroon cast, and when she saw me, they narrowed thoughtfully.

"Hey, Jacko, is this the kid you wanted?"

A big man with small, pale eyes, a toothpick clenched in his teeth, came to look at me. He dressed as rough as any of the men laying wire or manning the cameras, but through all of the chaos, he was the only one who moved slowly, at his own pace.

"The studio never sent one of the kiddies over," he said with a shrug. "Think they're all working on that duster over in Agua Dulce, that big thing with Selwyn and Ramone. *Orphan Train* or whatever."

Maya made a face, which did not make it less beautiful. She pointed a red nail at me.

"Well, she'll do fine, won't she?"

Jacko looked dubious, and she turned to me. Her eyes weren't cold at all, they were melting chocolate, and she smiled with the weight of a blessing falling over my shoulders.

"Won't you, baby?"

"I will," I said instantly. "What should I do?"

"A real trouper, huh?" said Jacko with a laugh. "All right, we'll give it a try. What you're wearing will be good enough, but stash your shoes and socks somewhere."

The moment she got her way, Maya lost interest in me. An assistant came forward to straighten out the ruffle at the hem of her red dress, kneeling down like a supplicant, and I was left sitting on the curb and carefully untying my shoes and removing my stocks, trying not to stub my feet on the scattered pebbles when I stood up. A nicely dressed woman took pity on me.

"Here, honey," she said. "We'll wrap them with paper and put them right here so that you can get them later, all right?"

I'm glad she thought of it. My parents would have skinned me if I came home without my shoes, but I never gave it a second thought.

My dress, which Jacko had declared good enough, was a carefully mended calico that hung limp in the heat. It had been made for an adult woman, and though my mother had sewn in the curves, it still hung on me with an irregular kind of frump.

Orders must have been shouted from somewhere, because an

assistant director came up to me, thin as a whip, harried and distracted.

"All right, you start here. When Mrs. Vos Santé says, 'In all my born days, I never saw the likes of you, Richard,' you run around the corner. Go up to her and beg for change, all right?"

A shiver of shame went through me at his words. I knew what beggars were, people with desperate eyes and clutching hands, trying to grab for whatever extra bit of life they could squeeze out of the day. I looked down at my dress in confusion, because I couldn't understand what made it a beggar's dress, and I could see my bare and dusty feet underneath, stepping on each other shyly now.

The assistant director didn't wait to see if I understood. Instead he left me on my mark and ran to attend to other matters. Time slowed for a moment, solid like it can get when prep pulls out like taffy.

Then I heard the sharp, dry clack of the clapboard, rendering all else silent, and Jacko called out the magic word.

"Action!"

From my spot on the corner, everything seemed dim even as I strained my ears to hear Maya Vos Santé's words. She was talking with a man about cruelty and how a woman could expect to find nothing but in a world ruled by men.

The man said something utterly forgettable even in my memory, and Maya Vos Santé laughed. The sound was like drops of cold water running down my spine.

"In all my born days, I never saw the likes of you, Richard."

My cue, though I didn't even know to call it that yet.

I ran around the corner, stubbing my heel badly on a rock, but I didn't even stumble.

The moment I stepped into the camera's eye, I had entered some kind of magical circle. The air was thicker and somehow clearer, the colors more vibrant than they had been before. I had to stop myself from looking down at my hands, certain that they would be glowing against the umber light.

I stuttered to a stop in front of Maya and the actor. To me, they were both dressed like royalty. My mouth went utterly dry, and there were no words for them. *Beg*, the assistant director had said, but I didn't know how to do that.

I swallowed hard. The click in my throat was so loud that it should have been audible on the reel. The actor just frowned, but Maya was looking at me with concern and warmth, her face tilted to one side like a gentle cat's, so perfect I could have died.

"Please," I managed, my cupped hand coming up slowly.

"Oh, sweetheart," said Maya sadly. I thought I had ruined it all, that she was disappointed, and I would be sent away from this magical world. My eyes filled with tears, but then Maya was digging in her enormous black handbag.

"Here, baby," she said, crouching down to see me almost eye to eye. She pretended to tuck something into my palm, and then she cupped the back of my head with her hand, pulling me forward and pressing a cool kiss to my brow.

"I think you're the special one, Marie," said the actor, and Jacko bawled cut.

The air snapped back to normal, so hard that I could barely breathe. For a brief moment, I could truly see, and now someone had come along and slid transparent snake scales over my eyes. Everything looked so shoddy and so dirty that I could have cried.

I heard some muttering from Jacko and the man with the camera, and he looked up, nodding.

"We got it! Set up for scene fifteen."

Scene fifteen certainly didn't need me. Maya forgot about me the moment the scene was over, and I was bumped and jostled away from the center of cameras and lights, washing up finally next to the nicely dressed woman who had helped me with my shoes before. I noticed that she wore a silver cuff around her thin wrist, lovely, but so narrow that it could not be removed easily. The word WOLFE was emblazoned on it, and she caught me looking at her curiously.

"I'm under contract at Wolfe," she said with pride. "Seven years. It means that I can't take jobs with any of the other big three, and that they'll have work for me the whole time. I'm not in scene fifteen, but I'm in scenes seventeen and eighteen, which are being shot right after."

I was duly impressed. At home, the worst thing you could be was without work, and seven years of standing around in nice clothes seemed far better than pushing a blazing-hot iron that seemed to weigh as much as my little sister over an endless line of white shirts.

"What's your name?" I asked shyly, and her gaze turned wistful. She had remarkable eyes, one blue and one brown, giving her a cheerful, puppyish look.

"They haven't given me one yet," she responded.

I sat with her for the next hour as they shot scene fifteen, more complicated than the one I had been in and requiring more takes. That year, Wolfe put out close to three hundred pictures. Speed was key, and even if Jacko was no genius the likes of Dunholme or Lankin, he got the pictures through on time and under budget, better than artistry any day.

My new friend had been whisked away for a final tug at her wardrobe when my mother came looking for me. I saw her standing as confused as I must have been amid the lights and wires, the people all on their own tracks and us without. She looked frightened, slightly disgusted, and confused, and when she saw me, she stalked over, taking my hand.

"Where have you been? We thought you would be back . . ."

"Oh, hey, you the kid's mom?"

Jacko came up behind her like a bear, making my mother wheel around in shock. He looked rough, like a man who wouldn't bother with clean clothes from the good laundry, no one who came into our place.

He reached into his wallet and peeled out a few bills, thrusting them at my mother. My mother didn't move to take the money from him, and he scowled.

"English? You speak English? Christ . . ."

"I do," she said finally, her words clipped. "I will."

She took the money, even if she had no idea what it was for, and she never took her eyes off of him. If he was discomforted by her gaze, he never showed it.

"Good, good," Jacko said, crunching on his toothpick. He glanced down at me speculatively.

"She's cute. I'm shooting down here again in two weeks, the fourteenth. If you bring her back, she can do that too."

My mother only stared, and with a sigh, Jacko turned to me.

"I heard you, your English is great, ain't it?"

"Yes, sir," I said, proud and oddly ashamed at once. My mother's was just as good.

"Good. Well, you stick around, you do as you're told, and maybe someday, well, who knows, right? Could be you up there smooching the sheikhs, yeah?"

Something else called for his attention, and my mother was finally allowed to tug me away.

She opened her fist a block away to reveal two ten-dollar bills. It could be used to patch any number of holes in the laundry, and at the height of the Depression, there were many of those.

"What did you do?" she asked, stunned, and I looked down, suddenly ashamed.

I stammered out an explanation, too anxious and overexcited to lie, and her face turned stony. I could see pride warring with the money in her hand. To my mother, there were things we did and things we did not do. What I had done on the movie set ranged back and forth over that line, pacing restlessly.

To my surprise, instead of scolding me or pinching me, she pulled me into an alley. I could smell the starch and lye of the laundry on her, a clean but oppressive scent. The trains had run the night before, and her hair, hanging over her shoulder in a braid, looked like a strip torn out of the world.

"All right," she said. The money had disappeared into one of the secret pockets sewn into her shirt. "You don't have to go back if you don't want to."

"I want to," I said instantly, and she frowned.

Still, she gave me her hand to hold all the way back to the laundry, where I helped my sister fold clothes and wrap them up in crinkling paper. I don't know what she told my father, if anything. The money wasn't mine to keep, it wasn't real in any way that mattered to me. There were more important things.

That night, as I stripped down for a shared bath with my sister, Luli looked at me with some consternation.

"What's that on your forehead?"

I pulled down my father's little round shaving mirror to look. There was the faint silvery imprint of a kiss where Maya Vos Santé had kissed me. She hadn't left a trace of rouge on my skin, but she had left something else instead.

I couldn't scrub it away, and despite my sister's uneasy look, I didn't really want to. Fringes were in fashion, and the kiss was covered readily enough. It was not quite a scar, not quite a brand, but more telling than either.

IV

Even with it all, the money, the crackling atmosphere of the set, the kiss Maya Vos Santé had given me, I might never have longed for a star of my own and a place high in the Los Angeles sky. I don't know what else might have happened to me; I was too young when it all began, and I hadn't shown the twists and hooks that would have drawn other fates to me.

("Oh, you were always meant to be in movies," Jane said. "One way or another, you would have found your way in, no matter what was standing in your way."

"Is that a compliment?" I asked her.

"It's better than a compliment, it's the truth.")

Three weeks after shooting *Jackson's Corner*, my mother swore and thrust a crisp paper package into my arms.

"Hurry. The lady in the blue dress. She forgot this one. Run after her, or she'll think we lost it."

It happened often enough that I didn't think much of it, instead dashing out with the package under my arm. I glimpsed a lady in blue disappearing around the corner, and I ran after her, weaving my way through the crowd and keeping the package close to my body.

The woman was moving fast, but I knew she was the right one

because she had a paper bag printed with our logo—the character for "lucky"—on her arm. She was barely taller than I was, but she walked with the quick, precise steps of a regimental soldier, glancing neither right nor left.

My mother hadn't told me her name, so I couldn't call out to her. I didn't catch up with her until she paused in front of a small café on Carver Street. Her look of wariness dissolved when she realized that I wasn't a beggar, and she beamed when I handed her my package.

"Oh! This must be my cashmere. How silly of me to forget it. And, poor thing, you ran all this way to give it to me. Wait just a moment, let me give you a little something for your trouble."

I was wondering if she would give me enough to go to the Comique again, but then Michel de Winter appeared.

Michel de Winter was a relic from another time, a silent actor who came from the French stage. Just a few years ago, I had seen him haunting the smoky, shadowed streets of Bucharest, following a mysterious woman who dropped white flowers in her wake. It turned out in the end that he had been chasing Death's consort, and he had died, face twisted with agony, only to be resurrected in front of me now in a gray suit and green silk tie, the white strip of hair that had shown so bright in the old films gleaming in the afternoon light.

"You are late," he whispered, because the silent films had finally consumed his voice, leaving him only a shred to use.

"Darling, I am sorry, but look, I am here now, aren't I?"

When she spoke to me, the woman had had an easy way about her, pleasant but entirely unremarkable. Now there was a grandness to her voice, the sound of it bell-like, and people around us turned their heads, curious and unsure why they were curious.

I stared, tip forgotten as I realized that I was looking at Clarissa Montgomery, who just a few months ago had lit up the screen in *The House on Faust Street*. I felt as if the very breath had been pressed from my lungs, because she changed everything.

One moment, life was what it was, dull, busy, and common. The next . . . she had changed it. She wore her glamour like a stole tossed around her shoulders, and she cast it like a net over everyone who had seen her.

When I looked at Michel de Winter, old god that he was, I could see the worship in his eyes, a kind of helpless love that didn't even want to help itself. To see her was to love her, and a wanting rose up in me like an ache. I wanted someone to look at me like that; I wanted to change the world simply because I could.

Clarissa Montgomery forgot all about my tip, sliding her cashmere into the bag as she went to join Michel de Winter. They switched to his native French, their conversation fading quickly into the noise of the afternoon as they walked on.

I had seen Maya Vos Santé on set, that power sharpened to devastating purpose, but I had never seen it used in the real world. Simply by being herself, Clarissa Montgomery changed the afternoon from common to something I would never forget. From the way some of the people on the street were still blinking, whispering among themselves *Was that Clarissa Montgomery?* I could see that they wouldn't forget it either.

When my parents looked at me, they saw another mouth to feed, another pair of hands around the laundry. When people on the streets saw me, they saw a little foreigner, a doll to be played with and cooed over or pushed away from something I had no right to, which, judging by some people, was everything. Jacko saw an easy way to appease Maya Vos Santé, and Maya Vos Santé saw a prop that she wanted and had been denied.

I wanted what Clarissa Montgomery had, the ability to take those looks, to bend them and to make them hers, to make the moment hers, to make the whole world hers if she wanted. I wanted that, and that want was the core of everything that came after.

By the time *Jackson's Corner* came out, I was something of a regular on Jacko's sets. He knew that I had a family, so he never tried to pull me into the pack of changelings the studio kept around for that sort of thing. I was no Baby Joy or Baby Gemma either; I was only able to do the kid parts for some six or seven months after *Jackson's Corner*. I started to grow, painfully and by inches, as tall as my mother by the next year.

After a picture or two, I started to figure out my way around. When I look back at that time, which seemed to last forever but now I know was barely more than an hour on a summer afternoon, I could slap myself for what I thought I knew. I thought I was wise for knowing not to cross the circle of the camera's eye, for knowing which crew members would smile at me and which would curse. I thought I was doing very well to know that while most of the people I met were real actors, some few were empty props who could not talk and could not move unless they were directed to do so. I brought my own lunch, never made trouble, and when I was hurt or tired, I only stood straighter and hoped that no one ever noticed.

I saw the thin and crying girls who haunted the edge of the set, looking not for the lead but for Jacko himself. I watched one morning, silent and unnoticed as a ghost, as Jacko took one girl aside and talked to her in stern and fatherly tones.

"Look, you ain't hurt. Not really. Not like some of these mooks would hurt you, right? Stop crying about it. You got a long life ahead of you. Stop crying. You're going to be fine."

He forced money into her hand, and she stumbled away like a dog that had been struck a glancing blow by a car. He looked after her anxiously until she was out of sight, and then, shaking his head, he returned to the set.

My sister and I went to the Comique to see *Jackson's Corner* when it came out. I would never have known what movie I had appeared in if I hadn't heard the name mentioned after my short scene.

It was bread and butter fare for the time. Maya Vos Santé was a woman with a past, looking to make amends, and the male lead turned out to be Raymond Reeves, forgettable but with a fairly admirable profile. The movie was like any I had seen, but suddenly I recognized the set change to Baker Street, which in this movie served for the streets of Hell's Kitchen.

My body jerked like a fish on a hook when I heard my cue again. The camera found my skinny form pelting around the corner barefoot, and I watched, face flushing red as I skidded to a halt.

"Please," came a childish, piping voice through the Comique's tinny speakers, and my arm by my side itched as its twin rose on the screen.

It was exactly what Jacko had needed it to be, drawing pathos and wistful sighs from an audience that was just as likely to spit on a beggar as give her money. More important, of course, was Maya Vos Santé herself, kneeling down to kiss my forehead.

In that moment and out of it, I felt the brush of something true there, something larger than life and far better. She was generous, she was pure, she was a woman with a past, but her heart was still kind enough to wrap around a skinny little beggar child. She was a benediction, and again, I felt strangely and mysteriously blessed.

None of Maya Vos Santé's films survived, of course. They were lost in the great fires that took so many of the kings and queens of Hollywood. There were some rumors about hers, that *Jackson's Corner, Dream of Wild Days, She Demands Her Way* and all the others were sacrificed to John Everest's revenge, long after she could do anything to stop him.

She disappeared before her films did, and there weren't even any rumors about it, none that I heard. Women disappear, and even if you are famous, it can happen without a sound, without a ripple. I have to assume that one night, when the stars were gleaming overhead, she met a devil on the road like so many of my friends did, and he offered her a spread of cards, flipping them between his pale fingers. Alcoholism, born-again reverence, madness, a quiet cottage, a noisy car wreck, a lonely house on the edge of the desert, a book she could use as a tomb, a single line etched in the boardwalk, they would have flickered by, and taking a deep breath, she would have closed her eyes and chosen.

V

When Jacko wanted me, he would call my mother or send over a runner if it was very last minute. I was at school less and less, ostensibly helping my parents at the laundry, but if the truth were told, I was waiting on the phone call that would, for a few glorious days, free me from the endless shirts and trousers of Hungarian Hill.

Once Jacko asked after my sister, but she was developing a horror of my other life. When my mother carefully brought up the idea of joining me for one of my days on set, Luli cried and cried, hiding in the closet with the door pulled behind her as she had not in years. By turns, she clung to me and hid from me as if she was unsure about what I was becoming. To be honest, I wasn't always sure either. There was a warmth and a weight deep inside me, something strange and new.

There was Su Tong Lin, of course, whose star you can still see gleaming softly and demurely near the meridian. I hear her star in Paris is brighter by far, and the one in Mumbai even more lovely. She grew up in the Chinese circuses, from which vaudeville was an easy jump and the silent movies even easier. She was born to the life, and though she might have mended a sleeve here or darned a sock there on the road, she certainly never pushed an iron in a room so hot she could have fainted.

My mother understood somewhat, because she would come with me to the set when she could, but day by day, my father watched me, puzzled and increasingly aggrieved. He came to see me on set exactly once, when I sold flowers to Genevieve Dumar. It was a good shoot, and I even got a couple of lines that Jacko made up for me on the spot. He had developed a kind of absent affection for me, passing me candy or the odd hair bow as a treat. That day he gave me lemon candy that tasted like sharp sunshine, and I held it in my cheek until it melted to memory. After the day was up, Jacko ruffled my hair and handed my mother another ten. My father stood behind my mother the whole shoot, face stone and shoulders straight, but I could see a storm brewing on his face every time Jacko came near me.

It didn't break until we got home. He struck me a glancing blow across my cheek, sending me reeling to the kitchen floor.

He shouted in Cantonese, and by then, it was nearly lost to me. I heard the words "disrespect" and "bitch" and "whore." He might have struck me again if my mother hadn't wrapped her strong arms around his chest and dragged him back.

I clapped my hands over my ears and shut my eyes as they fought. She shouted in her broken Cantonese, and his words were faster, snakes and lightning accusing her, accusing me of all kinds of evil.

I opened my eyes just in time to see him raise his fist to her, and without a flinch, she had a kitchen knife in her hand, up and pointed straight at his throat. Her hair was ashen gray that day, but my father's skin hung in soft folds around his neck and his arms were thin and ropy with sagged muscle. His powders lost their potency in the West, and now he was showing it.

My father instead turned around and stalked to their bedroom, slamming the door behind him. The sun came out, the air was thin enough to breathe again. The only sound was my sister's high wail as she hid under the kitchen table. My mother hesitated, leaving her there for a moment to come to me.

She turned my face side to side, and nodded with relief. No bruise, no bumps, that was good, because I needed to shoot again the next day.

I knew better than to ask why he had done what he had done. There was always the feeling like I was getting away with something when I ran down to where Jacko and the crew were shooting. That I would need to pay for it in one way or another made a kind of dull childhood sense to me. To my surprise, my mother tried to offer me an explanation anyway.

"Your father was humiliated," she explained, petting my sister's hair. Luli had come out sniffling, clinging to my mother and watching me with eyes that were strangely baleful in her young face.

"No one said anything to him," I protested, and she nodded.

"That's right. No one did. Back in Guangzhou, he was a big man, even if he was a second son. People asked after him, and no one would flatter and praise his daughter when he was standing right there, not even offering a word to the man who had raised her, made her everything she was."

I scowled at her words. I went to school haphazardly at best, but all my lessons featured white boys and girls making themselves, dragging themselves out of this ghetto or that coal mine, rising above. None of them looked like me. I couldn't see any well-dressed man being impressed with my industry and offering me my very own orange orchard to run, but the lesson remained.

My mother could see this rebellion in me, and she tapped me hard on the head, not quite a blow, but not a loving thing, either.

"Your father and I made you," she said sternly. "We feed you and care for you. We named you. That's not nothing."

Every time the gap between jobs got too long, I would think that it was over, that my brief career in the movies was done. Everything else would be the laundry, hot steam, filthy clothes, and my father glowering at me forever.

Things with my father continued to fester for a while. He had never had much to do with me before. With my sister, I was solidly part of my mother's domain, her problem, her responsibility. Now that he was truly seeing me for the first time, not another pair of weaker, more willful hands or an ungrateful mouth he had to feed, I could feel his attention on me like a scouring light. His regard was nerve-racking and predatory, even if he never struck me again.

I started to lose weight, and after I woke from a sound sleep to see his silhouette standing in the doorway in the dead of night, I stopped sleeping as well.

When I showed up for *Darcy's Sons*, I looked so terrible that Jacko paused over me, the toothpick working furiously in his mouth. I was certain he would send me home, braced to leave without a tear in my eye, but my heart was a stone in my chest. At last, he bent down so he was eye level with me.

"Hey, CK, stop looking so glum, okay? We'll get you fixed up."

He sent me to the makeup girls for the first time, telling them to do what they could to make me look good again. Their magic was an older one, and as the youngest prodded at the dark circles under my eyes, a calm man with a warm smile stirred a mixture of French chalk, almond oil, and carmine on his portable double boiler. The eldest, all black slacks and matador jacket, glared dubiously at the solid cakes of dark mascara she guarded in a chest not unlike my father's medicine cabinet.

I was a strange case, orange and ocher and tan when they worked with peaches and strawberries. Maya Vos Santé had the same problem, and she brought her own imp to set, a chattering thing of smoke and fire that had mascaras and lipsticks tinted by some mysterious witch from Palo Alto. After the war, Jane would have a shade called Incarnate created for me, a perfect true red without blue or orange in it for my lips under the lights. Incarnate became my signature color—properly ours, but in the books and on the screen, it was mine.

The makeup girls made me presentable enough for Jacko, but then I was delivered up to my mother at the end of the day with a face full of paint. She helped me scrub it off, and though I eventually grew used to it, that day I felt as if I had been basted for the roast.

My mother took action then. She rummaged in the lost laundry pile until she found a tattered gold silk scarf and four small buttons. As my sister and I watched, she sewed the silk into a pair of rough bags, stuffing them with scraps and a lock of hair, one for my sister and one for me. The bags were tied off five times apiece, one head, two arms, and two legs, and then she dressed them with scraps cut from my and Luli's old dresses. For Luli, my mother used one she had just outgrown, but for me she had to go digging for a dress that I had worn years ago.

I thought of the hair that I had given to the Comique. I had wondered off and on what they did with it, and now I had cause to be very nervous indeed.

My mother didn't have to do much after that. She left the dolls around the house, in Luli's chair while she was at school, in my bed when I was working later in the evening for Jacko. It was almost ridiculous how easy it was.

Soon enough my father was placid and easy, crooning over a pair of quiet dolls instead of growling over a pair of terrified girls. He stroked the Luli-doll's hair, he sat mine at the table and praised her for her dutifulness. Once I even saw him pick the dolls up and hug them as he had never hugged us.

I saw what he saw sometimes. Out of the corner of my eye, there was a perfect version of myself flitting around the corner, avoiding the rooms where I was because, apparently, she didn't like the real me either.

My mother's magic was a patchwork of the mountain lore her father had picked up in Colorado and half-remembered charms from her own mother. The doll versions of Luli and me never grew, and they never left the apartment, not even when my father finally died of a heart attack, the year I turned twenty-eight. My sister and I had come home for Lunar New Year, and my father simply stood up, hand over his heart like he was giving the pledge, and then collapsed gracefully to the ground. He was dead long before the ambulance arrived. As we followed the shrouded stretcher out, out of the corner of my eye, I saw two little doll-girls, hand in hand in the dim hallway, their faces solemn and their button eyes hard. As far as I know, they are there still, haunting the new condos that have taken over Hungarian Hill, haunting the new people with scents of starch and lye, not quite ghosts but no longer merely dolls.

VI

Of course I had a name. I still do. It's mine, and now I keep it in a carnelian box, hinged and clasped with gold, carved to look like a creamsicle egg. It's Chinese with an ugly American cognate. I take it out and look at it sometimes. It fits like something made for me, though the maker didn't quite know my measurements and guessed at the colors that might suit me.

Jacko called me the Chinese Kid, or CK when he was being whimsical. I thought it was affection or plain American disinterest, but a caterer explained it to me one hot June day.

"That man doesn't do anything by accident," he snorted. "He's making sure that you don't belong to the studio, not yet, not until he can get a good fee for bringing you in."

I must have looked confused, because he sighed and explained between setting out large trays of sandwiches.

"If he has a name, he's under contract to reveal it to the studio. Once he does that, he doesn't get to decide what pictures he has you in, you get lumped in with all the other little changelings that roam the lot."

The caterer was called away, but I was left frowning. My job, as much as I needed it to breathe, had been simple until then. I showed up, I did as I was told, and my mother received a few bills shoved in her hand at the end of the day. I was fourteen and had been in and out of Jacko's productions for two years by then. Though sometimes a month would go by without work, leaving me feeling a little like a fish gasping out of water, most of the time he wanted me every two or three weeks.

Nothing stretches like time when you're a child. I would resign myself to being a laundry drudge for the rest of my life, and then Jacko called.

"Hey, can we have CK for a couple days at the end of the week? Dress her in something Chinesey, all right?"

"CK, CK," my mother muttered, picking through the pile of lost clothes. "What an asshole."

Jacko still wasn't sure how much English my mother spoke. She used her words as sparingly as five-dollar bills when she was around him. Some part of it was a lifetime of keeping every advantage close to her chest, but I'm certain some of it was watching Jacko turn bright red as he had to halt his day to explain something to her.

I know it crossed her mind once or twice to see if she could hold me back for more money. I would have bitten and cursed and run away to the set, but that wasn't the only thing that held her back. The studios were a strange and treacherous place, and my mother lived where safety meant being beyond notice, out of reach, invisible and unknowable. That I got paid out of Jacko's own pocket kept me apart, and that satisfied her just fine.

I tried on all sorts of ridiculous names. Every child does. I crossed the names of my most attractive classmates—Betty-Joan, Ruby, Eleanor Jane—with street names and the names of politicians, creating less the names of famous actresses than ugly chimeras for the crew to laugh at.

None of the crew used their real names either. No one was a Francisco Jimenez or a Paul Chen. Instead, they were all Lefty, Biggs, Shakespeare, Gato, and Pashka, things you would call a kid or a pet of some kind.

Verde explained it to me one day while we split a sandwich.

"It's union rules," he said proudly. "When you're an apprentice, you use an egg name that some old lady in Burbank spits out. After you graduate to journeyman, like me, the other guys get together and give you your work name."

"So why are you called Verde?" I asked, curious, and he frowned.

"If you can't tell right away why someone has the work name they do, don't ask 'em," he told me.

"Oh, I'm sorry," I said, and I looked apologetic enough that he continued.

"It's for our own protection, see?" he said. "If the studios get ahold of our real names, if we walked in there without union protection, I mean, Santo Christo, who knows what they would do?" He shook his head, closing his hand around something in his pocket. I knew that it was a little iron icon of the Virgin Mary. There was iron in the cameras, the dollies, and the scaffolding, but only the techs carried iron like that.

For *Looks Like a Stranger*, I was meant to be sitting on a barrel, peeling an orange in the background as Irene Leonard slapped Lewis Herman across the face. The turquoise Chinese jacket that my mother made for me stretched tight over my shoulders, my breasts, and now even my hips, but it would hold for another few shoots, she thought. I had outgrown two others since I passed my sixteenth birthday, and past seventeen, it looked like I was going to outgrow a third.

I took my spot because the barrel was out of everyone's way, and I bounced the orange I was meant to be peeling in my hand.

I noticed with some amusement that Lewis Herman was watching the orange, or at least he was pretending to watch it. His eyes followed the fruit before flickering towards my breasts, jerking back when I bounced the orange a bit higher. I'd been fending off boys on Hungarian Hill since I was eleven. I certainly wasn't afraid of Lewis. I amused myself by tossing the orange from hand to hand, making his head swing back and forth.

I didn't see Irene Leonard come around the corner, dressed to kill in Schiaparelli and as steady on her heels as a panther is on her paws. I caught a glimpse of her white-and-black houndstooth jacket just as she caught me by the arm and dragged me off of the barrel.

"No!" she said to the world at large. "This isn't happening. Dewalt, where the hell are you?"

I pulled back out of her grasp, staring in confusion at Irene Leonard. She was another one who didn't really make it. She did *Looks Like a Stranger*, a handful of others, and I believe she's still hanging on somewhere in the orange groves. She was lucky enough to get a tart line and a close-up in Walter Busey's *Fires in Heaven*, and she can probably ride that forever if she's careful.

Once she had grabbed me off of the barrel, she turned her gaze around the assembled crew imperiously. I glanced at Lewis, but he must have thought that I was looking for help. He only looked at his feet, his hands shoved in his pockets in a way that ruined the lines of his suit.

Jacko moved at his own pace, almost wandering into the tense scene as if he happened upon it by accident. It seemed a miracle that he could shoot well over fifty movies a year when he never seemed to move much faster than a bison's wander, champing his toothpick amiably.

"What seems to be the problem, Irene?" he asked, and she pointed at me.

"Tell me why I'm doing this scene with your Chinese sexpot in the background. What kind of 'local color' is she supposed to convey, Dewalt? We're in fucking Los Angeles, not the goddamn docks in Singapore."

Jacko was unmoved by her appraisal, and I wish I could say the same. My face turned red with heat, and then I went cold. If I hadn't become an old pro at staying still to get the shot, I know I would have curled up to cover all the parts of me that the crew was now inspecting with interest.

Instead, I stood up straight, tilted my chin up like I was told so often to do, and stood my ground. Running away, I knew instinctively, meant that the circle would be broken and I would never return. I might be allowed to do so, but I'd be crawling back, echoes of this humiliation curving my spine, suiting me only for roles in service and, as Irene said, the goddamn docks in Singapore.

"I swear to God, Dewalt, do you want me to walk right off this set? I will, don't think I won't!"

Jacko's small blue eyes took her in, and then he looked at me. In the back of my mind, I realized he was weighing me against the star of the picture. I braced myself. I was not going to cry if they kicked me off because my breasts were outgrowing my jacket. I wasn't.

"All right, everyone, take five," he said, shrugging. "Irene, kid's out, now go have the makeup girls do up your eyes. They're running. CK, come on."

Irene threw a victorious glance around the set; she wasn't even looking at me. After all, I wasn't a rival to be vanquished. I was a poor background decision that she had gotten fixed.

I fell into step next to Jacko, who walked me around the set towards the rear street, picking up a wrapped sandwich for me on the way.

"Your mom waiting for you somewhere around here?"

I shook my head, watching him carefully. There were calculator keys clicking in his head, weighing one decision against another, one loss against another gain. I waited to see what his calculations would come to.

"You know, you're creepy when you just stare like that, CK."

"So?"

"Blood as cold as the Atlantic, you," Jacko said, shaking his head. "Su Tong Lin could melt steel, but that ain't you, is it?"

It didn't seem like it needed an answer, so I didn't give it one. I liked being cold as the Atlantic, somehow monstrous and untouchable.

"How old are you?"

I was so startled by the question, I told him the truth.

"I just turned seventeen last October."

Jacko actually winced at that.

"Shit. All right, we can work with that, I guess. Look, I need you to go home and stay there until after Halloween."

I looked around at the fair March day, disbelieving.

"What are you talking about?"

He suddenly loomed larger than I had ever seen him. He towered over me, and there on Allen Street behind the set, I realized how very alone we were.

"You run around here like butter don't melt in your mouth, but I know what you're after," he growled. "You want to be in movies? You want to make the big bucks, set your star above the horizon? You tell me no, and I'll know what your face looks like when it's lying."

I reared back, but he grasped me by the wrist.

"I picked you off the street like a shiny penny, and I won't say you can't be a star. You want to see your name up in lights? Do as I say. Don't ask why, keep your mouth shut, and I'll take you up there. I'll drive you up the hill to meet Oberlin Wolfe, and yeah, you'll get all of that. Just do what I say *now*."

I schooled my face to the stillness it took on when my father screamed at me. He must have thought he read acceptance there because he finally let me go. Jacko reached into his wallet and counted out a short stack of bills, enough for two weeks of work and paid to my own hand rather than my mother's.

"Good. And don't get any bright ideas of wandering up to the studio on your own. That way's a wracked path, and there are more dead virgins on it than there are hairs on a hog's back."

I took the money mutely, and I stared at Jacko so long that he finally growled and stalked back to the set.

If someone had been walking down Allen Street then, they could have just plucked the money out of my hand, a flat hundred dollars and more than I had ever held.

Finally, I tucked the money into the secret pocket my mother had sewn in my jacket and I headed back to Hungarian Hill.

Jacko promised that he would return in seven months, but I wondered what his promise was worth. All I knew was that I never got anywhere without knowing why, and now it was time to make some inquiries of my own.

VII

I went home and gave the money Jacko gave me to my mother, and when she asked me what had happened, I just walked out again. I spent the next few months sulking in a daze, helping out at the laundry with an ungrateful twist to my mouth and doing everything that was asked of me with a barely disguised disgust. My mother was so exasperated with me that it wouldn't have surprised me if she made another doll so she could replace me again, but my sister was hopeful.

"Come on, sissy, I'm going out with some girls from Ord Street. You can come with us . . ."

She was easy to ignore, but she never gave up. When I finally raised my head to see her, I realized that she had grown just as I did, fifteen to my seventeen, and in matters that didn't concern her dark home or her sulking sister, bright as a penny.

I didn't want to go with her to whatever silly games she proposed, but it did finally sting me into doing some work of my own. There were plenty of people willing to talk about Wolfe Studios and Oberlin Wolfe himself in Los Angeles, and that's the way he liked it. The greater the stories grew, the larger his little piece of Eden, and the more we talked, the less truth there was to be found.

I went around to the Comique, where I sat on a stool in the ticket taker's booth while she worked. She never bothered to offer me her name, but once in a while, some sibling—recognizable only by their height and beauty and the neon light in their eyes—came by to ask for this favor or that. She offered advice on heartbreak, handed out quarters from the till, and once or twice she opened the broom closet door to give them passage on to someplace with a lowering purple sky and grass tall enough to reach over my head.

"Where can I go to learn about Oberlin Wolfe?" I asked her, opening up the broom closet door only to be confronted by brooms and the scent of lemon cleanser.

"Read *Variety*," she said, not looking up from her paper, and I snorted.

"I don't want to read *Variety*, I want to know."

"Ask nicer, then."

"Will you please tell me where I can learn about Oberlin Wolfe?"

"Ha, no."

I was about to storm out when she looked at me over the top of her paper.

"Oberlin Wolfe is bad news. They all are, you know that, right?"

"I'm not stupid," I said, and she sighed.

"You're not one of mine, not even close. I don't have any responsibility to you."

"No one does," I declared, and she made an exasperated face.

"I guess you really think that. You want to know about Oberlin Wolfe, why don't you go ask Daphne Grove?"

I frowned.

"I don't know who that is."

"You think I'm going to do your work for you? You're lucky I talk to you at all."

She wasn't wrong, and I remembered to thank her before I left.

Daphne Grove wasn't in the phone book, and no one I asked on Hungarian Hill or off it knew about her. In desperation, I went to the library. They'd won the battle against allowing Black patrons, and I had to wait for two days until the librarian who thought I was white enough was on duty.

The directions she gave me took me east, and I hitchhiked out with a milk truck heading that way before dawn. I kept the driver company as he told me about how he had been a banker in Oklahoma when times were better, before the dust devils came in and turned his money to grit, and he let me out in a suburb where the houses were farther apart than I was used to and each yard proudly bore a straggling tree.

I walked along the street slowly as the sun came up, and when I came to the address that the librarian found for me, I stopped on the cracked sidewalk. Beyond it was a cluster of short trees, their branches thin and sharp, the trunks stood so close together a dog would have a hard time twisting through.

"You're Daphne Grove," I said with disgust, stepping from the cement onto the bare soil.

I was, we were, came the answer from the rattling branches and the stiff knifelike leaves. *You should not see me like this, all bare. Come back in spring, when I am clothed and lovely.*

Chitalpa trees in spring bore frilly pink flowers, ruffled like the bottom of a dancing dress, and I reached up to touch a branch.

"Did you dance?" I asked in spite of myself, and the branches dragged against my hand, dry and sorrowful.

I danced, and I sang, and they all wanted me. There was no one more perfect than me.

I didn't even sing, and I didn't know how to dance. I swallowed.

"What happened?"

They wanted me too much, and so they decided that no one should have me. Oh, beware, beware of the wolf and the mountain and the oath.

"How do I get to see Oberlin Wolfe?" I asked, and it was probably just and fair after that that I got a slash of branches over my head and on my shoulders, driving me back to the sidewalk in a flurry of blows. I yelped, covering my head as I ran, and the grove, angered, lashed at me, still reaching for me even after I gained the pavement.

I spat out half a leaf, glaring at what was left of Daphne Grove. I wouldn't be her, so I caught a ride back to Hungarian Hill.

I stayed away from the Comique for a while, bitter and afraid the ticket taker would laugh at the cuts on my cheek. I had no idea how to get any star to talk to me. There were powerful spells and watchful dogs to keep me off the studio lots, or I would have tried sneaking in, and the changelings, wild and nervy as they were, would as likely eat me as help me. In the end, I was stuck at home, where it finally occurred to me that even the great stars of Hollywood needed their clothes washed and pressed.

I thought I was clever when I offered to start running laundry out to my parents' patrons, or at least, the rich white ones whose names impressed me on the ledger. My mother was suspicious of my newfound industry, and when she could, she made me take my sister with me, riding on the handlebars of the battered, rusty bicycle loaded down with ill-fitting panniers full of shirts and trousers.

"Stay out of my way," I told her, and her she rolled her eyes.

"Like anyone wants to go deliver people's underclothes. Just drop me off by the reservoir."

"What are you doing by the reservoir?" I demanded, suddenly alert. "It's dangerous, you're going to get into trouble."

She turned to wink at me.

"I won't tell if you won't."

I bared my teeth at her, but I let her off where she asked, pedaling alone up a long street of houses that had once been something special. There was a haunted feeling here, and I left the bike propped up against the stucco wall, facing towards the street for an easy exit.

I rang the bell and listened as the church bell chimes echoed through the house. There was silence, and then there was a slow rustling step approaching, slippers sliding along the hardwood floors.

The door inched open, and I put on my best smile.

"Mr. Nikolic," I said, and the old man who peered out from the cracked door glared at me.

"Niko-litch," he ground out in a harsh and whispering voice. "It is Niko-litch."

"I'm sorry. But I have your shirts from the laundry."

"Ah, good. Give them here."

I deliberately took a step back from the door, and his eye narrowed, the corner of his mouth I could see drawing down in the corner.

"You used to work for Wolfe Studios," I said. "You used to be Count Zakharov."

A snorting sound like a horse getting ready to rear.

"*That* name you get right. Of course."

Now I was looking for the silvery quality of his skin and the ink black of his hair. Like Michel de Winter, the color had been leached from him by the old hungry cameras, but unlike de Winter, he didn't have a house in the Palisades and the adulation of millions to make up for it. He was a poor old forgotten lothario on a haunted street, and I tightened my jaw.

"I watched you in *Count Zakharov's Last Ride*. The one with Marvell Peyton."

"So? Who cares now?"

I knew the answer: no one did.

"How did you do it?" I asked, holding his shirts so he could see them. They were a good bribe, crisp charcoal Egyptian cotton, the points of the collar as sharp as arrows and the French cuffs ironed to a nicety.

He sneered at me through the crack in the door.

"How do you think? I killed a thousand, I killed ten thousand—"

"—and God will look down and smile," I said, finishing Count Zakharov's most famous line for him.

"So you remember. So what? One more stupid foreign girl, what do you matter?"

My lip curled back from my teeth.

"One more stupid foreign man, what do you matter?" I snapped in return, and he showed me his teeth as well in something like a smile.

"We are both foreign and strange," he said. "I suppose that means we must be friends."

I didn't want to be friends, but I stepped a little closer as he opened the door further. Now I could see that he wore some great old brocade robe edged with fur even in the smothering heat. The cameras were better now, I told myself. They had tamed them down, fed them better.

"Come here," he said imperiously. "Give an old man his shirts."

Peter Nikolic wasn't old, though at the age of seventeen, nearly everyone over thirty seems to be. He would have been in his fifties that day, but he was already something forgotten and dismissed to his echoing house on his haunted street. There might easily be another half dozen like him, watching us from their own cracked doors and afraid of the sunlight.

I edged closer, and I cried out in shock as the door flew open and his hands landed on my shoulders. He was suddenly taller than he was a moment before, tall like the other Ukrainians who came to Hollywood to make their money on the silver screen before their accents excluded them from the talkies.

"Such a beauty never was born within the walls of old Petrograd," he crooned, his mouth too close to my face, his acidic breath husking over my cheek. "Do you know those words, foreign girl? They wrote it up on the cards as if I spoke them, but I never did."

"Let me go," I cried, struggling uselessly before I remembered to fight. It took two solid kicks, like kicking a limestone block, and I stumbled back when he let me go. There was a step just behind me, and I toppled back over it into the dusty yard on my back. The fall bumped my tailbone, and the scratches from where he had dug his fingernails into my shoulders flared with hot pain.

Peter Nikolic stood in the doorway, his skin flaming silver, his eyes like cigarette burn holes through the world. He wasn't old for the moment, not with my terror ringing in his ears. He was great and grand and silent, Count Zakharov come to see the world burn for his Esma, and I stared at him in wonder.

Then the door slammed with an old man's mocking cackle, and I got slowly to my feet. The scratches on my shoulders would need peroxide if I didn't want them to get infected, and in a sullen rage, I picked up his shirts from the ground, pedaling back to the reservoir to throw them in.

Luli found me as I started back, and she hopped up on the handlebars as if we had arranged the whole thing. She smelled like turpentine, and I saw that her nails were filthy, ragged and torn with blue paint dug in so deeply she'd have to go after it with a pocketknife if she cared to clean it at all.

"Good day?" I asked, momentarily forgetting to be acidic, and she flashed me a bright real smile.

"Yeah."

After that I gave up on actors. Desperate for some kind of traction, I went to the waterholes where the crews gathered, rough places that only existed after dark. I dressed in shabby, baggy clothes, and I listened more than I talked. It took months, but finally, I heard something I could use. There was a trolley to Aspen Hills, and I was on it the next day.

These days, Aspen Hills is all tattoo shops and Friday-night enchantments, but back then, it was a quiet neighborhood, overgrown and smelling of the oleander and jacaranda that smudged the streets with creamy white and icy purple.

I got off the trolley and walked slowly along the cracked sidewalk, looking for the house number that I had gotten, all unlikely, from the phone operator. At the last, I didn't need it at all because I came to a large house in faded turquoise with a brass plaque on the low stone wall that surrounded the property. For a moment, I ran my fingers along the raised letters reading HAVERTON'S HOME FOR FORMER ARTISTES before I opened the black iron gate.

When I opened the glass-and-mahogany door, I was first met with a smell of linseed and lemon, almost strong enough to over-shadow something bitter and slightly acrid underneath. The stout woman behind the counter gave me a stern look as I approached, but she didn't question my presence, not even when I asked for Mrs. Hezibah Wiley. She only nodded towards the staircase to my left and told me to go all the way up.

"You should have brought flowers," the receptionist said. "She favors those who bring her flowers."

I learned about Mrs. Wiley from Martilo, who ran cables on Jacko's set. He was a big man with an enormous black mustache, and one night, he told the bar about the great Hezibah Wiley, who had become Eleanor Bloom and then turned it all away. He was some kind of relation of hers, a second cousin or something like that, and the pride he took in her, for both achieving and then leaving, was obvious. He said that these days, she had returned to her old name—what she called her real name—and she lived in Aspen Hills.

The staircase was longer than I thought it was. The steps were steeper than the ones at the laundry for all that they were polished wood, and bare, which seemed to me a dangerous thing for the housing of pensioners. The striped wallpaper to either side of me was relieved by a museum's gallery of color process, sketches, tin-types, daguerreotypes, and even the odd sketch or small painting. The ones closest to the ground floor were nearly modern, shots from movies that I had seen when I was just a little younger, but further up, I saw older ones, ones I had never heard of, going right back through the silent movies to the bright printed handbills for vaudeville acts.

At the very top of the stairs was a door with a pattern of iron nails pounded into it, and I realized Mrs. Wiley was kept or kept herself in the attic rooms. At my knock, a restrained Mid-Atlantic accent called for me to come in, and taking a deep breath, I did so.

The rooms at the top of Haverton's Home for Former Artistes were bright, windows thrown open to let in the California sunshine. There was a riot of green plants everywhere, Eden heaved onto the fourth story, and amidst it all, Mrs. Wiley herself was nearly lost to view.

She was a small woman with an ancient smiling face, reminding me of an orange that had been forgotten on the windowsill and left to wrinkle and dry. She sat at a small table with a half-finished game of patience in front of her, and she watched me with eyes that seemed as sharp as splinters. It was impossible for a woman as ancient as she looked to have been in the movies; the film industry wasn't old enough yet to have true elders, not even among the strange and dark ones who owned the studios, but she sat in front of me like a marker of something older and wilder.

"You didn't bring flowers," she observed.

"I didn't know to do so," I said. "I came for information."

"Then what did you bring me instead of flowers? I can see that you are no fan of mine, no worshiper."

My parents taught me not to come calling empty-handed, and I hadn't. Silently, I laid out a pack of cigarettes, a stack of novels, and twenty dollars, which I had held back from Jacko's final payoff.

Mrs. Wiley hummed in satisfaction. She stowed the cigarettes and the cash somewhere in her voluminous purple caftan, piled the books on a table to the side, and nodded at me.

"I suppose someone taught you manners after all. All right, push me to the balcony and we'll talk."

I realized that she sat in a wicker wheelchair, which had been all but hidden before she gathered her caftan around her body. I cautiously pushed her to the open balcony, and turned to her there.

"All right. For what you gave me, I'll tell you how things are. If you want me to tell you what you can do, that will be more. Yes?"

"Yes," I said. I wondered grimly if I was being scammed, but I had few other options. I wasn't going to wait for All Saints' Day, not when Jacko was playing a game I could barely understand.

I told Mrs. Wiley what had happened, and somehow it turned into the story of everything that had come before. I told her about the laundry, and Jacko's films on Baker Street, and about Maya Vos Santé and Irene Leonard and all the rest. Through it all, she watched me with those bright, bright eyes, and I didn't think I had ever been watched like that before. Jacko was interested in what I could pretend to be. My mother watched me and silently worried about what I wasn't. Mrs. Wiley looked at me searching for what I really was, and what she saw made her nod and smile grimly.

"Well, first, let's talk about your man Jacko," she said, tapping one hard finger thoughtfully on the cement balustrade. "He's easy. If he had said to the studio that he had found a likely looking girl that could be the next Su Tong Lin . . ."

"I don't want to be Su Tong Lin," I interrupted petulantly, and she smiled.

"Shut up, sweetie. It doesn't matter what you want, but I do agree. She was as soft and beautiful as sunlight, and that's not you.

"If he had given any hint to the studio that you existed, you would have been snatched up and a paper-child contract with a few hundred dollars tied around her neck left in your place."

I thought of the silk doll that my mother had made to replace me for my father. I think it was then that I decided for certain that I never wanted to have children, not if they were so disposable, so very easy to replace.

("They're not," Jane said to me gently. "They're really not."

"If you say so."

"You weren't, either," she said, and we had to stop talking for a while.)

"Jacko would have gotten something nice for you, I think," Mrs. Wiley said, inspecting me carefully. "A choice picture, his pick of the stable, even a few good years, yes, but I think he saw something else he wanted more."

Her eyes went distant and hard, and her free hand closed tight into a fist.

"He wants a queen all his own. He's smart enough to know that he'll never be a king, not in his own right. He's no Oberlin Wolfe, no. However, queen's consort? That's a good road. That's easy."

"Consort to a queen . . ." I said hesitantly, wondering at the words. There was something ugly about the idea, and Mrs. Wiley nodded with a goblin smile.

"Oh, I think you have the right of it. He would hitch his star to yours, and my dear, I do mean *hitch*. You're the girl he made, the one he fed on small parts and food service sandwiches. He's dazzled you and brought you into this world, because he didn't have to shoot all of those pictures on Baker Street, and I daresay that there are a dozen girls prettier than you walking around on Ord Street."

It hurt less than you might think. "Pretty" was a word that could come before "chink bitch" just as easily as anything else. There probably were girls far prettier than me on Ord Street, but their parents kept them at Chinese school and temple, refusing to let them roam.

"He has plans to dangle you in front of the studios as the fresh new face—they get you if they keep him. He probably has a few on the line, and you're the most likely. If you found out about me and came here to get information, I can even see why. In a year or so, he'll probably marry you. Would you like that, I wonder?"

I certainly would not, and the disgust must have shown on my face. It made Mrs. Wiley laugh out loud.

"Smart girl. If he's not dragging you up, he's dragging you down."

That wasn't why I was so put off by the idea, but that didn't matter.

"So I can be a studio changeling or Jacko Dewalt's wife. Is that all?"

"Of course not," Mrs. Wiley said. "I sneaked into the midnight dances without a patron at all, and I had Wolfe, Everest, and Aegis all bidding for my hand by the end of the night."

"I don't dance," I said disconsolately, and she laughed at me again.

"We're not talking about you right now, dear. I danced so well that I could be dancing still if I hadn't grown sick of it, but of course by then Elgin Aegis owned me from the chalet in Le Havre to the beautiful little bungalow in Brentwood. He owned my teeth too. Unfortunate legacy of a childhood spent eating gravel in my bread, I'm afraid, and they were rotting out of my head by the time I was twenty-four."

She smiled at me with her perfect teeth, and I knew with a shiver that they had been magicked into her mouth from someone who lived where I lived now, and had nothing but two lines of inflamed gums and a pocketful of cash.

"How did you get away?" I asked, because of course she wanted me to.

"As I said, Elgin Aegis owned me, but the studios are strange and hungry things. Sometimes, I think they're more than the men who own them, or that those men are just the faces and the lures. No, I gave him something he could never have if I stayed with the studio."

She drew up the edge of her caftan, and now I could see her legs ended at the ankle. The skin there was shiny and pink with old scar tissue that had been lovingly nourished with soothing creams, and it was so unexpected that I nearly started to cry. I swallowed it back, meeting her eye again stonily, and she nodded at a shelf immediately behind us inside the glass doors. From where I stood, I could make out a pair of wooden feet, beautiful, carved by a master's hand and polished until they shone. A series of leather straps showed that they were meant to be fastened to the wearer's legs, but even I could see that they were not for dancing.

"Do you think they keep yours on a shelf as well?" I said without thinking, and my hand went up to my mouth. Cold as the Atlantic, but that was monstrous even for me.

There must have been something of the monster in Mrs. Wiley too, however, because she leveled a look at me that was tolerant and amused.

"Oh, I wouldn't be surprised if Elgin Aegis fed them to that marble lion he keeps at his house in Big Sur. He didn't want a pair of feet that had been so calloused and scarred that you could barely tell they were feet, after all. Ugly things, even before I turned forty."

"Then what?" I asked. I was still reeling. I would see worse things at Wolfe, but at seventeen, this made me ache.

"Aegis got my ability to dance like Eleanor Bloom, one more thing that no one else had. It was worth letting Eleanor Bloom die for that. Eleanor Bloom is dead."

"Long live Hezibah Wiley?" I hazarded, and she smiled, triumphant.

"Yes. Perhaps you'll do all right. I lost the mansion, the apartments, the horses I never wanted, the husband the studio made for me, but I have money at least, a pension that will last as long as I do. I clip a little here and there—people still love *Biloxi Belle*— and that might be a lot longer than anyone dreamed. Aegis didn't scoop me hollow and set me to nodding like he did to poor Pearl Winston and the Kardov sisters. Do you know, I read in the paper they trotted the Kardovs out for that one thing last year, *The Lights Over* whatever? What a sight they must have been, batting those big black eyes and nodding along so easy."

This could be you, an ominous voice whispered in my head. *This could be you if you were* lucky.

I ignored it, because some needs have always been stronger than dread or sense.

"All right then," I said. "How do I get in?"

"There are the auditions, of course," Mrs. Wiley said, smiling like an angel. "They come around and give every girl in America her chance at the limelight, the starlight, and the stars."

That was the line they said on the radio whenever the studios went on their big talent hunts. I gritted my teeth, because they weren't for me or Maya Vos Santé or Su Tong Lin. Su Tong Lin was discovered in vaudeville, and Maya Vos Santé had had herself delivered to Oberlin Wolfe rolled in a carpet like Cleopatra.

"Dear, I have told you how things are. Now I can tell you what you should do."

There were a dozen plans in my head, but they would all take time. I knew that if Jacko Dewalt got wind of any of them, he would shut me down as quickly as a man would step on an ant. If I tried to believe in any kindness he might have shown me, all I had to do was to think about the girls crying around the edges of the set, sent on their way firmly with some cash in hand.

"All right," I said, bracing myself. "What do you want?"

"Twenty years," she said immediately, and I stared at her.

"Oh, I'm not a lawyer," Mrs. Wiley said at my startled look. "I'm not going to take twenty years now and leave you at forty, and I won't pop into your life when things are doing well and live twenty years of your best moments. I'll take twenty at the end. That's enough for me."

She had said she clipped a little here and there, and with her stories and her wits, I could see how she could get by for quite some time.

When it looked like I might balk, she smiled slyly.

"You're already betting on a small piece of forever," she said.

"No one goes into the studios expecting to be out in five years with a nice paycheck and some good stories."

Twenty years against forever. I had been told that you needed to believe in yourself, believe in your wits, your looks, and your luck against the titan's weight of the world. I decided in that moment that I did, and I nodded.

"Done. Twenty years for a plan that will get me in to see Oberlin Wolfe."

Mrs. Wiley smiled almost proudly, and she directed me to push her back inside the apartment she had earned by wanting to be free more than she wanted anything else.

"Put a kettle on, will you, I'll be making a cup of tea."

I rummaged in her small kitchen and returned to find her busying herself at her desk. She pulled out a pale peach notecard and she wrote my name and *twenty years* on it. Her handwriting was a rolling, elegant script, one beaten into her, I later learned, at parochial school. My own writing was chicken scratches, and the calligraphy I learned had been left behind like Chinese school years ago.

"All right, dear, now give me your hand."

I shrieked when she made a small cut on my wrist with her penknife, but she wouldn't let me draw my hand back until my blood saturated the little card with my name on it. She was stronger than she looked, and we both watched as my blood darkened the cardstock.

Mrs. Wiley finally let me go, ignoring my growl as she placed the bloodied card at the bottom of a fine porcelain teacup. She filled the cup with a whoosh of hot water, and the water tinted brown with my blood.

I didn't feel any different when she finished it, and she didn't look any different either, but she smacked her lips and proclaimed herself satisfied.

"Now," she said. "I'm going to give you a name . . ."

VIII

My shadow paced in front of me on the sidewalk, only tottering slightly on my high heels. I looked stretched out but sharp on the pavement. I had a brief hallucination of my shadow reaching out in front of me, long and thin to wrap its fingers around the throats of the people sleeping in the houses on either side of the broad, clean street.

The streetcar was too polite to run into Jacko's neighborhood, dropping me off almost six blocks away. I was painfully aware that if I was unlucky, the LAPD would have plenty of questions for what I was doing in West Adams Heights, for which I had no real answers, at least not ones I could tell them. Instead I walked briskly on the sidewalk, head up and spine straight. I didn't look like I belonged there, but if I moved fast enough, I would be someone else's problem, and that was good enough.

Jacko's Mission Revival two-story hulked in the dark. Yellow light came from the ground-floor windows telling me that he wasn't asleep yet, and I was relieved to see no cars in the drive except for Jacko's own cream-colored Cadillac.

A sudden rustle from the oleander bushes that stretched out from his neighbor's property made me hurry up the drive, and before I could lose my nerve, I rapped hard on the red door.

Jacko appeared quickly, a square tumbler full of something amber still in his hand. Out of his usual clothes and dressed in a gray sweater and slacks, he looked softer, but a thundercloud gathered over his brow as he recognized me.

"CK? What the hell are you doing here dressed like that?"

The dress I was wearing was lucky bright red, clinging to me until it fell in soft folds around my knees and tied at the collar with a small, kittenish bow. My mother recognized the woman who had dropped it off as Fighting Frank Mulligan's mistress Donna Schafer, and since they had both died in a shootout in Santa Clarita, she probably wouldn't be back for it.

I smiled widely, showing all my teeth and making him blink.

"Don't I look all grown up?" I asked, spreading my arms out and doing a short spin. "Are you sure you won't reconsider?"

I nearly sang the last word and stumbled as I did it, so close to Jacko that he had to reach over to steady me or let me fall. He left it until the last moment, but he did catch me, and when he set me on my feet, he smelled the beer that I had gargled and spat out on the corner after getting off the streetcar. The stuff made my teeth feel fuzzy, and the small trickle that found its way down my throat made me want to retch, but I smiled all the same.

"Jesus Christ, CK, your mom know you're out like this?"

He slid an arm around me to help me in, and I slumped in his arms, soppy and silly. I pressed my flushed face against the wool of his sweater as he absently cursed my loose limbs, letting him do the work of wrestling me out of the tiled foyer and into the sunken living room beyond it. My head lolled against his chest as I giggled at nothing. Beyond my lowered eyelashes, everything was a red-and-gold blur.

With a heave, he unloaded me onto a leather couch before stepping back. I reminded myself not to pull down my skirt or slide my legs together. Instead I lay where he had left me for a moment before hauling myself to my feet. He regarded me warily like a stick of dynamite that might go off in his hand.

"How did you get all the way out here? We're a long way from Hungarian Hill."

"I get around, Jacko," I said with a laugh. It was the first time I had said his name. "There are parties . . . that I can go to. My mother doesn't have to know."

I lunged forward, making him pull back in shock. He scowled when he realized that I was leaning towards the sleek radio given pride of place at the front of the room. I flipped it on with a careless finger and then spun the mother-of-pearl dial, sending the needle whizzing through stations. KRLV had just started doing late-night broadcasts a year ago, and most of the other stations followed along. I settled on something with a bright beat, trumpets and drums, and I ignored Jacko's wince at the sudden noise.

"Come on, dance with me. No hard feelings, right?"

He blew exasperated air through his lips, but he stepped up when I offered him my hands. He was light on his feet despite being so big, and he guided me easily around the living room. There was something in his eyes that glittered, and I knew better than to think that it was worship or love. This was possession. I was giving him a taste of what the future might hold—*queen's consort, that's a good road*—and he wanted it.

I was never a very good dancer, even after lessons, and back then all I could do was watch the older girls practice with each other in the alley behind the laundry. He took me for two turns around the room before he let go, turning the radio down and shaking his head.

"Come on, CK, you know better than this. I told you. After your birthday, this winter, we'll go up to Oberlin Wolfe's office, you and me . . ."

I pouted and turned the radio up again. Dora Franklin's brassy voice declared she would never love another man in black, the horns practically crying for her.

"I don't want to wait," I whined. "Everyone else already sees me as grown, why don't you?"

"Christ, it's not what I see or don't see, it's the law, ain't it? You wanna be one more changeling that they drug up in the morning and down in the evening? You don't."

"I just want to know *when*," I pressed as if he hadn't told me the answer on Baker Street. "I want to be a star, Jacko . . ."

My body crawled with spider legs as he looked at me up and down. He was weighing something in his own mind. How far could he go? What could he get away with? Stars were good girls, but anyone who thought they came up without some dark fingerprints on white silk slips and some foxing around the edges was a fool. Jacko wasn't a fool.

"You're going to be a star, CK, didn't I promise?" he said, coming up to stand in front of me. "You're going to gleam up in the sky."

"You did," I said, ducking my head bashfully. "You know, you hear awful things about girls who want to be stars. People that make them promises."

"I mean what I say, CK," he rumbled. "I'm not going to be one of those guys who strings you along for two-bit gigs that end up on the cutting room floor."

No, he had other plans for me, and I knew that if I accused him of that, he would tell me that I should be grateful. Other girls might have been.

"Tell me what it's going to be like when I'm a star," I whispered dreamily, taking his hands in mine. It kept them away from my body for the moment, but their touch, hard as horn despite the lack of callousing, made me shiver.

"You? You're going to go right to the top, CK," he said, swallowing a little. "Mansion up in Bel-Air, wearing fur every winter and Egyptian cotton every summer. You'll be painted a mile high up on the movie screens, staring into the eyes of Hal Fosse or Brock Williams, right? People will look at you and get fireworks where their hearts should be and diamonds in their eyes."

"Tell me more," I said encouragingly, and he nodded, eyes lidded and strangely unfocused.

"*Variety* will write you up. Dottie Wendt will interview you at the Knick, and she'll hang on your every word as you tell her about your childhood in Paris, the finishing school in Algiers, the man without a name who broke your heart in Florence. Men will want you, girls will want to slit you up the front and wear your skin . . . God, you're so beautiful."

His hands twitched, and my heart jumped. I walled off my panic behind brick and stone. I could hear it clawing at the mortar, breaking fingernails and bloodying fingertips, but it couldn't reach me. I wouldn't let it. I held Jacko Dewalt still instead.

"You'll leave Su Tong Lin in the dirt, no one will care about her crying maids or her Shanghai courtesan anymore. They'll be watching you instead, watching you on the screen as you kiss the boys, sneak them the keys to your father's lair, die for them and rise just in time for your next premiere. You'll live a hundred lives in front of the unblinking eye, and you'll be perfect."

He pulled his hands away from mine, sliding them up my arms. His eyes were wide, and he looked as dazed as I felt. Somehow that was worse. When he was like this, he might do anything. He might curse himself later, but that was later.

He drew me to him, hands not hurting but firm enough to remind me that they could. I leaned back but kept my face as still as stone. Every minute mattered, every second, every . . .

A crash echoed through the silent house, breaking the moment into a thousand pieces as something no doubt priceless shattered on the shiny tile.

"What the hell—"

Jacko started for the back of the house, his study, where the crash had come from, but the spell was broken and I didn't have to pretend. I threw my arms around his waist and dug in my heels. He was so surprised by my attack that he stumbled.

"Goddamn you, get off," he snarled. "There's someone in the damn house."

There was, and I had to keep him away from her for as long as I could. I clung on to him so hard that we both toppled over. We hit the tile with a meaty thump, him on top of me, but he scrambled away. I lunged after him desperately, filling my hands with the wool of his sweater and hauling back hard. It was good Scottish wool, it didn't give. I kept him on the ground for another moment before it occurred to him to turn on me.

"Get the hell off, damn it," Jacko roared. His fist drew back, but he must have believed what he said about my future because it landed as an open-handed slap. I saw stars, but my hands stayed clenched. The second one caught me high on the cheekbone, the edge of his hand grazing the corner of my eye. The pain of that blow made me loosen my hold, and it was enough for him to scramble up. He stepped on my hand carelessly, making me gasp, but then he was thundering to the back of the house.

I staggered up to my feet, holding my injured hand tight to leach away the pain. The blows left me dizzy, but it was already clearing up. I stumbled back to the study as the radio blared Lou Ryan to the strangely still air.

The study was a mess of broken glass and upended drawers. Jacko stood in the middle of it like a man whose house had blown away. He turned a furious baleful gaze to me, and in that moment, queen's consort or not, he might have strangled me.

"You don't know my name yet," I said quickly. "But you know Jenny Lynn Steel, don't you?"

He reared back as if I had thrust a burning brand at him. I had always thought him pale, but now he went pasty, the red blood under his skin drained away.

"What the hell do you know about Jenny Lynn Steel?"

"I know that she should have been the next Josephine Beaufort, and that Oberlin Wolfe doesn't know why she's not. I know that she's still living in Pescadero with her parents. I know that they're happy when she talks or looks around or gets out of bed, but that those days are getting fewer. I know that you had pictures of her in your desk. Special pictures. Ones that you couldn't stop yourself from taking, could you?"

"I never took any of you," he said defensively, and I almost laughed.

"Because I'm not tiny, pretty, and blond. It doesn't matter, does it? I'm lucky because I don't get your motor running. You're lucky because Oberlin Wolfe never has to see those pictures at all."

His face took on an angry sneer.

"Of course you've got a price."

"Of course I do," I agreed stonily. "I want to see Oberlin Wolfe after Halloween. Not as your discovery. Not as your ticket, not as your goddamn mare. Tell me, what were you going to say when you realized that I wasn't going to marry you?"

I saw Jacko's mouth drop open, and then he closed it again with a snap. He looked like a man carved out of rock, like a mountain ready to fall.

"You would have," he said, his voice flat. "One way or another, you would have. Christ, who have you been talking to?"

"Doesn't matter. I won't have you, and because you planned all of this without letting me in on a word of it, and because I have your life in an envelope, you're going to get me an appointment with Oberlin Wolfe. Then you are going to stay the hell away from me."

There was a long moment where I could tell that Jacko was measuring the distance between his hands and my neck.

"November third," Jacko said finally. "Eight A.M. I'll send a car for you, and you'll give those pictures to the chauffeur. Believe me when I say I don't want to see you again, either."

"I'm burning those pictures, and I'll send you the ashes," I said. "Trust me."

"I don't have a choice, and you know it."

Jacko glowered at me, dangerous even if brought to bay. I would have to spend the rest of my life watching out for him, Mrs. Wiley said, or at least, the rest of his life. That was fine.

My back could feel a dozen needles from his gaze as I walked to the door, and then once I was out of sight, I headed west, back towards Hungarian Hill.

IX

My mother and father had gone to bed hours earlier. As I entered the apartment, the doll ghosts whisked around me balefully, angry as always when I disturbed the peace of the house. I ignored them.

Luli beat me home, waiting for me by the single orange bulb burning in the kitchen. Beside her sat an envelope filled with photographs. The envelope was closed, but I knew as well as I knew the lines in my own palm that Luli had looked at the pictures inside. I pulled them out anyway, fanning the half dozen shots like a poker hand on the table.

Jenny Lynn Steel, the Sweetheart of Anaheim. She gleamed on the black-and-white prints like starlight. There was something in her wide dark eyes that could stop an army, but the sweet curve of her mouth said she was all for you. Jacko's obsession with her seeped into the shots he had taken, the cruel magic he had worked. How easy it must have been, because he had found her just as he had found me, nursed her on small roles and promised she would be a queen.

The camera took all of that from her, some of the shots perfectly clothed, and some nude. Clothed she was shy; nude, there was a desperate bravery in her eyes, and so he took that too. Those photographs took the shine out of her, and now what was left was a woman in bed in Pescadero, wondering what had carved such a hollow inside her.

I made a strangled noise and swept the pictures back into the envelope, shaking as I did so. I didn't want to touch them one minute longer than I had to, and I shoved them into the space between the stove hood and the brick wall behind it. Luli watched me, and I could see a hint of relief that I was as disturbed by the photographs as she had been. We weren't going to speak of it, and I was grateful.

"Well?" she asked instead.

"It worked," I said, kicking off my heels. My feet ached and felt swollen twice their usual size even from that short walk. Mrs. Wiley had said that her famous feet were ugly from years and years of dance, and that night I thought I could see how it started.

"You still need to give me the fare I spent on the streetcar," Luli reminded me, and I groaned.

"Get it out of my purse," I said, and when she made no move at all, I hobbled up and pulled out the money myself. Luli counted the coins up carefully, rude in China and California, before stowing them in her pocket.

Luli had grown as well as I had, but no one could say that we had grown into anything alike. She decided that my father's shifted eye was more a blessing than neglect, and she helped out at the laundry as little as I did.

Now she lounged at the table like a union teamster, dressed in canvas pants that hung off her boyish hips and a man's shirt untucked and unbuttoned to show the thin singlet underneath.

"Thank you," I said suddenly, and I walked around the table to hug her, wrapping my arms around her from behind as she sat on the kitchen chair. We weren't a family that touched each other like that, but I had seen it done enough times in the movies. At first, she was as stiff as a doll made of wires. Though she never hugged me back, she did finally loosen up. Luli tilted her head back to look at me, a slight smile on her round face.

"Been waiting for you to say that," she said cockily.

It struck me with the force of a blow how beautiful my sister was. She had lived, like my father and my mother, in a peculiar blind spot for me for years. If I wasn't on set, I wanted to be. I was in a waking sleep at home.

But it was true. My sister at fifteen was a beauty. When Mrs. Wiley talked about girls prettier than me on Ord Street, my sister could have been one of the ones she was thinking of. In her boys' clothes with her rough-cropped hair and too-old-for-her smile, Luli would make people sit up and take notice. If she would look down and blush, she would be made in the model of Su Tong Lin. Her voice, a little husky and with a funny upturn at the ends, would have broken hearts.

I must have looked at her for too long, because she tilted her face, still looking at me upside down.

"What? What are you thinking now, sissy?"

"Come with me," I said impulsively. "Come with me when the car comes on November third. We'll both meet Oberlin Wolfe, and I'll tell him all about you . . ."

My sister exploded from my embrace so hard that the chair tipped. It would have clattered to the floor, making an enormous racket, if I hadn't caught it on my hip.

"Don't you dare," Luli said, her voice deadly serious. "I don't want to go anywhere near any of that crap."

There were still some things that could make me flinch, apparently; I drew back as if she had reached out to pinch my arm like my mother sometimes did. I stared at her in shock, making Luli shake her head.

"I didn't say anything when Ma made a doll for me as well as you. I mean, I was sad about it for a while, because I thought I should be, but in the end, whatever, right? He wouldn't let me run around like I do, and eventually he would have gotten after me just like he got after you.

"And I think you mean well, because that's everything that you've ever wanted and more, but, no. No way in hell."

"But why?" I asked, unaccountably hurt.

She looked at me for a long moment, and then she shook her head. Just then, she felt far older than I was and far more wise and tired.

"Because I don't want it," she said roughly. "That sounds like hell to me, and the studios are evil. They'll murder you to see if you get up again, and if you don't, oh well. Where I go, they don't do that."

"Where do you go, Luli?" I asked, thinking of the paint under her fingernails.

She grinned, suddenly shy. The realization that she was far more beautiful than I was was like a shower of gold over my head, heavy and gilded.

"Do you really want to know?" she asked diffidently, but I could see the eagerness in her face.

"Yes, very much so."

She led me back to her room, where she pulled down a thick scrapbook. I sat down on the edge of her bed next to her, another thing we never did, as she opened it.

It was full of sketches in ink and drawings in colored pastels and crayon. They were beautiful on their own, but even I could see that they were plans for something else. I started to ask what, but then I saw a picture that I realized was familiar, its blues and golds an explosion of some alien sky.

"Luli, is this the mural on Mrs. Ramirez's store?"

Her brilliant smile told me everything I needed, and now that I looked down, I could see the smudges and smears of old pigment on her dark trousers.

As she pointed out the details I had missed, the little bird that served as her signature, a curl in the blue that recalled the ends of our mother's braid, I thought with relief that Luli was going to be fine.

X

It was an agonizing two-month wait for November third. I read everything I could about Oberlin Wolfe in the magazines and in the papers, I went to watch Luli paint a mural on our old Chinese school, I helped at the laundry, but everything was beginning to feel stretched and flat. I didn't belong to this world anymore, and as I approached the border to another place entirely, my parents' house took on a wavering quality, like something seen through glass.

The end of October offered a bit of a respite in that Hungarian Hill hurried to the annual work of preparing for the dead. Most of our neighbors hung up garlands of marigolds in welcome, and all around us were the brightly painted skulls to make the dead feel at home. Those whose dead came to visit them walked boldly out in the street on Halloween, arm in bony arm as they went to the places they had enjoyed while they were living. Everywhere, people sang, songs for all and songs that could only be heard long after the meat had fallen away from your bones.

At the laundry, we locked the door and lit up the red bulb over the family altar. Our dead were a long way away, but the bulb told them they would be welcome if they came. My mother sat by the window keeping an eye out for her father, who slept under the Colorado mountain, and my father said nothing to anyone, perhaps ashamed that if his dead came, his wife and daughters couldn't speak with them.

November third dawned bright and terribly clear. I dressed in Donna Schafer's red dress again, and in my fresh-polished heels, I waited outside for the car from Wolfe Studios. The dead were gone, I was still alive, and I had worn myself out being frightened and nervous over the last few months. There was nothing left to me but an aching calm.

The car that arrived for me was sleek and black, as funereal as it was grand. It felt like a joke when the man in the uniform opened the door for me, but I nodded regally at him before taking a seat inside.

Watching out the window of the car was as good as a motion picture itself. The mean, dark buildings of Hungarian Hill gave way to houses and stores that were taller and cleaner. We drove up into the hills, and the low buildings grew grander, became gleaming shops, and finally became that rarest of things, space, open space, enough space to think, to run if you wanted or to be alone.

There were a pair of silver wolves guarding the entrance to the studio. They gleamed in the light, and the gears that powered their long limbs and their powerful jaws moved just as smooth as life. The driver paused, opening the window to let one poke its broad head in. I heard it sniffing curiously even as the other gazed at me with blank mechanical menace. Then in tandem, they both went and lay down again, the geniuses inside that powered them growing cool once more with nothing to attack.

"Thank God," the driver muttered. "Last month they tore the top off of a taxi."

"Was the taxi trying to get in?" I asked, and the driver shrugged.

"Who the hell knows. Those two don't need much of an excuse, that's for sure."

Wolfe Studios was a disappointment at first. Unlike the palatial homes and verdant parks we had passed, it looked no different than a set of warehouses piled on top of each other. Here and there, I saw people wheeling around trash cans and dragging along racks of equipment, and somewhere far in front of us I saw a flash of strange and silver light, but otherwise, it looked as dull and dusty as any other place I had ever been.

That doubt gnawed at my heart until that silver light returned, this time shooting straight up into the sky. It disappeared, invisible in the autumn sunlight, but it would gleam at night, and there would be a new name on the marquees, a new immortal where before there had been darkness.

People rushed out into the street to see, and the car ground to a snail's pace.

A moment later, the crowd parted to reveal a slender white girl, her butter-gold hair dragged down her back and her dark blue eyes vivid with mascara and panic as she ran headlong through the on-lookers. The shoulder of her Roman robe slouched down her arm, revealing her lacy bra strap underneath as well as some of the strapping that kept her breasts almost flat to her chest.

"Oh, oh, oh," she cried, her mouth a dark cavern in the middle of her face, and instinctively, I knew that if anyone mortal touched her then, they would only burn.

She turned, and I could see the dark blood that spilled down her side. When they pulled the cloth away, they would find her skin miraculously healed.

"Who is that?" I asked, stunned, and the driver shook his head, as startled as I was.

"I should know," he muttered. "For someone like that, for . . . I should know."

He didn't. No one did, not then, but they would.

She paused in front of the car, and despite my Atlantic cold, I shrank back. I had seen some of that incandescent glow before, scraps of it on the actresses with Jacko on Baker Street, the polished and tamed gleam of it on the picture screen. In person, it was blinding, something that could kill you.

Her wild eyes met mine. I couldn't look away. I never wanted to. I had never wanted to worship before, but now I wanted to sink down, to pray, to give thanks and fear and love. My hand was on the door handle.

Before I could stumble out into her splendor, a pair of tall men approached her cautiously. One had a robe, and the other a carafe of water so cold that steam rose up from its wet sides.

There was a moment where we all verged on destruction, and then she allowed them to cover her. She sipped at the cold water, and she became human again, if she ever could be human again. They led her away, leaving a worshipful crowd behind her, but before she vanished, she looked back over her shoulder. Her eyes met mine, and there was the tug of a claim on my soul.

When she was gone, I pushed that claim away as hard as I could. I felt feverish, my body too warm, my teeth chattering together. It was as if there were a hook through my heart, and for now, she was letting the chain attached to that hook play out through her fingers. Someday, she would tug and I would come, and the idea horrified me and fascinated me all at once. For now, all I could do was try to rip that hook out, but I might as well have ripped out my heart.

"Something else again," said the driver, shaking his head as he started to drive. "Maybe that's good luck for you, though, huh?"

Or maybe that was all the luck to be had in the world for the day, and to hell with me. I had not been raised to think of luck as an infinite resource.

He drove me up to a building that looked a little grander than the rest, stepping out to open the door for me again. He said something kind, I think, but I couldn't hear him. Instead I stood as straight as I could, and I walked in through the double doors.

There was a brisk-looking woman at the front guarded by two enormous security men, and she looked on me kindly enough.

"Oberlin Wolfe's eight o'clock? You made it just in time. Take the elevator all the way to the top."

I almost expected one of the security guards to peel off and accompany me, but it struck me again that this was a normal day for them. Of course hopeful girls came to see Oberlin Wolfe every day. Some of them showed up again and rose as stars, and far more stumbled back to the car trying not to blur their mascara with tears. Some others still, rumored but persistent, never returned at all.

The elevator was glass and brass, and the Black woman at the panel smiled at me. She looked like she was a woman made for smiling, but the job only allowed her so much.

"Top floor, please," I said, painfully aware that I should have tipped her and knowing very well I had no money in my purse.

She didn't seem to hold the tip against me, only murmuring good luck as I went in. The elevator stopped in a surprisingly close lobby, far more cramped than I would have imagined for the office of one of the three kings of Hollywood.

The woman who sat behind the desk here looked at me far less kindly. She was a beauty as well, but that was becoming almost normal to me. More important was the bored, predatory glint in her eye.

"Mr. Wolfe's eight o'clock? I'll let him know you're here."

"Of course," I said stiffly.

She didn't say anything else so I took a seat. I didn't see her speak into her intercom, but I assumed that something had happened.

Half an hour later, I no longer assumed that, and the only thing that stopped me from getting out and pacing was the not-so-secret amused glint in her green eyes. There was a little smirk there, something unpleasant, and I gritted my teeth.

When the carriage clock set on her desk chimed nine, I got up and approached the desk again.

"Please remind Mr. Wolfe that I am here," I said politely.

Her laugh was a high treble of contempt.

"Oh, sweetie, that's not how that works," she said. "This is your big day, but for Mr. Wolfe, the fact that he's here at all is just a pain in the ass."

"What are you . . ."

Before I could get another word out, the intercom crackled to life.

"Janet, is the girl here?"

"She is, boss," said the receptionist sweetly, savoring her informality in front of me like a piece of candy. "Shall I send her in?"

"Yeah, and call at Lou's for some coffee too. The usual."

The look she gave me was triumphant, but I didn't spare her another glance. I would rather go back to the laundry than try to make a receptionist job into something to hold over other people.

"Mr. Wolfe will see you now," she informed me. The receptionist pressed a button, and the wooden panel in front of me slid open.

When I entered the office of one of the most powerful men in Hollywood, I flinched from the light. The entire wall facing the entrance was glass, and the morning sunlight came spilling right in. I learned much later that that was on purpose, a choice Oberlin Wolfe had made so that when anyone came on his turf, they were dazzled by the light in front of them and so that he could see them with the harsh glare on their features.

There are still plenty of pictures of Oberlin Wolfe around if you know where to look. He's part of Hollywood as much as he's still part of the studio that bears his name, and even now, he walks the back lots, eyeing his empire as if daring it to disappoint his legacy.

He was a tall man, lean through his years of riding and war, and his pale hair, worn long in his youth, was now cut brutally short, just a silver glimmer over the shape of his skull. His features were sharp and slightly alien, and his fingers looked as if someone had tugged them out ever so slightly, making them appear long and spiderlike while they tapped impatiently on his desk.

I stood in front of the desk, hands at my sides. For what felt like an eternity, he didn't even look at me, and then finally, as if on some unseen signal, he heaved himself out of his chair and around his desk, lurching towards me.

If I had imagined any kind of hovering preternatural monster, I was wrong. The monster in front of me turned out to be a very normal one, especially if you grew up on Hungarian Hill. The clothes were far finer than any of the ones that ever came into the laundry, and the alcohol was probably nicer as well, but it was familiar enough that I put up a hand to stop him when he came too close.

Wolfe snorted, brought up short. This close, I could see that his eyes were fixed somehow. They were pale and beautiful, but they were terribly, terribly still.

"So you're the one I got that terse little note from Dewalt about a few months back," he mused, more to himself than to me. "He sounded pissed off. Did you blackmail him?"

I thought that I had learned to keep my face still, but he saw my surprise there, and he laughed. For such a handsome man, he had a strange cough-like laugh. I couldn't smell any cigarette smoke on him, but it was like a crow's caw.

"Ha, thought so. Dewalt doesn't do a damn thing for a woman unless he's in bed with her or she has him by the balls. You made an enemy before you even walked in here."

"I'll probably make more before I'm done," I said with a shrug, and that made Wolfe laugh again.

"Smart, but I don't know if you're tough enough to back that up."

"I am," I replied with a confidence that I had borrowed from Mrs. Wiley. I would never be adorable and bubbling over with praise for myself and others. Instead, I was still and cold, and I had to hope that was enough.

"All right, let's look at you," he said with a sigh. "I had to crawl out of the bodies after the Wild Hunt for this, might as well see if there's a scrap of you that can be useful."

I could see at least some of Jacko's revenge now. Whatever the Wild Hunt was, it had left Wolfe exhausted and irritable, not a wonderful time for an actress to cross him.

He circled me lazily, eyes traveling up and down my body. If he could have reached out to bite me, I'm sure he would have. When he casually reached for my breast, I knocked his hand away, but I didn't shout. I only glared. Mrs. Wiley had told me to expect something like that, but she needn't have bothered.

There was a chance it would enrage Wolfe, but instead he only narrowed his eyes. He pressed closer to me, not touching, but close enough for me to feel how amphibiously cool his skin was and to smell the way the reek of alcohol and something musky hung off of him. I stayed as still as I knew how to, shrinking back from my skin until it felt as if there was another inch of space between us. He hadn't touched me, so what was I going to cry about?

He looked deep into my eyes, and then I saw what was wrong with his. The pupils never moved, either to shut light away or to take it in. It prickled something in my hindbrain, telling me that if Oberlin Wolfe had ever been human, he certainly wasn't any longer.

He finally pulled back as if bored with me, and he propped himself back against his desk, letting some of the papers piled on it fall to the side.

"All right, smile. No, not like that, silly bitch, with your teeth, show 'em off."

I did as he said, and he frowned.

"At least your own teeth will do. You're not one for the comedies though, are you? Pretty, but a little dead."

I shrugged because I couldn't think of any real defense for that. He smiled at me, and I kept myself from saying that he could hardly do better. He picked through the detritus on his desk until he came up with a single lavender sheet.

"All right. Read this."

I fought the urge to start reading as soon as it was in my hands. Instead I read it over silently before beginning.

"In all my life and ever after, I do not understand why my parents should have sent me to Grieverly Hall upon their deaths, nor why they deemed my Uncle Crispian a guardian for a young girl newly bereft of her parents . . ."

It was a Gothic piece, all Mid-Atlantic accent that could turn ridiculous if you took your mind off of it for one moment. June Della Ray had done something very similar, and I mimicked her calm instead of my own, hopeful virtue instead of cold.

When I was done, Wolfe looked perhaps more interested, and he fished out another piece for me.

"Here. Again. Put your body into it this time. I'm not running a goddamn reader's theater here."

I read the piece over, and a rough fury stirred inside me. I looked up at Wolfe, who smirked at me. This was nothing to him. He only wanted to see what I would do.

I looked over the piece again, and then I stepped discreetly out of my heels and sank to my knees. I could have told myself that it was just acting, but every star in the smoky Los Angeles sky knew better. For better or worse, it was always you there.

"Please," I said softly. "If you ever had a heart, if you ever felt anything for us. If you ever thought of me, please don't do this."

The words felt like scraps of buckram in my mouth, too stiff and dry. Wolfe was turning away, and suddenly there were tears in my eyes. I tilted my face up so they would run from the corners of my eyes rather than making a muddy wash of my mascara.

"I've never felt this way before," I continued. "I hate it, and you don't care, do you? I was just an amusement to you, a toy . . ."

Rage and hate were better than that soft cloying sweetness, but the tears kept falling. I met Wolfe's gaze squarely as I spoke the words, and he was still there when I finished. I held the pose, and then I rose to my feet. Stepping back into the heels, even if it was like walking on knives, restored some of my self-possession.

"Nice," Wolfe said thoughtfully, and I had a little more of his attention than I did before. "The bit with taking your shoes off, though, over the top."

"I couldn't kneel with them on," I said with a shrug, and that won a dry, barking laugh from him.

"Well, all right then. We have people that can teach you better. You seem like you got a bit of a stick up your ass, but I don't know, maybe that's what people want now."

For a moment, I dared to think that I had won my way, but Wolfe stepped towards me.

"All right, now give me a kiss," he said, and he opened his mouth to show teeth that were too sharp by far. Something small and animal in me froze with terror. I didn't know what came next, but it made my stomach lurch with fear.

"You came here without a patron," Wolfe continued pleasantly. He seemed to grow with every step that he took, and where he had been long-legged before, now there was something unearthly about the length of his limbs. His mouth seemed to stretch far in front of his face, and oh but his teeth were stained and old.

He came forward for every step that I took back, and as I retreated slowly, his smile only got the wider.

"You go through that door, and you've lost," he informed me. "You know that, don't you?"

He took up the whole room, and I saw flashes of the real Oberlin Wolfe then. He was a beautiful man in slim-cut slacks, but behind him, or perhaps slightly off to the side, there was something far older, and far less human. I thought he was a common monster when I came in, but if that were true, it was because I had only seen a fraction of his form. He was large and knotted like the roots of some kind of terrible tree. He was sharp-toothed, and he was very hungry.

"Give me a kiss, China doll," he said, a growl in his voice.

Without thinking, I lifted my hand, pushing away my fringe. The kiss that Maya Vos Santé left there glimmered silver, and for some reason, it sat Wolfe back. He leaned forward—bent down on knuckled fists—and my hair stirred as he sniffed at my brow. Deliriously, I thought he would lick it, and my skin wanted to crawl right off of my body.

Wolfe bent his head down, and a sound came from him like barrels rolling down in hell. It shook the room, and I put my hand back against the door, not to run but only to steady myself. I realized that he was only laughing.

"Clever thing," Wolfe observed. "That's not something I can get for myself anymore." Maya Vos Santé was gone by that time. One day she was making movies out of Wolfe Studios, splitting her time between Jacko Dewalt and Lance Dunholme, and the next you couldn't remember when you had last seen her name on the marquee. There were rumors, but nothing you could hang a fact on, and though her movies would keep for another few decades in the vaults, she left nothing behind.

Gingerly, as if afraid that I might lash out at him, Oberlin Wolfe closed the distance between us again. He was tall enough to lean forward and place his lips over the silvery mark on my forehead. At the touch of his mouth against my skin, I shuddered. It felt like nothing at all, only a kind of coldness and a kind of loss. My throat was full of something thick and viscous, and when I was finally able to swallow again, Oberlin Wolfe looked human.

One languid hand came up to touch his lips, and he regarded me carefully. For just an instant, there was something fearful in his gaze, or a confusion as to what I was and what I was for. It certainly wasn't the first time someone had looked at me like that.

Then he turned away from me with a shrug. Whatever I was was taking up far too much of his time.

"Well?" The word slipped out before I could stop it, brash and demanding.

He glanced back.

"You still here? Yeah, fine. We'll give you a try. Two hundred and fifty a week to keep you for the next three years. That's traditional. You can stay in the dorms unless you want to run home and live with Ma and Pa at night. We'll get you trained up, and see what we can make of you."

"No maids," I said, thrusting my chin up. "No funny talking, no fainting flowers." At the very end of my meeting with her, Mrs. Wiley had laughed when I asked her what I could expect from the studio.

"From any of them? Lies, damned lies. Self-interest. The only thing you know is that you don't know a goddamned thing. Ask for the sky. Who knows, but they might give it to you."

Wolfe turned and stared at me. Right then, he looked like nothing more than a harried man who wanted me to go the hell away so that he could finally deal with his hangover in peace, but even with this face, he could force a fall before I had even begun to rise.

"Crucified god. What the hell am I supposed to do with you then?"

I shrugged.

"Find something. Of course you can."

That was a challenge, and Wolfe's kind, they seem designed for them. It was a weakness, but whether it was a weakness for them or for us, I never decided. He laughed his coughing laugh again.

"Fine. And what do I put on the press releases, Miss Ambitious?"

"Esme Ling," I said.

"No, dumb," Oberlin Wolfe said. "Another."

I flushed a dull brick red and gave him my second, and then my third and fourth choices.

"Hey, aren't you meant to give me a name?" I asked after the tenth one I tried.

He dropped something into his water to make it fizz and threw it back with a wince. His smile was the furthest thing from humor.

"You want things your way so bad, this is what it's like," he said. "If I had my way, you'd be Lotus Bell or Spring Green or some damn thing like that."

He threw himself back into his chair, raising his hand at me like a bandleader about to strike up a tune.

"Go on. Give me a name."

Lena-Barbara-Seana-Marlene-Darlene-Sandra-Pearl-and-Emerald

Time stretched like a piece of taffy. I stood on Oberlin Wolfe's rug, and names fell from my lips like rose petals, and then like rocks. I felt as if I stood there for hours, giving him names that he shook away. My throat went dry, and my voice turned to something rusty and hard.

Janet-Wendy-Susannah-Elizabeth-Sarah-Michelle-Candice-and-Edie

He wasn't doing it to torture me, or at least he wasn't doing it just for that. If he could have given me a name to get me the hell out of there, I believe he would have. Instead, he watched me with a face made of stone and teeth that were hidden and sharp.

Mila-Ophelia-Juliet-Coral-Eglantine-Rue-Lacey-Winifred-Pauline-Elle

I drew up names I didn't even know I knew, scraping my throat until it was raw. I even think my own real name was in there somewhere, as dismissed and forgotten as all the rest.

Doreen-Isabela-Lark-QuinnJoanBetteMarilynGayleLoretta . . .

Somehow the names still came, even as I clenched my hands, digging my fingernails into my hot palms. My voice was a drone in my own ears, and I might have stood there forever under some strange spell if Oberlin Wolfe hadn't raised his head, nostrils flaring and a slow smile splitting his face.

"Luli," he repeated. "Good. You can keep the last name, Wei, isn't it? Luli Wei. That's you. Now get the hell out of here. Janet will do the rest."

I stumbled out of the office with a terrible ringing in my ears, and every step I took I knew that I had done wrong. Somewhere across the city, my sister was crying, though she didn't know why. The excision and graft was so brutally quick and thorough it had made ghosts of us. The way we were was dead and gone. Now there was only Luli Wei and her sister, an anonymous girl on Hungarian Hill.

Janet gave me a load of contracts to fill out. It didn't matter what they said, because Wolfe and I had done the song and dance, kiss and christening. It was done, and I was Luli Wei.

I was going to be a star.

ACT
TWO

~

I got lost my very first day.

Cars were for queens, and so on the day I was scheduled to move into the dorms on Wolfe Studios, I did it by bus, carrying four stuffed shopping bags. The twine handles cut into my fingers, but those bags contained everything I owned, from dresses to shoes to jewelry. I had left nothing at home but my family.

The metal wolves at the gate gave me a cursory sniff before ignoring me, and the guard behind them did much the same. Then I was in Wolfe's own country, and even the noise of the street and the smell of dust and hot asphalt behind me was faded into insignificance.

The information desk was closed, and the entire studio had a strangely hushed sound as I walked deeper. I knew that there was a small town's worth of people working within these walls, but I couldn't see them or hear them. Even as I walked, a strange sleepiness fell over me, and my shoes grew tighter and my bags heavier.

I woke up when a blue Packard raced by, nearly hitting me, and I looked up just in time to see a girl's pale face pressed against the glass, distorted and strange. That woke me up, and taking a firmer grip on my bags, I kept walking.

I've heard that John Everest built his studio like a wheel. His own tower took the center and the lots, the dorms, production, editing, props, and costumes all spread around him like spokes, turning to grow his power. It seemed to me that there was no such organization at Wolfe Studios. I passed by closed lots as big as warehouses, an unmanned commissary that promised sandwiches and lemonade, and dust and dust and dust.

I hopefully followed a trio of girls all dressed in green velvet, but they disappeared into one of the lots, the steel door closing behind them with a permanent click. I turned around to backtrack, but then I was nearly swept off my feet by a crowd of people in togas and tunics leaving another set. Sword-and-sandal epics were big that year, and the crowd pulled me along and then spat me out by an artificial pond bordered by trees I knew couldn't grow in Los Angeles. They were too tall, their green leaves too plump with water.

"You're not supposed to be here any more than I am," I said to one, but yet, here we were.

I started to turn from the water, but then a splash rang out. Something had tumbled in on the far side, and I froze, my heart beating faster as I scanned the ripples. I didn't know how to swim—no child on my street did—but I could lower my hand, perhaps, or a branch?

For a moment, I thought that the water had played a trick on me, but then the glassy surface broke over a long and sinuous curve, something rising like an enormous smooth stone before sinking down again.

I saw the curve hump through the water twice more, and then, to my shock, a face pushed up out of the depths just a few yards from where I stood. I caught an impression of dark hair tangled with glass and trash, a dark round eye, and a mouth that opened like a wound to reveal teeth, so many teeth and too many teeth. It was something, I realized, that had been thrown away, dropped long ago and never picked up again. Then the water was as smooth as a mirror again, but I could see a dark shadow in it, swimming towards me, hungry and strange.

Underneath my sweat, I was icy cold, and I backed away from the pond. I let the trees close around their secret again, and as soon as I could, I turned on my heel and ran. I didn't know what lived in that pond, whether it was a drowned ghost that refused to leave or some pet of Oberlin Wolfe's, but I didn't want to find out. Didn't want to see that round eye or those teeth again.

Somehow, my mad dash away from the thing that lived in the pond had taken me right where I needed to be. I learned later that I wasn't the only one who had problems getting to the dorms, and though that was the worst it ever was for me, there were still nights when the turquoise doors and pale stone were obscured by smoke and dust, leaving me to sit still and stay quiet until the world chose to right itself again.

I was given an uninterested glance and a key by the matron, and told to avoid the elevator, because it didn't really work. I climbed up four stories to my room, and when I closed the door behind me, I felt a brief and vicious stab of triumph.

This place and this moment were mine, no matter what else happened. I had come to Wolfe Studios with no patron and no strength but my own. This terrible little room with the peeling linoleum was mine, from the fan that gently shifted the heat to the niche in the wall that held a forgotten saint, to the drugged and bandaged white girl sleeping on the couch. This studio which would try to devour me in a dozen different ways was mine, from the wolves to the pond I would never be able to find again, to the dust that scourged the paint from the signs.

It was all mine, and as strange as it was, as dangerous and as odd, that victory seized me and never let me go.

Eventually, hours after sunset, after I had arranged my few things in the dresser of my tiny bedroom and then rearranged them again to make it look as if I had more, the girl on the couch stirred. She was the suite's only other occupant, taking the room across from mine. She moved as if she were under water, but she leaned in my door and asked me if I wanted coffee. Her voice was deep and hoarse from her sleep, accented with strange stops.

I said *yes* cautiously, and she brewed something strong and smooth, handing me mine and drinking hers standing up in my doorway. She was dressed only in a short nightgown that stretched tight over her large breasts and round belly, and underneath it, I could see the bandages that wound around her hips.

Dazed as she was, she caught me staring and shrugged, her shoulders moving like smooth rocks.

"My tail," she said, as if she were passing the time. "They said I could not have it any longer."

Greta Nilsson was my roommate my first year living in the dorms. She was from Sodermalm in Sweden, where they say the girls are so beautiful that no man can resist them. In Sodermalm, the most beautiful girls are monsters, hollow-backed or cow-tailed, and no one thinks it strange at all. Oberlin Wolfe heard of Sodermalm. When he sent a scout out there, the scout was wise enough to speak with the old-timers on the mountain, and so went out armed with a rope blessed by a priest.

With the rope, he captured Greta as she sat sipping her coffee on a bench by the water. He led her all the way back to Los Angeles like that, shedding her navy blue coat, her mustard scarf, and her warm boots as the sun grew hotter than she had ever seen. A girl with a hollow back would have been a difficulty, but a girl with a cow's tail was no trouble at all.

I drank the coffee she gave me sitting on my bed with one bare foot tucked under my thigh. I wasn't good with other girls. I felt strange around them, all competition tangled with a desperate urge to please and belong. My new roommate didn't look like a girl I would have fought with or a girl that would draw my eye over and over again without my quite understanding why. She watched me as I watched her, and she spoke first.

"Did they bring you from China?" asked Greta curiously. "You came of your own will—are things so very bad there?"

I shot her an irritated look.

"I came from Hungarian Hill," I said coldly. "You can get there on the trolley if you want to walk a mile."

A few miles, but it might have been a world away. My mother never left our few city blocks. My father never left the laundry anymore.

"Who wants to hear about a girl from Hungarian Hill?" she said. "Did you work in a laundry or a restaurant as well? Come up with something more interesting."

I bridled at her words, but her tone was calm and sweet. There was no malice there or contempt. When I looked closer, it was as if her eyes tracked a different world than the one we all saw, one that was slower and more vivid by turns, something that might have made sense in the high mountains of Sweden but certainly didn't translate to bright Los Angeles.

That day, I ignored her strange words. I might be ahead of the graduated changelings who clambered all over the dorms like newly hatched lizards and the open-call starlets who had had their names stripped away, but my feeling of elation at being at Wolfe Studios tangled with the fear of how far I had yet to climb. In the weeks since my meeting with her, Mrs. Wiley's bloodstained tea-cup and satisfied smile crept into my dreams. Twenty years, that was a lifetime, it was my life back to my birth and beyond, and I was realizing it was no small thing I had gambled away. I was in a hurry, and I had no way to start.

When I didn't answer her, she entered my room without speaking and leaned down to face me. Her movements were graceful in spite of the bandage swathed around her, but she missed the balance of her luxurious tail. She was foreign to me just as I was foreign to others. She had a round moon face, her heavy breasts straining the loose shirt she wore. Under it, I could see the slight hang of her belly and her heavy thighs. She had a lunar beauty rather than a human one, and people looking at her could drown in it, still confused by the pull of this one fat and lovely girl.

"We are in this together, right?" she said. "Shall we be friends?"

"Is it really that easy?" I asked. I wanted to sound tough, but it came out slightly wistful instead. I didn't have friends. I had never really felt their lack, or at least that was what I told myself.

She smiled sweetly, and took my hand in hers. She smelled faintly of milk and honey and something warmer as well. Later, I realized that she was still very much on painkillers when we were having this conversation.

"Of course it is, min skatt. Nothing's hard but life, eh?"

III

As it turned out, there were plenty of things that were hard. The girls and boys in the dorm, we were interchangeable parts, ones that needed to be tuned and supple enough to step into whatever gap or crack that appeared. Some had patrons who could speed the way, but the rest of us were relying on sheer shine and determination to bring us to the attention of the casting directors.

Mondays Greta and I made our way to the dance classes of Mme Benoit, who taught out of a squat and dusty building off the set. She wore a pair of supple red leather shoes, a strange combination of ballet slippers and tap shoes, and when she danced, the whole world stood still. She could not dance without crying, and it was unnerving to hear her lecture us on attitude, cambré, and turnout with her cheeks wet with salt water.

Tuesdays both Greta and I had to study with the diction coach, a man we only knew to be German because of his name. Greta was purposefully obstinate with Herr Hochstetler, but I steamrolled my native accent as flat as a sheet of gold leaf. I had told Oberlin Wolfe no funny accents, and I meant to hold up my end of the deal. That was where I lost the very last of my Cantonese, and it died with a soft aspirate, a consonant rhotic.

On Wednesdays we were meant to educate ourselves, taking advantage of the various tutors and facilities that Wolfe Studios provided. Greta largely used the time to doze in our sitting room, and for my part, I drifted fretfully from fencing lessons with the cast of *Robin Hood* to comportment for the cadre of girls who were earmarked—quite literally, with a pearl earring—for the period dramas. There were so many options that I felt unraveled. So many ways to improve meant that I was lacking in all of them, and I dropped weight at an alarming rate as I spun from ballroom dance to makeup lessons.

"No," Greta said one morning, as I looked over the mimeographed schedule we had been given. "The only thing you are learning today is to like my cooking."

She was clever. She didn't make me any of the rich and creamy foods that she remembered from Sodermalm. If she had, I would have been sick and likely wasted away to one of the thin ghosts that haunted Lot C, rattling in their skins and lit from within with a yellow-green hunger. Instead she made me broth and kroppkakor, dumplings filled with potatoes, onions, and pork. They awakened my appetite, and then she could give me salted raw salmon, dark bread with herring and mustard sauce, and even rice pudding and ham. My mother's cooking had been indifferent, but under Greta's direction, I grew sleek, my angularity smoothed away and my hollows filled out.

On Thursday, singly, in pairs, and in large and mistrusting circles, we read for the casting directors, everything from dusty Westerns to Regency romances. To my growing anxiety, they never knew what to do with me, scowling whenever they opened my file and saw the restrictions that Oberlin Wolfe himself had noted there.

"I don't see what we're meant to do with you," said one man. I remember how his pomaded hair gleamed like the back of a cockroach. "What are you *for*?"

I didn't say anything, but instead I put my response in my glare. *Isn't finding that out your job?*

It was particularly bad when I got close. One Thursday, they were seriously considering me for a walk-on bit in a Western, someone needed to cry out a warning before she was shot from the street. The casting director wavered over the matter, and then shook his head, giving the part to one of the nodders that lined the back of the casting rooms instead.

Abigail McKinnon had been white with slick black hair, my height and my build—we could have shared clothes if anything had remained in her that cared about clothes. The nodder that was left after Abigail got pregnant and refused to give up her baby got more work than I did.

~

Have you ever seen a movie where a part was simply filled? There's no life or wit to the person spilling the drink, or running from the riders, or smiling in the crowd scene, but they're there and you don't notice until much later how stiff they were, how awkwardly they moved.

The nodders were too expensive or too dangerous to make in great numbers, or something like that, because I don't doubt that otherwise Wolfe would have made for himself a kingdom of them. Even after what was lit up in them had been extinguished, they still took direction, even if they did it clumsily and badly.

Greta had no better luck than I did for all that Wolfe Studios had sent a scout after her. She said her lines with a drawl that was just short of insolent, and she seemed to move as if she were underwater. I heard one casting director wonder aloud whether Greta had been allowed to keep taking her morphine long after she should have stopped. But Greta wasn't drugged, she was grieved, and then grief became her trademark when they cast her in *The Belles of St. Desmond*.

Except for one incandescent shot, where Greta turns to Brandt Hiller and tells him she doesn't care for men of his kind, *The Belles* didn't last. It disappeared, lost to fire or fortune or sabotage, but for a year or so after it premiered, it was enormous. Women went about slurring their words as if they were drunk on sloe gin, an ugly imitation of Greta's husky accent, and men let their hats droop down over one eye in imitation of Brandt Hiller. It spawned a series of imitations, all darkly lit and gloomy, none of them with even the transient grace of the original. The vogue would end when the war broke out, and Wolfe Studios would turn to bright musicals and war propaganda, but that Thursday, we didn't know that.

When Greta returned to the apartment that night, I was a stew of jealousy and resentment and guilt. It's hard to resent someone when you're eating the potato dumplings they left you, but I tried. She didn't deserve it, however, and I resolved to do my best and to put on a glad face when she returned.

Then she opened the door, and all feigned gladness fled to make way for shock.

Greta stumbled in as if she had found our rooms by accident, her fair hair falling like a sheaf of fanned newspaper across her brow. There were two red spots of color high on her cheeks, and her eyes were too bright and glassy. She looked like a hunted animal. I locked the door and checked it twice before I turned back to her.

She had perched herself on the tall stool in the kitchen, her bare feet tucked primly underneath her and a tall glass of akvavit in her hand. It was strictly contraband, purchased from a sly Japanese girl who seemed to come and go as she pleased, and I glanced at the door again.

"Greta . . ."

"It is *terrible*," she said in her round and rolling voice. "I have fallen in love."

She tipped the glass back, and when it came back down, there were enormous diamond tears running down her face.

IV

Friday, I'm sure, was meant for something, but whatever it was got lost in Friday night. Friday night was when all the walls came down, and Wolfe Studios shifted that slight bit to make it something other than a series of sound stages and back lots in the middle of the Hollywood groves. Something about Friday dropped the boundaries down like silk banners. The hunt rode on Friday nights, not like they did on Halloween and Midsummer, but we could hear their horns through the clinking of champagne glasses and the laughter that rose in an attempt to hide them.

If we were clever, we would have barred the door and stayed inside, but I think if we were that kind of clever, we would never have walked past the great silver wolves at the gate. Deals were struck on Friday nights. Directors had their heads turned by clever girls and beautiful boys. A Friday night lover could be a formidable ally on Monday morning, and they said that children conceived at the Friday night fires went on to be stars in their own right, heroes and ringmasters, politicians and beauty kings.

Once, a girl in our dorm saw something enormous and horned devour a darkly beautiful girl with a lisping Castilian accent. The next Monday, I saw that same girl in dance class, a calm and silver light in her eyes, and I wouldn't have bet a single cent on whether she was more or less than she had been.

The Friday fires never became normal. I remembered one girl, tugging her pearl earring restlessly, who said that they existed outside of time. If we went walking too far into the dark, the studio would turn into earthwork halls and stone circles, unmoored and drifting in the dark and the smoke. A boy with a delicate mustache and wild eyes said that the fires were the reason for the studios in the first place, that it all went on to keep the fires burning. He jumped into one, nothing to sacrifice but himself. I remember his mother coming to pick up his name from the receiving office, carrying it out in an envelope. She was lucky to get that.

I had never gone to the fires before Greta was cast in *The Belles,* though she had ventured down there once or twice. I was putting it off for some reason, perhaps waiting until I had more than castoff parts to show for it. I still hadn't proved myself in any way that counted, but that night, Greta needed to wander and to move, or she might have frayed herself to pieces with stress and weak tears.

There were tides of old clothes washed around in the dorms, discards and left-behinds, and though it was rare for Greta to find anything that would stretch over her hips or her breasts, I did somewhat better. That night, she simply wrapped herself in yards of pale mulberry silk, pinning it here and there and in the end emerging awkward and strange but beautiful. I did well for myself in a shapely dress in newly fashionable black. No one else would touch it because it belonged to a girl who committed love suicide with a grip ("screwing below the line," as Evelyn Drake said, and I was glad when she was exiled to Aegis in exchange for an Indian girl with a Brooklyn accent), but I wasn't in love with anyone, so I knew I would be fine.

"Stay with me tonight," Greta insisted. "I do not want to be alone."

I still hadn't figured out what had happened to Greta the night before. I knew she had been brought in to read for Joseph Spengler, and then she would have been tested against whatever male star they were showcasing. I tried to ask her, but she only pinched her mouth into a painfully thin line, shaking her head.

It occurred to me as we skirted the edges of the fires that for Greta, human though she looked, love might be something very different. I was old enough to see love wreck other girls, with pregnancy, with drugs, with a longing that could never be quenched, and the idea that Greta's kind of love might be more destructive yet terrified me.

Tonight she clung to my arm as if I was a knight in shining armor, and whenever someone got too close, she buried her face in my shoulder. Most of the people we passed looked on her with contempt, fat and frumpy in her cocoon of silk, but a few looked with wonder at the gleam that peeked through. They never noticed me at all. I might have been her nurse or some old friend brought up from the valley to see the secret fires.

A few of the girls who lived in our dorm called us over, and when I shot her an inquiring eyebrow, Greta nodded. The sky was just losing its last traces of blue, and the fire they had gathered around was small and furtive. They seemed to be hiding, and the smiles the girls there gave us were shy. Studio changelings, I thought. They had been brought up in the shadows of the fires. They had scraped out a kind of life there, and they knew how to keep safe against the long nights.

We sat with them though neither of us could understand their strange and sharp language. It sounded a little like Cantonese, I thought, and French, and it mingled with some kind of punctuating hand sign that fluttered like small birds. One of them passed me a flask with a giggle, and shrugging, I took it. The first sip was unpleasant, pure burning with a crisp honey and herbal aftertaste that made me think of my father's tortoiseshell cabinet. I passed the flask to Greta, who took a long pull immediately, gasping a husky laugh when she was done.

"Uisge beathe," she said with a smile. "It's different than what my cousins gave to me, but good. Thank you. Thank you."

She passed it back to the tall girl with the dead pale skin and black hair, but the girl passed it back to her. As Greta took another long sip, I looked at the girl sharply, but her gaze was perfectly level. There was no gloating plan or lust for humiliation in the girl's eyes, but I didn't trust her. When she would have given Greta a third drink, I pushed her hand away.

"You can't keep her safe, you know," the girl said in English. Her voice rang like small bells, echoing and tinny.

"Of course I can't, I know that," I growled. "But she doesn't need any more of that. Drink it yourself."

Greta tugged my sleeve as I was staring the girl down.

"Come," she said. "I want to see more of the fires."

Her words were a bridge. A part of me didn't want to cross them, wanted to run straight back to the dorm, or even, shamefully, back past the gates where the wolves Sinister and Dexter kept out those who were not supposed to enter, but never cared for who wanted to leave. In front of us was something dark and burning, the future I wanted more than I wanted to breathe, and I nodded.

"All right. Let's go. But slowly, all right?"

Plenty of people have written about the Friday fires. When Perry and Amity Fitzwarren came west to trade their glamour for fairy gold, they danced through them like king and queen, untouchable until, of course, they weren't. Even Amity couldn't capture the way the flames looked more red than they should have, how the heat ebbed and flowed like the tide. There was always a full moon hanging over the lots on Friday night, outshining the one that hung in the sky for everyone else, and once I looked up to see a lunar face looking back at me, and laughing with a kind of cruel indifference.

We were too new and frail to rule one of the fires ourselves. They were courts in miniature, the fires where directors and actors could pretend to be Oberlin Wolfe himself. With Greta on my arm, we skirted the roistering fire of Alan Watt, in the prime of his career with his stunt horse Etta at his side. She wore a human form that night, her horse hide thrown over her shoulders like a cloak, but we could see the white around the dark of her eyes and knew she would kick if anyone came too close. James Kenfield languished at a low fire to hide the tremors in his hand and the deep lines that addiction had carved into his face. He reached for us, me or Greta or some ghost of an actress he had known a lifetime ago. We left him too, but not before a studio changeling crept hopefully close. I turned my head to see her grow taller and thinner, her features turning almost hawkish. Lorena Fairman, I thought, or maybe Shelley Du Lac. Ghost queen to a dying king, and it made me shake a little.

Greta felt the tremor go through me, and it was as if she forgot that I was the one who was meant to be looking after her. She stroked my arm and squeezed me close.

"Poor lamb," she said, and she tipped up to plant a soft kiss on my forehead, bare since Oberlin Wolfe had stripped it of Maya Vos Santé's kiss. "Let us find a safe harbor. We should not wander all through the night."

Where? I might have asked her. We were in the heart of the fires now, and behind the beat of the drums, the horns sounded, brassy and cold. On Saturday morning, everyone would be back in silk pajamas, sipping mimosas by the side of turquoise pools that hid nothing in their depths, but it was not Saturday morning yet. It might not be Saturday morning for a long time.

Greta took the lead now, guiding me on a weaving path through the dark. More than once, I heard a voice call my name from the darkness and the flames. Once it was most likely Jacko, once it might have been Jane or Tara, calling through darkness and time.

It could have been fame or fortune in the form of a director or an actor who liked the line of my body, the curve of my cheek. It could also have been something barbed and hungry, no predator like Oberlin Wolfe but something that made its way stealing scraps that no one would notice. Often, there's no way to tell until you can count the teeth.

Greta led me right past those calls, her head turning neither to the right or the left. She knew her place. It wasn't here, but she knew it, and that gave her a kind of strength.

I am still not sure if she had a destination in mind. As far as I could tell that night, she was only leading us deeper to a place where the darkness between the bonfires seemed to drag at us, close and stifling.

Just when I wanted to tug her back towards the edges, something shifted, and I heard a soft voice calling to us.

"Oh it's Greta and her girl, come here, come here . . ."

The voice was bright and sweet, but there was a resonance to it that couldn't be resisted, not then. Greta smiled with a strange kind of relief, and unerringly, she drew me forward.

This fire threw back a wall of heat, but still there was something cold to it. There were far more women gathered around it than men, and the men had a watchful, wary quality to them, like nothing I had quite seen revealed before. The people around this fire fell softly on each other like leaves drifted together on the ground, but there were sharp eyes on Greta and me, trying to see some marker that I couldn't sense myself.

I looked up at the girl seated on a low couch covered with fine brocades, and I recognized her. I had last seen her stumbling in the lot, her star's gleam obvious even in the November sky. She was naked then, and now she only wore a sheer white silk dress, scattered with glass beads to give it a hard shine.

Emmaline Sauvignon kept her own private and peculiar court

around a fire that looked like a fallen star, and a distant drum that echoed my heart beat faster.

I moved haltingly towards her, eyes wide, and if she had called my name in that moment, showed me in any way at all that she recognized me, I would have fallen dead on the spot. Everyone who you have ever seen painted up on the screen thirty feet high, loving or laughing or hating or warring, every single one has this potential in them as well, a trick for being worshipped and a taste for the divine.

Instead, Greta's hand on my arm kept me steady, and Emmaline only looked at me with a friendly smile.

"Hello," she said. "Are you Greta's girl?"

"She is her own," Greta said with a shrug. It was, to me, a daft thing to say, but Greta's language was like the way she moved, slow and strange, insisting on its own way. "Shall we stay?"

Emmaline paused, and I could have dropped into the abyss of that moment. Then she smiled and glanced around her circle.

"Make some room, Greta and . . . who are you, dear heart?"

"Luli Wei," I said. The hesitation before I said it was gone. It was almost mine now. I heard my sister had become a Mary. You could go practically anywhere with a name like Mary, and I wondered if she had made the best of it like she had made the best of the little button-eyed dolls.

"Beautiful," she said lightly. "Make some room for Greta and Luli. Shove over, will ya?"

She hadn't been at Wolfe Studios much longer than I had been. Sometimes, the Minnesotan farm girl still came out. Her last name used to be Lundstedt, and perhaps that was why Greta knew her, some quirk of ancestry or cold reaching further than warmth ever could.

The circle opened like water for us, and re-formed with us a part of it. It was seamless in a way that seemed more magic than the wolves or the distant horns, and I sat on a cushion with Greta leaning against my side.

"Jillian was just telling us about how her meeting with Abelard went."

The dark-haired girl sitting close to Emmaline's knee laughed, shaking her close-cropped curls in calculated modesty. She pressed closer to Emmaline, and immediately I disliked her. I excused it with a dislike of lapdogs in general, but even then I knew the truth.

"Oh, well, I was terrified out of my wits, you know? One of the studio changelings told me that the chair you sit on in Mr. Abelard's office was like a barber's chair, and that he could flip it back so that whoop, you went down on your back with your legs up . . ."

Someone from the circle made a disbelieving noise, but before Emmaline's sharp eye could search them out, one of the men spoke up. With his rough clothes and slight, scarred face, I knew he wasn't an actor, and Evelyn Drake's sly voice whispering about screwing below the line hovered traitorously in my mind.

"It's true," he said flatly. "And there are binds underneath it could keep a bull elephant down."

The silence after that was sharp but not unsympathetic. Emmaline nodded at Jillian to continue.

"So the day before I went walking down to the south back lot where they were shooting *Aegean Winds*. I don't know what I was doing, just walking because if I didn't get out of the dorm, I would have gone crazy, you know? When I came by, they were on break, or at least that's what they called it while Mr. Keene yelled his head off at Paul Wineland."

A giggle went around the circle. Even I had heard about Paul Wineland's famously slow manner of both speech and action. It dripped like honey on the screen, and he made bank for the studio, but it was like putting tinder to the torch when paired with Keene's equally famous temper.

"I figured that if anyone asked what I was doing, I would say I had just dropped off some coffee for someone, but no one did, so I kept looking around. It was getting dark then, and they only had lights over Mr. Wineland. I guess I'm pretty lucky there was no cliff there or I might have slipped right over."

Her giggle was nervous this time, and Emmaline placed a comforting hand on her head. Paul Wineland might have been known for his slow manner of talking, but Emmaline had a quality for stillness. She could wait out an age, and sooner than that, Jillian started talking again.

"So I'm walking along the coast, and before too long, it feels like the lights are a long way behind me, and I can hear the water crash below and feel the wind howling above."

No one doubted her here. Strange things happen on set.

"And this woman is sitting on the rock, and she's wrapped up in something purple and shimmery. She asks me for something to eat, because she's so hungry, and I give her some cookies I was saving for later. She eats them, and then she says to me, 'I can see you're a girl with a problem.'

"Well, I am, and I tell her about Mr. Abelard, and she thinks for a minute before telling me to sit down next to her, because she's got a plan.

"The next day, I go to Mr. Abelard like he says, and golly, but I'm sweating something fierce. I didn't even have seven shirts like the lady on the rock told me to get. I had to borrow from my roommate and our friend in the hall. So I walk into his office, and it's just like a forest in there. He's got trees in pots, so many that they block the window, and in the back is a real fountain made of rock with the water cycling through and little golden fishies swimming in it. It's so beautiful, and I'm sweating and scared and about to puke, but he just looks at me like he's going to swallow me up in one bite.

"He starts to gesture at the chair, but then he stops and looks at me for a minute. He can't figure out what's wrong, but he just tells me, 'Pretty girl, take off your shirt.'"

Jillian giggled again, her fingers knotting through her short hair and tugging. Again, Emmaline's fingers soothed her, and she continued.

"So I do it, and while he's still wondering why I've got a shirt on underneath, I tell him, 'Mr. Abelard, take off your skin,' just like the woman says. For a minute I thought he was going to have a heart attack, but he grits his teeth and picks up a knife from his desk. It was a weird thing, iron, and they don't like iron, do they, Emmaline? Wasn't that a strange thing for him to have?"

Emmaline shrugged, but I could see she was filing that information away.

"Mr. Abelard might just be a different kind of monster," she said, her voice calm enough to hide a great deal of trouble underneath.

"He tears himself open, and oh, it looks like it hurts. His skin was smaller than I thought it would be but it thumped when it hit the ground. The carpet was dark, or else I might have seen how bad it was and fainted."

"But you didn't," Emmaline said softly, and Jillian fairly glowed.

"So he's wearing something cheaper underneath, and his hair's slicked down like something newborn, and he says to me again, 'Pretty girl, take off your shirt,' and I do, and there's Chloe's pink seersucker blouse. I say the words to him again, and he has to pick up the knife again.

"This keeps going, and we hit my camisole. My heart's thudding so fast, because what if I got it wrong, or what if that woman tricked me, you know? I came this far, and maybe I should have sneaked another shirt on . . . Well, I take off Amanda's silk embroidered shirt, the blue one, and underneath, I'm down to my slip and my skirt. I say it one more time, 'Mr. Abelard, take off your skin,' and he cries! He starts blubbering and asking me not to do it."

She paused.

"If I had had an extra shirt on, I might have taken it back," Jillian said meditatively. "I'm not . . . I'm not like them. If I had my shirt on and not just my slip . . ."

She shrugged.

"I didn't. I insisted, and then he's down to his skin and I can see it all. I can see how he used to kiss up to the bigger boys in school so they didn't bully him, and how much fun it was to bully the littler boys. I could see how he put his mom in a home so he never has to think about her again, and a boy he stranded out on the prairie in the middle of winter. I saw all of it, and above all, I saw how *little* he was.

"With all the skin off of him, he was just this blubbering weedy sloppy mess, but the woman on the rocks told me that if I stopped there, he would just regrow his skins. In six months, a year, two years, he would be big Mr. Abelard again, in the nice suit and with the chair that can bind down elephants."

"So what did you do?" I asked, my tone hushed. I had almost forgotten what a little lapdog she looked to me. These were the lessons I had been craving while I learned how to walk in high heels and how to speak so that I sounded like I had never worked for a living. This was how to survive in the Friday fires and the ashes they left behind.

"I did just as the lady said. I picked him up from the floor and threw him on the desk. He has these trees in pots all over the office, and I pulled my knife from my purse. I cut a few good switches, and I start beating the hell out of him. I beat him so hard that I think my arm is going to fall off. Even when he's howling fit to bust my eardrums, no one comes in."

"They're used to yelling from the office," offers someone else, and the circle nods sagely.

"Well, I wear out the switches, I just want to crawl away and sleep forever, but I'm still not done. I'm so tired, but I drag him to the rock fountain. I throw him in and I wash him. I didn't have a board, so I have to beat him against the rocks until all the nastiness is gone. It took a while."

Jillian paused, and tilted her head so that Emmaline could tousle her hair gently. She luxuriated in the attention before she continued, but I couldn't fault her this time, caught up in her story.

"I wrung him out and threw him over the ledge of the fountain to dry. After that, I don't know, I guess I slept? I went to the couch at the back of the office, and I curled up there. It was nice. Comfortable. When I woke up, he was Mr. Abelard again, but not the one I had met.

"He was shrugging into a stiff, shiny new jacket, and though he's still big, there was something different in his eyes. Maybe this was who he used to be, or maybe I chased him out, and something else came to live inside him instead."

She shrugged, supremely unconcerned.

"'So you must be Miss Waldorf,' he says with this big smile. 'I'm Ronald Abelard, and I'm so pleased to meet you.' Well, I sit down in that chair that he don't even know how to flip anymore, and we talk and talk for almost three hours. I have a three-picture deal now, and that's three pictures before Midsummer, mind you. I've got a new place all to myself over in Brentwood, and he says that I might have an even better contract waiting for me after this, and I got it all while keeping my slip on."

She finished triumphantly, and the circle burst into applause, myself included. Ronald Abelard made Jillian Waldorf's career, and though her star is quite small, it is very bright. The man himself drifted away on some easterly wind, and the nastiness he left behind crumbled to ash on some back studio lot.

"I wonder what would have happened if you had sat behind his desk," I said without thinking, and Jillian's sharp eyes turned to me.

"Is that what you would have done?" she asked, a hint of contempt in her voice. "Skinny as you are, I bet you couldn't have dragged him to the fountain or slammed him down to get all that awful off."

It was on the tip of my tongue to tell her that of course I could have. I had been dragging heavy silk dresses and pure wool suits through the wash since I was a child. Then I shrugged because that kind of truth mattered very little here, at least to me.

"I don't know what I would have done," I said, meeting her eyes. "You were very brave and very clever. I hope I could have done the same. But I still wonder what would have happened if he had opened his eyes and the first thing he saw was you sitting behind his desk."

"Nothing good," Greta proclaimed, and because it was her, I smiled a little.

"You never think there's anything good," I said, and the strange tense moment with Jillian passed. She leaned her head against Emmaline's knee, and I tried not to be so jealous, because now I knew it was just jealousy.

Someone else mentioned the courtyard in front of Mr. Abelard's office, a famously ugly place, and when Jillian described the statue and the iron fence and the flowers that grew there, Emmaline looked surprised for the first time.

"Five pointed petals on a short stem?" she asked. "A rust-red center?"

"Yes," Jillian said, too startled to be calculating. "Just like that. In a few pots."

"Oh, love-comes-home," Emmaline said faintly, and the whole circle drifted a little closer to her. When she noticed, she looked up and for the first time, she seemed almost embarrassed.

"Love-comes-home, that's what that flower is called," she said. "It used to grow all over my family's estate. They're spring flowers, and every year, without fail, they bloomed just a day before I was sent off to school. Like my home was saying good-bye."

Even then I didn't really believe it. There was a story behind

Emmaline and love-comes-home, called kickweed back in her native Minnesota. I never got it, but all I needed was that wistful look in her eyes, a longing for something that somehow, she didn't have.

Someone muttered about Abelard being able to make it summer all year round in his courtyard, and someone else countered that they could all do it, turn back the season and make it shine or snow.

"I bet we could get love-comes-home for you, Emmaline," Jillian was suggesting. "I know this florist on St. Immanuel's Way, and he does all the flowers for the big weddings . . ."

I saw the tolerant look on Emmaline's face and a trace of pain there that made me strangely hungry. I wanted to erase that pain, and I wanted to be the only one to do it.

"He's not going to have love-comes-home," I said. I hadn't meant to speak up at all, and without consideration, my voice was scornful. Jillian turned to me with a stung look that narrowed when she realized she had no idea who I was. I was no one to be careful around, no one to placate or smile for.

"What do you know about that anyway?" she asked. "Do they have a lot of flowers at the restaurant?"

Greta stirred almost as if she had woken up just for this statement alone, blinking large eyes in the firelight.

"They would not here," she said in her slow and amiable way. "That flower, we have it at home. Needs warmth in the ground, but it will not bloom without a first frost, you see?"

She thought for a moment before continuing.

"You could do it, I suppose. Warmth of this sun, refrigerator. But no one would. It is not so beautiful."

Greta made her way at Wolfe Studios as if she didn't care about anything, because she didn't. That gave her a peculiar kind of power, often imitated but never perfectly, because if you imitated her, you cared. For Greta, they had already taken away her tail, and now she didn't see what else anyone could take from her.

"I suppose it's not," Emmaline said with a half laugh. "You're very right, Greta. It's only a humble little thing, after all."

"We know it grows in one place in LA," I said.

It was a peculiar moment. I had stepped back from myself, a foot or more. Greta was still leaned against me. The fire still warmed my face, and it was my voice echoing around the circle. The real me sat back in the shadows as if astonished.

"Yes, in Mr. Abelard's courtyard," said Jillian. "He doesn't do anything for anyone, not just for asking."

"Maybe if it was Emmaline doing the asking," said a narrow person draped in a robe from last year's musical, *Midsummer Madcap*. Someone from the costuming division, I thought absently, judging from the borrowed look of their finery.

"She's not going to have to ask at all." From a foot behind my body, I got a sense of curious dread. I knew what was going to happen because it was me, after all, but if I could have stopped myself, I might have.

"And why not?" asked Jillian.

"Because I'm going to go get them for her myself. Tonight."

The circle broke into excited murmurs, almost as good as applause. The sound woke me up a little; at least it sent goose bumps up and down my arms and brought a flush to my numb face. My heart was beating fast, and somewhere, that drum echoed in me still. Greta squinted at the fire and then at me as if I had turned into something that she didn't recognize.

"Pull the other one, it's got bells on it," said Jillian, but she looked uncertain. She gathered closer to Emmaline as if suddenly unsure of her place. Emmaline's hand landed in her curls, but carelessly. Her voice cut through the chatter.

"You mustn't," she said seriously. "It's far too dangerous."

("Oh, she must have liked you right away to feed you a line like that," laughed Jane.

"Don't be such a bitch, she said she was sincere."

"I'll bet she was, but I don't write lines like that *not* to see people do the stupid thing.")

I thought I could drown in the sweetness of her voice. From where I sat, I swayed closer to her, and then I stood up. With a grumble of protest, Greta rolled away and looked up at me with some irritation, but I ignored her. I couldn't help it.

"Of course I will," I said. I sounded confident. "You wanted it, and you should have it."

Emmaline's lips parted, and it threw fire deep in my body. She couldn't help what she was, and I couldn't help what I was. We were stories that should never have met, or stories that only existed because we met. I still don't know.

"Please," she said. Only that, and I turned away from the fire, breaking the circle.

I walked into the darkness, and then I realized that Greta was walking with me. I looked at her in surprise. She sighed.

"I told you I do not want to be alone tonight," she grumbled.

After a moment, I took her hand, still walking.

"I don't either," I admitted, and she laughed a little.

V

It would be easy to think that the studio directors, lords of the court, kept their offices in towers hovering high over the tumult. Oberlin Wolfe did, but there was no one like Oberlin Wolfe.

Ronald Abelard instead kept house in the east courtyard, along with Emerson Lankin and the Mannheim brothers. They were bigger business than Jacko Dewalt, and they kept their own counsel. Though they liked to give out otherwise, they were all human, and they fought those humble beginnings with cypress moss, a garden plot full of spiky foreboding plants, and a fountain that featured a crucified Jesus in bronze. As the famous society writer Dottie Wendt said a few years later, too Bosch for words.

It was not a long walk to the east courtyard in the daylight, but the way was longer in the dark. I had at least grown used to the ache of high heels now, and Greta kicked hers off, swinging them in her free hand as we walked.

The fires were behind us. The darkness was absolute save for the sodium lights high above.

"Do you know what you are doing?" she asked gravely, and I shrugged. I knew what I had to do. I had to bring flowers to Emmaline, love-comes-home for her head and her hand. What happened before that, I wasn't sure about. I had a bit of knowledge about picking locks with a sliver of metal or plastic, and if necessary I was narrow enough to slip into places that most never imagined. The bridge to Emmaline crowned in flowers that I had given her was shaky, but I told myself it would hold my weight. I might not have actually believed that story, but I needed to at least pretend that I did to get to the end of it.

Greta sighed again, shaking her head. She looked more like a sacrifice than I was comfortable with in her cocoon of shimmering silk. Her hair was falling down out of its pins, and if it were not for the pale resolve on her face, she might be one more girl drunk and debauched in the Friday fires.

"I want you to go back," I said, stopping under the relative safety of a lamp. "You don't need to be involved in this."

She arched an eyebrow at me, perfect scorn and affection in equal measures.

"Are you going to go back?"

I shook my head. I couldn't say that I had already stolen my sister's name, I didn't know what I would be if I took more from Greta, who thought she had lost everything. Instinctively I understood that there was always something more to lose.

"Then we are going."

We walked into the darkness again. There's nothing so absolute as the absence of artificial light, and the distant sounds that we heard made that darkness even heavier. Once we heard the horns of the hunt, and we both hid behind a dumpster, waiting for them to go by. There was the roar of the engines, a mad baying that seemed too shrill to be that of a dog pack, and a laugh that filled the world. We huddled behind the dumpster, pressing ourselves against the brick until it was silent and we could move again.

A little after that, we stopped short because we heard a sob a short distance off, feminine and despairing.

"Are you all right?" Greta called, and the sob cut off short.

"P-please . . ." The sob came again. "Please . . ."

The sound was so desolate that I started towards it, but Greta pulled me back with a shake of her head.

"What is it? What has been done to you?" she asked.

"Please . . . I need help, please . . ."

"Explain," Greta demanded, and I blinked at the harsh note in her voice.

"Please . . ."

She shook her head, taking my hand more firmly.

"Come on," she said, and she walked on.

"What was that?" I asked, glancing over my shoulder. My stomach turned at the desperation in that voice, but the farther we walked from it, the easier it got.

"Doesn't matter," she said. "She wanted us to go into the dark, but she would not say why. Too many things like that where I come from, and they lead to death. Death in the mountains, death in the swamp, but it is all death alike."

Sooner rather than later, we came to the east courtyard, where we both breathed a sigh of relief. There was something overblown about the Gothic dreariness of the courtyard, lit from all around by bulbs with a dim violet filter. It was a story compared to the reality of the darkness between the fires, but I reminded myself that stories could still hurt and kill. The gate was shut but not locked, and we walked in as easily as if we had appointments.

We found roses and columbine in the east courtyard garden, as well as whispering stalks that rattled as we passed and something that chimed like bells, but until we came closer to Ronald Abelard's office, with its brass plaque inscribed with his name on the door, we couldn't find love-comes-home.

The little flowers were lovely, but nothing special. I wondered briefly if Abelard came from someplace like Greta and Emmaline did, where the rusty-hearted flowers meant home, and then I decided that I didn't care at all. I pinched off the stalks close to the dirt, grateful for my sharp nails. I could never have kept them so long at the laundry. I had only plucked a few stems when I glanced up to see that Greta was gazing at the roses.

"In for a penny, you might as well," I said, and she broke one woody stem with a soft laugh.

That was when we heard it, a rustle at the gate, a sound like a groan for water. We both froze, and I bent down, ready to grab another handful of flowers and run.

"What are *you* doing here?" asked Greta, and her voice was sharp, as if someone had come into her courtyard and not the other way around.

"Caroline?" The face was male and slightly breathless, but the name wasn't a guess. That was the name they were throwing around for Greta, Caroline Carlsson. She answered to it about as well as an iron teakettle would, which was to say, not at all.

"No," said Greta sharply. "That name is ridiculous. My name is Greta."

"Greta . . ." The tone was worshipful and wondering, and now I stood up, bewildered at what was going on.

Brandt Hiller was just twenty-four, and he looked younger. There was something tender about his face and the way his blond hair fell into his eyes, something soft and sweet and touching even to me. He had played eager young sons for a few years, and just that summer, he had graduated to young romantic roles.

"No," Greta said, stalking towards him. "Get my name out of your mouth."

I watched, mouth slightly ajar, as Greta walked towards this young man that looked like a willow branch in the violet light of the courtyard. I didn't think I had ever seen her approach anyone with that kind of resolve before, and the missing piece clicked into place.

"Is that . . ." I hadn't meant to speak at all, but Greta glanced over her shoulder at me.

"Yes," she said, her eyes bright.

He was perfectly still as she approached him, and I saw the uneasy shadow of something I recognized in his eyes. She could have been coming towards him with a knife or a railroad spike instead of a rose in her hands, and that would have been just fine as long as she kept coming. She trampled moss and flowers under her feet, and when she came up to him, he took the white rose from her hand.

"Please," he said, and Greta must have known why he said it because she reached for him and drew him in for a deep kiss. It went on so long that I looked away, and when I looked back it was still going.

When Greta pulled away, she was turned so that I couldn't see her face, but I could see his. It was as if he had lost himself but gained something so profound that it was worth it, worth it.

Greta glanced over her shoulder at me. She looked more than beautiful. She looked wild, and this was the part of her the studio wanted, that it could never touch. It would never show up on film or on command, worthless to them, and I shivered at how rare it was to see at all.

"This won't take long," she said curtly. "Pick your flowers."

She took him behind the fountain, dragging him by one hand. He stumbled after her, losing a shoe in the process, and because I didn't have anything to do besides what she said, I picked as many of the flowers as I dared. They looked patchy when I was done, but not so devastated that someone would get in trouble, I hoped. The more time I had to think, the more I could see destruction radiating out from what we were doing.

I bound the stems together with a garter. My stocking drifted down but that didn't matter on Friday. I looked like a wasting bride with the bouquet in my hands, but Greta was right, and it didn't take her long. My head jerked up when she called me, and warily, I rounded the grotesque fountain to find her bedded on smashed greenery with Brandt Hiller resting on one shoulder. They hadn't taken off their clothes, but Greta's skirt was hiked up to her hips, Brandt's trousers undone.

"Put that down and come here," she said, indicating the side opposite from Brandt.

She was wild and strange, but I went to her without fear. I placed my bouquet carefully on the ground, and I came to rest next to Greta, leaned up on one elbow and with my back to the fountain.

She sighed with satisfaction, butting her head against me. There was still that anger wound through her, but it was calmer now, not so desperate or grieved. As I watched she patted Brandt's cheek until he came awake.

"Cigarette and lighter," she demanded, and he fumbled them out of his pocket.

He lit three narrow cigarettes, taking the last for himself. Three on a match means the last one's dead, but nothing came out of the darkness looking for him. The smoke was sweet and sharp at once, floating up over our heads.

"I'm sorry," Brandt said presently, and Greta shot him a sideways look.

"Why?"

"Because I don't belong to you."

A strange set of emotions crossed Greta's face, and she narrowed her eyes.

"Yes, you do," she said. I was older when I learned about the skogsrå, Greta's people. Hollow-backed, cow-tailed, they would love their men until they killed them, and that certainly meant that they owned them. What it meant for a girl with no tail, brought back from Sodermalm on a rope, no one really knew, but Greta knew her way best.

Brandt shivered under her gaze, and her arm tightened around him.

"What are you afraid of?" she asked, her tone softening.

"Oberlin Wolfe, and you should be as well," he said. He tugged down his winged collar, and shining at his throat was a silvery kiss. Greta reached for it with a finger, and pulled back with a hiss as it sizzled. Brandt flinched, but it was an old flinch. It hurt him every day.

"You're not supposed to be here, are you?" I asked suddenly. "You sneaked away."

"I came looking for you at Emmaline's, and they told me you had come here," he said, sparing a shy glance at me. I could see where it would be easy to love him.

"What did you sneak away from?" demanded Greta, and he lowered his eyes.

"I left the hunt," he said reluctantly, and I half sat up in shock when Greta let out a laugh of disbelief.

"To come looking for two girls picking flowers. That man will eat you alive." Oberlin Wolfe was always just "that man" to Greta.

"I don't care, I found you," he said defiantly, and Greta shook her head, still smiling.

"So I own your heart, and that man owns the rest. How strange, how strange."

"Oberlin Wolfe owns everything here," I said uneasily, and Brandt shook his head, refusing to meet my eyes.

"Me more than most," he said, fear and sadness and a kind of awful pride to it as well. I understood better than I wanted to. If you couldn't be a king, king-consort wasn't a bad road. Of course that's if the king wasn't just as likely to devour you as to drape you with jewels.

Almost as if they had been summoned by their mention, we heard the baying of the shrill hounds and the brassy cascade of horns. I stood up, ready to flee with flowers in my hand, and Greta rolled smoothly to her feet, her silk falling down over her hips like smooth rain. Brandt got up more slowly, but he straightened his clothes with the deliberation of a knight strapping on his armor.

"Stay here. Stay quiet. Don't *look*," he said. The last sounded like a plea.

Greta nodded, and she pulled him close, kissing him right over the burning mark that Oberlin Wolfe had left. It must have hurt, she hissed with the pain of it, but when he pulled back, his eyes shone.

He walked towards the gate to the courtyard, and Greta pulled me into a crouch behind the fountain. I made an irritated sound when she covered my eyes with her hand, but she only laughed.

"You are human, min skatt, and thus frail."

She was right. I could hear Brandt walking through the courtyard, and I heard the hounds still, and the horns go silent. There was a murmur of voices, and when those went still as well, I knew who had come forward.

"You ran, beautiful," said Oberlin Wolfe. "Why did you come here?"

"Does it matter?" asked Brandt. "You found me."

"Running's cute when you're new," said Oberlin, and there was a rattling menace in his tone. "I thought you were past that. Do you need to be taught again?"

I would have turned into a tree with fear, but to my astonishment, Brandt laughed. Greta jerked in surprise at that as well, and her expression was more fascinated than it had been a moment before.

"Teach me, don't teach me. You are going to do as you like, aren't you? Don't pretend it has anything to do with what I do."

There was a rising growl that shook the earth, and then, abruptly, it stopped. Not just the growl, but everything was still, as if it were holding its breath or stifled some other way. Somehow, frail little Brandt Hiller had stopped the king of Wolfe Studios. Greta almost stood to look over the fountain, but I grabbed her and pulled her down. She glared at me, and I shrugged. I wasn't the only frail one behind the fountain. Oberlin could have torn her to bits as easily as he could have me or Brandt.

I counted to ten, and then Oberlin laughed. I heard relief in the answering laughs of the people he rode with, but nothing from Brandt.

"Lessons can be enjoyable I suppose, with the right pupil," Oberlin said, his tone expansive, positively daddyish. I realized with shock that the head of the studio himself had been beaten and fooled by the shy blond boy who could barely look Greta in the eye.

A shout went up, the hunt went off to find other prey, Brandt Hiller with them, and I fell against Greta with relief.

"I think I lost another twenty years off of my life," I said when it was silent again, and she laughed a little, tugging me to my feet.

"Come on," she said with a sly wink. "If you are lucky, you may find that the gratitude of a beautiful woman can restore twenty years or more. Especially if she looks at your rear as hard as Emmaline does."

I blushed deep rose when I realized what she meant and what she had assumed, but hand in hand, we walked back into the dark.

VI

Emmaline's fire was dim and low when we returned, and smaller as well. Some of the circle had stumbled away to bed, and others were stretched out in the orange light. Jillian curled up slightly separate and puppyish close by, and she didn't stir as we approached. Greta took a seat at the fire, rifling through the remnants of a cheese tray with interest as I came close to Emmaline.

She sat tall and straight on her chair, staring into the fire as if it held answers to her most secret questions. When she looked up, there was a kind of pleasure in her face that took my breath away.

"You came back," she said, and I tilted my head, a slight smile quirking my lips.

"I said I would."

Of course I had planned a speech on the way back, something cocky and off-hand, nonchalant without overlooking the danger of what I had done. In front of Emmaline, however, that melted away. Instead I offered her the bouquet with two hands, and she accepted it the same way, her face tilted up to mine, eyes bright and clear.

The flowers looked too humble in her hands, but she brought them close and buried her face in the white petals. She breathed deeply, one breath and then two and three, before looking at me again.

"Yes. Love-comes-home. It's what I remember."

"Good," I said, and I might have stood there forever if she hadn't shifted the flowers to one hand and offered me the other.

"Come sit with me," she said, tugging me down. I started to say that there was no room, but then I saw that there was. The chair she sat in, what I had thought of as her throne, was just large enough for two girls to curl into each other, locking like the whorls of a seashell. I leaned against the brocade cushions, my hip snugged close to hers, her arm resting around my neck.

In the dying light of the fire, she tugged a bloom from the bouquet, tucking one flower behind my ear.

"It was common as dirt back home," she said, "less common than good dirt. But then I came here, and I never saw it again until today."

"Do you like it?" I asked inanely, and she smiled.

"'Like' isn't the right word. It's not really that pretty, is it? Scrawny, gawky, strange . . ." I felt my heart crumble like mountains into the sea until she smiled. "More like I needed it, and I never knew."

She shaped the word "need" in her mouth so perfectly that I could almost feel the tip of her tongue touch the roof of her mouth. She laughed softly, and then she leaned in.

"God, but you're pretty though," she murmured.

We were so close together that the kiss was almost an afterthought. She was warm, and her kiss tasted like apple wine, sweet and dry. I was frozen at first, but then I chased her mouth, wanting more of the taste of her and the pleasure of her. My hand came up to touch her face, her hair, and she tangled her free hand in my dress. It was as if she wanted to hold me still, as if I might have run away.

The flowers were crushed between us, and now I could smell them better. It was a scent that was more fresh than sweet, even slightly herbal. She moved them aside, and wrapped herself around me more tightly.

I felt like I was being carried away, down into someplace held against the molten heart of the earth. There was something more than bodies here, though it was that too. More than having never been kissed, I had never touched another person before, not really, not in a way that mattered. We kissed and kissed until my mouth felt overused, like it would never need paint again, and I marveled at the softness of her mouth, her sharp teeth, the bones of her hand where she pressed it against my jaw.

I could have kissed her until the sky fell in, but it lightened instead. I looked up after what felt like only a moment to see that there were livid streaks of salmon in the sky. Greta stretched like a cat before coming over to collect me.

"I suppose it's that time," Emmaline said regretfully. She kissed the corner of my mouth as if stowing it away for me to savor later, and climbed to her feet.

"Will you bring her again next week?" Emmaline asked, and Greta shrugged with one shoulder.

"She's free to do as she pleases."

"Will you, then?"

I smiled, looking likely as dazed as I felt.

"If you'll have me."

She smiled at that, bright and vivid and sunny. She and Greta were stamped from the same mold, both fair-haired and blue-eyed, but where Greta was sultry in her flesh, Emmaline had shed everything to gleam like gold wire.

"Over and over and over again," she promised, and something in me quickened.

Greta finally had to take my hand and lead me back to the dorms. By then, Emmaline had her own place in the Palisades, all white columns and heart-shaped swimming pool, her own gardener, driver, and cook as well.

Greta and I fell into my bed together, hands clasped and staring at the ceiling. Love drew a darkness out of her, but to me it was only a warm sweetness, desert honey poured down my throat.

VII

Summer was the realest time in Wolfe Studios. In summer, everyone was working, running, building or hustling at one thing or another. There was no hiding in summer, not when there was always a picture to cast and new stars to launch into the sky. Most fell down in the autumn, but some climbed even higher to light the solstice.

Even if the casting directors didn't quite know what to do with me, they were figuring it out. It wasn't much better work than I had had with Jacko on Baker Street, posing in the backgrounds, smiling or sneering on command. I ignored the whispers that it was my exotic race that put me into *Kensington Grove* and *They All Do Fine*. I didn't care if it was true or not. All that mattered was that I was earning my way, earning my star, a bit of silver at a time. I was the messenger girl dressed as a boy in *Her Surrender, Her Claim*, I did high kicks in a cabaret scene for Emerson Lankin's *A Night in New Orleans*, and I died beautifully in Lukas Waite's arms while he pondered war and its devastation in *A Terrible Light*.

The bit part in *The Lying Wife* could have been worse, but that was about all I could say for it. It was my job to drunkenly flirt with Paul Winslow at a nightclub before he had an attack of conscience and pushed me back. Winslow was overenthusiastic about pushing me, and I landed on my rear twice before the director called for a scene change.

"Hey, good scene," Winslow said to me, and abruptly, I stopped giving the benefit of the doubt to any man who seemed to like pushing women that much. I glared at him and walked off set, ready to change and go back to the dorm, but a young Black woman in pale linen approached me instead, an assistant from her patent white heels to the leather folder she carried under her arm.

"Miss Wei, Mrs. Davis would like to speak with you."

People who had assistants didn't make requests, so I followed along, wondering who in the world Mrs. Davis was. The heroine of the piece was Marianne Cheshire, who was tiny and delicate and had to be hefted up on apple crates so she could be in the same shot as Winslow, but I had already seen her give him and the director an earful of hell over an unexpected costume change. Marianne might have wanted to chew me out for one reason or another, but she only gave me a friendly wave as she went by with two girls from costuming on her diminutive heels.

The dressing room I was led to had an extravagant star on the door but no name painted on it. The assistant who had summoned me knocked twice, and then opened the door a crack, leaning in to talk with whoever was on the other side. I heard a soft murmur, and then she pulled back with a nod.

"Mrs. Davis will see you now," she said, and mystified, I entered.

The dressing room was the same size as my and Greta's apartment and decked out in reds and golds. Brocade curtains had been hung up to hide walls that I knew were only plaster behind, and feathery sheaves of decorative wheat sat on either side of the grand velvet chaise where I found—

"Tiny Annie?"

The elegant woman on the couch, her hair covered with white fabric pinned with a bloodred jewel, draped in a silk robe that pooled around her and dripped richly to the rug, gave me a dry look.

"Is that who I look like right now?" she asked.

It wasn't, and I bit my lip in chagrin.

"No, it's not. I'm sorry," I said, and she snorted, rising to a sitting position with a dancer's grace. She had been a dancer before she came to Hollywood, but Hollywood didn't want her to dance, not with her dark skin or her curves.

"Why?" she asked. "I *am* Tiny Annie. That little idiot made me a rich woman."

She had, too. Tiny Annie ran along behind Belle Gwynn in *That Bayou Night,* fussing at her skirts, holding her when Marshall Gray broke her heart, and coddling her whether she was a little girl or a grown woman. She promised she would always take care of her baby miss, no matter what came, and white people had a hunger for Black women who would say such a thing.

She might have been called Opal, or Nelley, or Bessie Lou, but she always played Tiny Annie, played her so well and so relentlessly that no one else could claim the spot. When some other actress tried, the audiences didn't believe it, insisted on the real thing, and that was Louisa Davis.

Now Mrs. Davis stood, her copper robe falling in lush folds down to her toes. She was shorter than I was, her face as round as a pearl and her lips shaded in plum and outlined with the most delicate strokes of a makeup pencil.

"I wanted to get a look at you," she said. "I wanted to see the girl who said she was too good to play a maid."

I would have said it a thousand times to Oberlin Wolfe and just as often to the casting directors, but it made me ashamed to hear it now from Mrs. Davis. I stayed silent, and she examined me with a candid, caustic eye.

"I knew Su Tong Lin before she left for Paris," she said. "She was a real sweetheart."

I waited to hear her say that she was nothing like me, smarter and prettier too, but Mrs. Davis was silent.

Finally, she shook her head.

"I can't tell. I don't know what you're going to be."

"The casting directors don't know either," I said truculently, and she gave me a cold smile.

"Sure they do. They know just like they know I'm Tiny Annie and Susie is Lovely Peony."

"You're not," I said, obscurely shocked, and she laughed at me.

"Oh, we are," she said. "Tiny Annie got my family nice houses in Santa Monica and a string of businesses where I say what goes. Lovely Peony got Susie's sisters into school in the East, got her daddy medicine for his sugar. What makes you better than us?"

"I'm not."

"No, you aren't. But we all know why you have to say you are."

There was a brisk rap on the door.

"Five minutes, Mrs. Davis," said her assistant, and Mrs. Davis said she would be right out.

She pulled the red jewel off her wrap, and when she shrugged off the robe, she revealed a calico dress with a fantastically stained apron underneath. She went from statuesque to dumpy, from a woman who owned houses all over Santa Monica to a nursemaid who only wanted to care for her baby miss.

She caught me staring and gave me a dark smile.

"You better know who you are," she said, "because you don't look strong enough to be me."

Her lovely assistant escorted her to set, and I was left sitting on a crate by her starred and nameless door. It was as if a storm had gone by and left me somehow intact.

She was right. I wasn't strong enough to be her or Su Tong Lin, and whatever path I took, I had to keep to it, because I wouldn't survive falling off. I shook my head, because I couldn't afford to spend too much time thinking like that, and fortunately for me, it was Friday, and you didn't have to think about much on Friday.

On Friday nights, I chased Emmaline's fire, and we curled together on her throne, as close as two halves of an almond. I leaned my head against her silk-clad shoulder as she laughed and held court, relishing the wistful glares from the other girls almost as much as I liked the warmth of her body next to mine. With her, I was a kind of royalty, rare and envied, and it was a new kind of pride that was born in my heart.

One night, I searched in vain for her fire, but instead I found Emmaline herself, dressed in a sleek and shimmering blue ball gown with a froth of white organza at the hem. For a moment, I wondered if she was real at all, and then she smiled and held her hands out to me. The stars were in her eyes that night, not the fire, and I would have followed her anywhere.

"Where are the others?" I asked as we stepped into the darkness between the flames. She shrugged.

"Wherever they want to be. I was tired of playing queen tonight."

"What would you rather be instead?"

She smiled, not looking at me.

"I want to be with you," Emmaline replied, not shy, not demanding, but instead with a softness and a sweetness that could bring me to my knees. She was less than twenty-one then, not old enough to drink though we all did, young like we would never be again.

("Drama queen," Jane said, biting and affectionate.

"Look who's talking," I retorted.)

We walked hand in hand through the dark, and there was nothing to fear when we were facing the night together. We heard the rumble of the hunt, the distant drums, laughter and weeping and screams, and it seemed as if we were children wandering a playground jungle. The broken glass was smoothed so it would not cut us, and the fires danced just beyond our fingertips, glowing with warmth but never burning us.

She was shorter than I was, and I tucked her under my arm as we walked. Vaguely, I wished for a suit instead of the dress I wore, a gray Hartnell sheath beaded in ocean-like waves. Sometimes we spoke, but mostly we roamed. I carried my heels hooked in two fingers, swinging by my side, but she kept hers, her steps so disciplined they never revealed the ache.

Close to Lot 14, Emmaline gasped as if she had seen a ghost, and when she showed me what had startled her so, I realized it might as well have been.

The Ford Model A crouched behind Lot 14 like a skulking cat, already a little out of style and without the awkward charm of the Model T. I went with Emmaline as she stroked the curved headlight casings, brushing her fingers across the meticulously polished chrome handles.

"The Poulsens had one of these when I was little," she murmured. "All shining and black just like this girl. It was the grandest motor in town, and if Denny Poulsen liked you, he would take you for a ride."

"Did he like you?" I asked, unable to keep the jealousy out of my voice, and Emmaline laughed a little.

"Oh no. I wasn't popular in Waverly. I gave myself airs." She was making fun of herself a little, but there was a stiff pride there too, along with a thread of affection for the place and people who had birthed her. She dared me to say anything, and I was silent. Instead I touched the sleek car where she had, running my hand over hers to entwine our fingers.

One of us found that the door was unlocked, and with startled giggles we climbed into the rear, tumbling over each other in the small space. When we shut the door behind us, however, it shut out the rest of the world, the Friday night fires, the studio, all of it.

We watched each other, suddenly shy, our breaths catching like a jagged nail on cheap chiffon.

She moved first, lurching close and pushing me against the door. For a moment, I was afraid that we hadn't latched it securely and that I would go spilling out into the dirt, but it held and I held on to her, tangled with her, taking her weight on top of me.

"So much fucking fabric," she swore hopelessly, and I choked because she was right. In that cramped space, it felt like there was more fabric than girl, between her gown and mine, and there was no magic to help us now, nothing that would cut away to reveal us slippery bare and sliding over each other like slivers of soap. I was half-suffocated under her and her satin, and without looking, I stretched and grasped for the hem of her dress, finding it before pulling it up. Her leg felt taut and strong under my hand. I could feel the light fuzz of hair on her legs, unexpectedly soft. When I touched the tender hollow at the back of her knee, she giggled, pressing her hot face against my throat.

"What do you like?" I asked, as if I were worldly-wise and in a position to give her whatever she wanted.

"With you, anything," she responded. "Keep touching me there, baby, and just slide higher . . ."

She braced one knee between my hip and the back of the bench seat, and her other foot was on the floor. It felt as if there was a laundry's worth of fabric between us, and in the dark I couldn't see anyway, but touching her was heat and skin and nothing else I had ever felt before, even touching myself in the tub with my knees spread.

She made these soft encouraging noises against my cheek as my hand slid higher, and her nails dug into my bare shoulders when I found her inner thighs. It was hot, too hot, but in the dark, no one would see the steam on the windows. The sleek sweat let me slide my hand up between her thighs, and I made a startled noise when I realized that she wasn't wearing any underwear. Instead, there was only the wiry hair between her legs and an incredible heat that I knew matched mine. I suddenly wished that I knew what color her hair was there, whether it matched the platinum on top of her head, or if it was some darker secret. A little bit of pressure parted her, giving way to the sleek hot flesh between. At first it might have been sweat or arousal, but when I stroked up with the heel of my hand, she ground down against me, and it was definitely arousal.

"Stay right there," she murmured, and she started to kiss me almost desperately, mouth all over mine, my eyelids, my nose, my cheeks and my chin. I could feel her pearly teeth behind the kisses, occasionally pressing too hard against my lip or my cheekbone, but that small pain made me press closer to her as well.

I jammed my elbow on the bench seat, grinding up with my hand even as she pressed down on me. It felt as if she was everywhere over me, enveloping me, enclosing me. A dull pain traveled from my wrist to my elbow and my hand was faintly numb, but it all mattered so much less than how hot and wet she was and how good she felt . . .

Then every muscle in her tensed, and Emmaline pressed her face hard against my shoulder, her mouth opening in a soundless cry. Her lips and her teeth pressed against my bare shoulder, and suddenly I wanted nothing more than for her to bite me, leave some kind of mark that would stay long after we returned from the fires.

I let my hand fall down, the muscles in my wrist sighing with relief, and she came to rest half on top of me, her body almost pushing me off the seat. Our breath evened out together, and only then did I realize I had been breathing as hard as she was, that my face and throat were slick with sweat. My hand was sore, and I stretched my fingers slightly, marveling at how wet they still were and how good she was.

"Should we get up?" I wondered, and she butted her forehead against mine playfully.

"Not yet," she said, her voice raspy. "I've always been a girl who believes in going Dutch . . ."

For one blind moment, I had no idea what she was talking about, and then her hand was sliding the hem of my dress up to my hips. She had an easier time of it than I did, even if she still had to fight her yards and yards of skirt, and she parted my legs with her own bare thigh. I squirmed against her, startled at how strong she was while looking as delicate as a wisp of lace. Her thigh was warm and vital between my legs and when she pressed against me, I couldn't help locking my legs around hers.

Now it was my turn to cling to her, my face against the rise of her breasts and my hands doing endless damage to the fabric of her dress. I couldn't reach her skin with my hands, but she clung to me, murmuring soft encouragement that I didn't pay any attention to at all. I was too intent on her between my legs, how I could stretch and stiffen and grind until I was shaking, and she was endless patience, not budging until I was as helpless and pleasured as she was. When I finally cried out, it was less powerful than when I was on my own in the bathtub, but it took the heart straight out of me and threw it into the sky. My body quaked, and I lay in Emmaline's arms. It was the most important thing in the world, at least in that moment.

Her soft fingers covered my mouth, and at first I kissed them. Then I realized she was keeping me still, and startled, I listened. A rumble, a roar, and the sound of excited shouts grew louder. I gritted my teeth and reached to pull my dress down over my thighs, and then we held on to each other while the hunt rode by. Her eyelashes brushed against my cheek as she closed her eyes, and I held her tighter.

At last, there was silence, and we emerged from the car. I

wondered whether the world would look different after what we had done, but it was just the same. Instead, I looked at her and found a soft glow on her cheeks, and from the stunned way she looked at me, I could see she felt the same.

"Beautiful," she murmured, cupping my cheek in her hand. She leaned up to kiss me, more a blessing than a lover's token, and then stepped back, offering me her hand. We wandered the fires as if we were strolling through a park, and though we never spoke, sometimes we looked at each other in secret wonder.

I returned from the fires with my heart glowing and so full of adoration that I could feel it spilling out of me. I wondered sometimes how the whole world didn't seem able to see it, but Greta shrugged.

"That kind of love, it's invisible until you cannot ignore it," Greta said. She and I sat on the lip of the small balcony at the end of our hallway's floor, our legs dangling down over the four-story drop. Above us, the Saturday sun was just beginning to rise in the sky, and in the pool below, some studio changelings were already rehearsing their underwater routines for the synchronized swimming extravaganza that the Mannheim brothers were shooting on Lot 3. I saw that they had lost at least one girl to the fires, and they were frantically trying to close the gap.

I tilted my head towards Greta, who watched the swimmers with a kind of grim intensity, as if she could divine some kind of fortune or future in their graceful passes. She walked me to Emmaline's fire every Friday night, and she might stay, but more often lately, she walked back into the night. She came back solemn and strange from the darkness, so oddling that no one questioned her.

"And the kind of love that you have with Brandt Hiller?"

Her mouth turned down unhappily, and Greta shook her head without looking at me.

"That is something else," she said gruffly.

I left it alone, but I reached over to cup the back of her neck with my hand. I wondered for a moment if I had touched my sister like this once upon a time, when she was small enough to want comfort and I was still there to give it. It seemed unlikely, but I had learned the gesture from somewhere. Greta sailed like the moon in the sky, untouchable and cool even now. She tilted her head forward and exhaled softly, never taking her eyes from the swimmers.

VIII

There's no such thing as a natural rhythm when you can walk out of a winter morning on Lot 3 and walk into an Aegean sunset on Lot 8. Still, when I was with Emmaline it was springtime in a place I had never been, one she told me about sometimes after we lay exhausted on her enormous bed in her house in the Palisades.

"Waverly could fool you with how pretty it was in the spring. For just a week, love-comes-home comes up like drifts of snow, and just as fast, they're gone. I used to go walking out in the fields full of them, tucking them into my braids and dreaming of a day when there was someone to see me be so pretty."

"I see you now," I said, brushing my hand over her cheek.

I did. I could see the proud girl she had been and the beautiful and accomplished woman she was becoming, conquering audiences with one startled flash of her eyes, one soft gasp from her lips.

There was a girl you could sometimes find at the dorms who had a candle, and if you bribed her with jewelry or just the right lipstick, she would light it for you and lead you out of the studios late at night. That year, I followed her light through the clanking basements, through the orange groves, all the way to the Palisades, and when I knocked on the rear door at Emmaline's house, she came out with a smile to kiss me in the moonlight.

We barely noticed that there was nowhere for us to go. We had the fires, we had her bed, and we had the stories we told each other. We compared ourselves to the great queens who had come before us, silent and speaking, like and unlike us. We danced in the living room to the record player, kept low even with the door locked and the shades drawn.

I heard all of Emmaline's stories. Some of them were polished smooth, and I never said that I had read them before in the magazines and interviews she had given. They were still hers, no matter who had heard them, and she told me the rougher things as well, the ones that she would never tell to *Variety* and Dottie Wendt.

She told me about the kittens she had found when she was young, motherless and crying. She had tried to care for them, but all but one died, except for the biggest, who went on to be the most vicious mouser in the county. She told me about a boy from Greensboro who had taken her first kiss like a trophy, and how sometimes she wondered if that boy had it still, or whether it was passed on to someone who now had it all unknowing that it belonged to a movie star and not a shy girl from the county fair. She told me about the magic from her part of the world, how it came down from the Puritan witches who had gone west, and how every ear of corn could listen for the one who had planted it, if she only knew how to ask.

She told me she didn't mind being paired up with Cassidy Dutch, who was coming up fast in all the dusters with his easy smile and real skills with a lariat.

"He's sweet, and he don't get grabby," she said with a faint smile. "We go out, and he leaves me at the door with a kiss and a chocolate, like he doesn't know what to do."

I had heard Cassidy surely did know what to do if the girl was from one of the houses on the Sunset Strip, and he wasn't half so sweet either, but I didn't say anything.

We played house in the Palisades, and it was a moonlight kind of house, all shadows and drapes, naked skin and laughter. It wasn't real, but it was true, and even if I lost sleep from the nights I spent with Emmaline, it felt as if I had gained the right to walk yet another world.

With her, I had entrance to a moonlight place, not one lit by firelight or electricity, but something deeper and lusher and wilder. We talked and we touched each other, and the only consequences we acknowledged were in each other, in each other's skins and in each other's hearts.

Wrapped up in Emmaline as I was, I might not have figured out Greta's trouble at all if I hadn't come into our rooms early one night. I limped in sweaty and pained from dance class, grimly aware that my toenails would be limned with blood at best, if I didn't lose a few entirely. Mme Benoit told us of nights where her shoes had drowned in blood, when every step had been like a sword through her feet. I knew I had gotten off lightly that day, and that was its own particular terror.

I was walking gingerly on my sore feet, and perhaps that was why she didn't look up when I opened the door. Greta curled up on the couch like a hurt and miserable animal, and almost mechanically, she licked at something white and hard in her hand.

"Greta?"

She uncoiled from the couch like my tentative call had mortally wounded her, but I saw that she was careful to hold whatever it was behind her. When she recognized me, the ferocity drained from her face, and she gave me an aimless look.

"Oh, it is you," she said with a shrug.

I hobbled over to her, and when she might have tugged away, I wrapped my fingers around her wrist to draw it forward. I blinked because I recognized it. She resisted me taking it from her entirely, but when I drew my hand away, it was smudged with soft white.

"Greta, what are you doing with *chalk*?"

Sticks of thick white chalk were ubiquitous on the set. They marked at the lightest touch. They were used to set marks on the ground, to trace out the layout of new sets, and of course to score the clapperboards that heralded the beginning of each scene. It left an almost greasy mark in thick white, marring everything it grazed. The chalk wasn't hard to get; the question was why she even wanted to get it in the first place.

Self-conscious now, she wiped her clean hand over her mouth. I could still see crumbles of chalk dust at the corner of her lip and her tongue, two shades paler than it should have been.

"It doesn't matter," she said, shrugging, but I knew that wasn't the case.

"Did it look good to you?" I asked carefully. "Like you saw it and had to have it?"

"It doesn't matter," Greta repeated. "I only saw it and wanted it. It looked like it must taste good."

She showed me the chalk as if that would help me understand. There *was* something oddly candy-like about it, like it was an enormous buttermint; I knew though that I would only get a dry and bitter powder in my mouth if I tried a bite of it, and I doubted Greta had gotten anything else.

I sat down on the couch, and after a short hesitation, she joined me. For the first time, however, she was stiff, shifted so she curled away from me instead of towards me. A moment passed, and she sniffled. Awkwardly, I shaped myself to her. I was unused to touching her the way she touched me, but slowly she relaxed into it. We breathed together, letting the moment stretch until I spoke again.

"There was a girl on Hungarian Hill who ate paper," I said presently. "Her skin was black like good ink, and one summer, all she wanted was to eat pages from the pulp novels they sold at the drugstore."

Greta stirred against me restlessly, allowing my hand to drape over her side, over her belly. She had finished *The Belles* just a week ago.

"What happened to her?"

"In fall she gave birth to a little girl as dark as she was, but when my sister held her in the light at her first birthday, I could see words even darker on her cheek, her eyelids, her throat. Strange titles that you could almost but not quite read. She was beautiful just like her mother."

"Like that is any protection," Greta snorted.

"Better than nothing," I suggested. "And even if yours isn't, she'll be strong and strange and a wonder."

That made Greta laugh.

"Perhaps I will birth a stick of chalk and Wolfe will use her all up to put marks on the floor, where I should stand and talk."

"We won't let that happen," I said, "but we have to think fast. You're going to start to show sooner than later."

"We?" she asked, finally turning to me. Her eyes were red, but she was smiling.

"Of course," I said, knocking my forehead against hers. "Who else?"

There was a lot of fucking going on at the studios, and where you have something like that, you have babies unless you are very lucky and very careful. Though we all went about as if pleasure were paramount and consequences happened to someone else, there was a brisk trade in underground knowledge about what could be done if you suspected you weren't lucky and after when you found out you certainly weren't. A girl in our dorm knew a discreet doctor who would get you kitted out with a diaphragm, and everyone had a friend of a friend who knew the best person to scrape you out clean, leaving you only ill for a few weeks before you were back at class or on the set again. It was important to find the best. Every year, the fresh crop of girls lost two, or five, or seven, and though "peritonitis" or "appendicitis" might be put on their death certificates, we all knew which dark and bloody end they had come to.

They were mostly terrible choices, and being smart and lucky only meant that they were ours. We made them because otherwise it was one more choice that the studios could take away from us, and in the corners of my memory, Abigail McKinnon nodded away. I had heard that they gave her baby to some old lady in San Diego, some relation or another to one of the executives. Harvey Rose was Oberlin Wolfe's fixer in more ways than one, glaring at the world from behind his green-tinted glasses, and whenever he came by the dorms, girls' or boys', we knew that a big problem had to be fixed.

"I want to keep her," Greta told me over a cup of chicken broth for her and rosehip tea for me. Her calm resolve told me not to argue, and I nodded reluctantly.

"All right. I think I know who to talk to. We need flowers."

Mrs. Wiley beamed over the armload of sunflowers we brought her, and she sat us down at her table.

"I know Wolfe doesn't like his babies roaming so late," she said. "You two sneak out?"

"We've got time but not much of it," I said. We'd bribed a driver with a picture of Emmaline from the cutting room floor. He was still staring at it in the car on the street.

"Finding an abortionist was as easy as getting cough drops at Aegis," Mrs. Wiley said. "I can't imagine Wolfe is any different. I guess you want to keep her?"

"Yes," Greta said. She kept her hands away from her belly, but I could see her wanting to cup her hands over it, to protect her.

"Why?" Mrs. Wiley's tone was just short of cruel. "You want something to love you when no one else will? You think this'll get you your man?"

Greta growled at her, in that moment looking less human than she ever had.

"I want her because she is mine. Because she came to me, and I want to love her and feed her as is my right, the one my mother had to me, and my grandmother had to her."

Mrs. Wiley looked at her for a long moment before shrugging.

"All right, good enough. First, this other one here should have told you that there's a price. Twenty years off the end of your life is traditional."

Greta nodded grimly, and now I watched her go through the same thing I had, her blood soaked into the little card and Mrs. Wiley drinking it up like a dainty vampire.

"Good," Mrs. Wiley said when she finished, licking every drop so cleanly that there was no need for a napkin.

"So you want the child. What else do you want?"

"To go home," Greta said promptly. "I was brought here on a rope. I want my child to know the forest and the long night. I want her to have good fish and cold days."

"Hm. At least you don't want to be a movie star as well, I suppose . . ."

"And I want my man."

Mrs. Wiley's white eyebrows went up to her hairline.

"If you want your man, he should have been here with you, don't you think?"

Greta shrugged like a horse flicking its tail to remove flies. What Brandt Hiller was to her was different than what Emmaline was to me, what a human woman might have felt for the father of her child. He was hers, and that was what mattered. Mrs. Wiley must have intuited at least a little bit of that because she nodded.

"Well, tell me. Who's the lucky young sheikh?"

"Brandt Hiller." Greta paused. "I don't know his real name."

Mrs. Wiley made a snorting noise that turned into a laugh.

"Oh, you have interesting friends," she said to me. "Miss Ambitious and Miss Muleheaded, that's you two."

"What?" I asked when Greta only glared. "What's the matter with Brandt Hiller?"

"My dear, even up here in my tower, I know a few things. I know what *Variety* tells me because a darling child brings it up to me. I'm first to know when it rains because I am so high up. And I know, because everyone does, who Oberlin has to offer up to hell on Halloween."

Greta made a cry of alarm, and I froze, pricks of heat and cold running down my body and making me shudder.

"Is it true then?" I asked. "Is that what the Wild Hunt on Halloween is for?"

Mrs. Wiley shrugged.

"We're only human, and who knows the actual truth of it? Every year, they go riding, and every year, they give over one girl or boy to what's waiting in the dark. No one sees that girl or that boy ever again, and then there's a party that's never loud enough or wild enough to cover the fact that there's something that can take even from the likes of Oberlin Wolfe, John Everest, and Elgin Aegis."

"Who are they giving up this year?" Greta asked, but from the sound of her voice, Greta knew.

"It's always the one the king loves most," Mrs. Wiley said. "And this year, even I know it's Brandt Hiller."

She sighed.

"I can't give you your life back. I drank it up, and I wouldn't even if I could. But Miss Muleheaded, you have to know that taking back your man means crossing Oberlin Wolfe."

"I am not afraid of that man," Greta retorted, and I wished that I could agree. I certainly was.

"All right. There's one tried and true way to keep him back from what's waiting in the hills, an old way, and it's as sure as anything that doesn't have an ironclad contract with one of the three.

"You find him on the ride, you pull him away, and you hang on to him. They'll change him in your arms, anything to make you say 'enough,' and if you let go, well, then, you've lost."

Greta nodded, eyes narrowed. She trusted her own strength more than she trusted anything else in the world. Her mother could bend an iron poker into a perfect round wedding ring, she had told me. She could hang on to one skinny boy.

"And when he's a naked man again, cover him up, and then he's yours. At least, Oberlin Wolfe can't take him away from you. But do remember, Miss Muleheaded, that he'll still be there, and he will be mad fit to kill. I told you before, Miss Ambitious, how much they like to own things. Tell your friend about my feet, if you like, because I don't care to. You tell her and then you think hard about how much they like having things taken away."

There were another two months before Halloween. It was two months for Greta to pace, to refuse any but the briefest interviews as *The Belles of St. Desmond* was playing to sold out houses, two months for me to bounce away from my last bit part and towards something far stranger.

When they called me back for a second read in *Nemo's Revenge*, I figured it was another tiny part, background scenery or smoking a skinny cigarette in a dock scene. After all, they were paying me by the week, they might as well get something out of me.

Instead, the narrow young assistant led me into a room that was empty of everything except a long table where the Mannheim brothers sat, bored looks on their faces.

"Luli Wei," the assistant announced, and I turned to face them. They had a scatter of paper in front of them, and Scottie, the older one, handed me a printed sheet.

"Here, read over that," he said. "We're still waiting."

I wanted to ask *waiting for who?* but I only nodded and read over the script. I could feel them looking at me, but I had grown comfortable being a thing that was looked at, if not touched.

"Oh good afternoon, so sorry I was late, beg pardon, all . . ."

Harry Long entered a room as if there was always a crowd waiting for him, eager to hang on his every word and gesture. Most of the time, it was true. Unlike so many of the silent kings, he thrived in sound, and though there were always stories that he had a charm where his voice used to be, I didn't believe it.

That afternoon, he was one of the kings of Wolfe Studios, and his oak-dark voice rolled out to wrap us all close to him. He was thin but muscled with hair slicked back like black patent leather and a thin mustache that might have been drawn with an artist's brush. He was dressed in white—white shorts, white shirt, white tennis shoes—and all he was missing was the racket. We, the Mannheim brothers and I, forgave him for it because he was simply himself, and that self, that afternoon, was enough to be forgiven anything.

"Here's the page, sir," said Whalen Mannheim. "Whenever you are ready . . ."

He turned as if seeing me for the first time, and I like to think that it wasn't just theatrical manners that made his mouth drop open a little. I was dressed in a deep red blouse and a black silk skirt. I stood easily in the tall heels I had borrowed from a girl in the dorm, finally learning to ignore the pain in my feet.

"Well, as I do live," he said, and then to my surprise, he said something that I both recognized and didn't. Mandarin, I realized after a moment, not my nearly forgotten Cantonese.

"I'm sorry, I don't speak . . ." I said, an edge of real apology in my tone.

"Oh, a shame," he said warmly. "Beautiful language for a beautiful girl. Shall we begin, my dear?"

I felt an odd corkscrew twist of shame and embarrassment in my gut. I had worked so hard to be shed of everything from the laundry, and running into even a version of it here and now felt wrong, especially in the mouth of a man as well-loved and well-off as Harry Long. If he could speak it with only a wink at how exotic it was, why couldn't I keep it too? Then Scottie Mannheim gave us the setting, and thoughts of Mandarin and Cantonese flew from my head.

If you've heard of me, you know the scene. Captain Nemo has lost everything at that point. His son has been taken by the waves, his ship is a mess of metal and glass at the bottom of the sea, and his crew lost to mutiny. He stands up in the grotto under the waves and looks around in heartbreak and dismay.

"It's gone, it's all gone," he said, his voice trembling in fear and awe. His feelings are stark on his face, and they pull me closer, better than the hot water that streams from the undersea trenches, sweeter than the bright pop of roe between my teeth.

"How does it feel?" I asked him, drawing his gaze to where I crouched on the rock. I was small for my kind, my tail only ten feet long instead of the half mile my father boasted. Even my brothers could topple a fishing boat with nothing more than a swift shove. I was tiny in comparison.

"You're Atlantean," the captain said with shock, and the acknowledgment on his face was better than I had ever dreamed of. I had had plenty of time to dream as I recovered from the destruction of my home.

I slithered off the rock, pulling myself forward on my hands, never taking my eyes from him.

"I was," I said harshly. "Atlantis is gone now, son of the land, gone after you battled with my father and my brothers, tearing down the gold towers and glass domes. The ten-thousand-year dream is ended because of you and your arrogance, your hate."

"The gold towers that hid torture chambers. The domes where

you kept humans like pets and zoo animals," the captain said coldly. He couldn't help taking a step back as I slithered a little closer. I was so unlike him as to be alien, something so wrong in his world that it hurt to look at me for very long.

"My father and my brothers made a mistake," I said, looking up at him. Snakes were as low to the ground, but they knew themselves to be dangerous. "They thought you were beautiful animals, fit only for display, kept as darling companions to be spoiled."

The captain opened his mouth to speak, but I hissed at him, loud and warning. It was a noise I didn't even know I had in me until I made it.

"I will not make that mistake," I said. "You are a plague that must be destroyed."

I reared back, fangs bared . . .

"All right, that's enough," said Scottie Mannheim, and I blinked. It wasn't an undersea grotto. It was an echoing room in Southern California, and I was pulling myself along on the ground as three white men watched me. I came to my feet smoothly, my face impassive but red. There was dust on my blouse and skirt; I would have to have them cleaned before I returned them to the girl I had borrowed them from.

"That was good," Whalen muttered thoughtfully, but even as his brother murmured assent, Harry Long shook his head.

"Are you blind and deaf?" he demanded. "She scared the wits out of me. For a moment, I was certain she was going to rip out my very throat and drink my blood!"

He turned to me, and I was startled by the sincere pleasure in his gaze. He took both my hands in his, bringing them up for two dry kisses on my knuckles.

"Very well done, Miss Wei," he said warmly.

"We still have a few more girls we want to see," Scottie said, and Harry Long shot them an amused glance.

"Of course, Scottie. Of course, Whalen. But please believe me when I say that I know what a monster looks like, and Miss Wei has what it takes. I am certain that you have found your siren."

I thumbed through the script cautiously, waiting for the moment the siren fell in love with the grizzled captain, but I found nothing. She was a monster straight through. She never stopped trying to kill the man who had destroyed her world and killed her family, not until a stray bullet aimed at her enormous sea serpent caught her in the chest. She died hissing with hate, and I smiled.

"That was a tough sell," Scottie Mannheim told me with some pride three weeks later. "You know, it's hard to get the commission on board with killing a lady, even a . . ."

He trailed off, too kind to say "Chinese," but still dressed in the hideously long and heavy rubber tail they had to slick with Vaseline to get me into, I smiled.

"A monster," I said. "I know."

The chlorine of the pool made my eyes sting and my hair turn to straw, but every day, I looked forward to getting on set. I was eager to get fitted into my tail and to have a web of plastic seaweed scattered with seashells draped artfully over my body. I had to shout most of my lines because the machine that made the waves was terribly loud, and during the scene where the captain wrestles the siren for control of Poseidon's trident, Harry Long swung me into one of the plastic rocks so hard I saw stars.

He was aghast, carrying me, greasy legs and all, to his trailer to rest until a doctor could be found.

"It's just a nasty bruise with a bit of a gash in the center," the doctor said, poking painfully at my scalp. "Nothing terrible, she doesn't even need a stitch. Her hair will cover it, she's fit to work."

"Preposterous. She's not working for the rest of the day, I won't hear of it."

I started to protest, but he shot me a quelling look.

"You are not working hourly any longer," he said. "You are going to nap here while I speak to the Mannheims about restructuring that scene, and then I am taking you home for dinner, something light if you can't stomach much, and something ridiculous if you can. Don't fuss."

I lay back in the trailer, smiling a little as I heard Harry Long wave down Scottie with his stentorian tones. My head ached abominably if I moved, so I lay as still as a statue, examining the butterflies in my belly.

Oberlin Wolfe's voice echoed in my mind. *You came here without a patron.*

I wasn't going to be one of those girls who walked in wide-eyed and was surprised to find a wolf waiting in the place where wolves lived. I hadn't heard anything terrible about Harry Long, but he was a king, and all kings are wolves.

The question was, could I do it? He was old enough to be my father at that time, and I heard his joints creak when he had to throw me around during the fight for the trident. He was kind though, and I remembered the glow in his eyes when he called me a monster. In his mouth, it was a compliment, and I would much rather be a monster than a victim.

I already knew that men roused nothing in me, but Harry wouldn't be so awful, I decided. He was a gentleman, or acted like one, and I had never heard of him making trouble for any of the actresses he stepped out with after the fact.

As for Emmaline, in the fires, it was just us. We wouldn't talk about Harry Long, just like we never talked about her studio-spun romance with the star of the Westerns, Cassidy Dutch, or the pictures of the two of them on horseback at his ranch in Nevada, snugged up tight on the back of his big bay stallion. The fires were real. Harry wasn't.

I would make a different decision now, but I am a different person now. Nineteen is a long way from where I am these days, and there's no crossing that distance, none at all.

Harry came back, and I realized I must have fallen asleep after all because the sun was low in the sky. Greta would wonder where I was, but my hours had been strange since starting *Nemo's Revenge.*

"Come along, my dear," he said. "Up you get."

I let him usher me into the wrong-side passenger seat of his Bentley, a midnight-blue car that ate up the miles between the studio lot and his home in Bel-Air. He steered the car with a chauffeur's competence into the covered garage.

"Take the guest bathroom," he said. "There are some clothes that shouldn't be too shabby a fit for you in the closet there as well."

As much as my insides churned at what was going to happen, I was incredibly relieved to drag myself into the shower. The bathtub was large enough for me to lie down flat, and the hot water that hissed out of the showerhead seemed endless. I gingerly washed the dried blood out of my hair, wincing whenever I nudged my bruise, and I scrubbed the rubbery layer of grease off of my legs. I dried myself off thoroughly, dumping my clothes into the convenient laundry hamper, and I went out to find what exactly was waiting for me in the closet.

I'll admit that my imagination was lurid. I imagined leather or lace, circus outfits, Chinese dresses, even a rubber tail like the one that I had worn all day. I was confused to find nothing more than a few dresses, too large for me and out of date by at least twenty years, hung neatly near the front. They were well made at least, and I found a green wrap dress that I could belt tighter around myself. I couldn't find any shoes and had forgotten mine back on set, so I went barefoot.

I ventured out into the living room as cautiously as an old woman crossing a busy street, but there was nothing more frightening there than Harry Long in casual lounging clothes, barefoot himself and enjoying a glass of red wine.

"Do you drink?" he asked, and when I shook my head no, he smiled.

"Well, more of the good stuff for me, then," he said. "Come, Teo set out some food for us, and I'm famished."

He had a diction and an enthusiasm that could get away with saying things like "famished," and he led me to the dining room where there was a tray of delicate light food. Cold salmon, cold rabbit, crackers, cheese, fruit and vegetables, it looked delicious and my head had stopped aching to where I could enjoy most of it. Harry pointed out delicacies I had missed, explaining where that came from or why this was so rare, but otherwise we ate in companionable silence. I relaxed, and then I remembered what was happening, and I tensed again. I could feel his eyes on my throat, on the way the dress sagged on my shoulders to reveal my cleavage, and I came to a decision.

"What do you think of me?" I asked. Jacko Dewalt was right, I was as cold as the Atlantic, but if Harry Long had wanted someone warm and bright and bubbly, he wouldn't have taken me into his midnight Bentley.

I had given him permission to look, but there was something curiously antiseptic about the way he regarded me, amusement tempered with something like real compassion. There had been little enough of it in my life that it looked to me like pity, and I prickled a little.

"I think you are a lovely young woman with a bit of a taste for blood," he said at last. "I think you will work very hard to get a tenth of what other girls as talented as you will be given. I think that you could be a magnificent monster, if you don't forget that, after all, you are a monster."

"That . . . wasn't what I expected," I said. I wished suddenly that Greta was here with me, but she was home in the dorm, malingering and staying out of sight as her belly grew. I had been raiding the farm stands for her when I could, bringing back oranges and apples and great bouquets of dark lettuce. It was better than the chalk at least.

Harry's finely drawn eyebrow went up, and he smiled.

"Did you expect me to seduce you over oysters?" he asked, and I shrugged.

"I don't know why else you brought me here."

"Because monsters need to look out for one another," he said. "You are Emmaline Sauvignon's sweetheart, aren't you?"

I hadn't expected to hear Emmaline's name that night at all, and I jerked like a fish on the line.

"You know Emmaline?" I asked in shock, and he smiled a little.

"Of her, anyway. I know about the company she keeps. When she first came to Wolfe Studios, she was just a little girl from Minnesota who did very well at one of the auditions. She got tired of small roles and bit parts, and came to look for wisdom from my friend Helen Martel."

Helen Martel's star shone dimmed but still true. She had done a handful of pictures at the beginning of the talkies, and then taking the money she made, spun it into real estate gold. All anyone knew about her anymore was that she had a different property for every week in the year, and that she did not suffer fools.

"Emmaline and Helen Martel . . ."

"Perhaps. But I didn't think that you would hold it against her, given what you thought coming here."

That was different, I might have said, but of course it wasn't.

"No, I only wanted to enjoy dinner with a young woman who is going places and also to say sorry for landing you such a blow today."

"It was nothing," I said, and he laughed.

"Stoic to the last, I see. No wonder you make such a good siren."

"You said you were a monster yourself, that we should look out for one another . . ."

He tilted his head to one side, but instead of answering, he only said, "Ah, there's Teo now."

Teo turned out to be a smiling young man with thick black hair and a slightly babyish face. They spoke fluent Spanish together, and Teo smiled at me.

"Glad you liked the food I put out," he said diffidently, and I felt a little dizzy.

"You're Mexican?" I asked, startled, and Harry smiled, a little more bitterly.

"Venezuelan, not that it makes a difference here," he said.

"It does back home," Teo added, taking the food out of the grocery bags and putting it away with the ease of long familiarity. When I saw him pull an apple from the bag and bite into it, one hip hitched against counter and watching me with a friendly and curious look, something locked together in my head.

"Monster in more ways than one," I said, understanding, and Harry nodded.

"Monsters to others perhaps, but at home we are simply ourselves. Best you learn that early on."

They fed me, which still meant a great deal when memories of long and hungry afternoons weren't so far behind me. My mother made it a matter of pride that we all had dinner together, eating late enough in the evening that our stomachs rumbled, but during the day we were mostly on our own.

Teo and Harry chatted lightly about the price of fish at the good market, who was sleeping with whom, the charms that Harry kept up around his house to turn back ill wishes. Someone was pregnant, someone had made an unwise deal with a devil and now even more unwisely flaunted the black fingernail that went with it. They included me sometimes, but were just as happy to let me stay silent. I ate their food and soaked in a kind of nourishment that I didn't even know that I had been lacking.

I had thought that the Friday fires were real, that what Emmaline and I had lived there and only there. Now that love leaked into the world I had to live in the rest of the time, came out in a fan of avocado on a white plate and a careless kiss as Teo passed behind Harry to collect the dinner plates.

Harry told me I could stay the night, but Greta would worry, so I told him no. On the ride home, I was silent, feeling full of a new kind of wonder. Harry and Teo didn't belong to the Friday fires. In Harry's house in Bel-Air, they belonged only to themselves.

When I walked into the room, Greta was still awake, on her side on the couch, reading a magazine with a scowl as she sounded out the odd difficult English word. She raised her eyebrow as I locked the door behind me and leaned against it.

"You've met someone," she guessed, and I came to sit next to her. In her flannel nightgown, she was as round as a pear.

"I have," I said. "A man, actually. Two of them."

"That does not sound like you," Greta commented, and I nodded and told her all about the house in Bel-Air, and the price of fish, and the different masks worn by monsters.

IX

Greta hid for most of September. Most of the publicity for *The Belles of St. Desmond* was already in the can, and after it premiered to raves across the country, Greta was in a position to have artistic fits. I brought her the papers that talked about her Scandinavian spates of darkness, seasonal megrims that turned the glowing starlet into a moon in eclipse. She laughed at them, and took up wearing a filmy nightgown left behind by a girl who had left to marry an orchard owner. It floated around her like a fog of dry ice, and it gave the dorm a reputation for hauntings when she walked the halls on restless nights.

Nemo's Revenge wrapped, but Scottie Mannheim told me to hang on to the rubber tail. *Return of the Siren* had already gotten a green light, and Harry and I were back together. He was all beaming pleasure to see me, and he took me home with him every few weeks. A shot of me getting into his Bentley appeared in *Variety*, under the headline "Captain Tames a Siren?" and Harry offered it to me, framed, with a flourish.

Emmaline had gone to Gstaad at the end of August, and the papers were full of her teaching Cassidy Dutch to ski, to enjoy wine, to simply exist in the privileged peace of the Alps.

"They love to see nobility," she said one night before she left. "Grace and generosity that elevates rather than degrades."

It was the only time she had come close to mentioning Dutch during the fires. She knew how to ski, and how to snowshoe and fish through ice as well, doing it all in a cold that I couldn't imagine in the California sun.

I read the magazine articles that had pictures of Emmaline flushed and triumphant on the slopes, and I missed her so much that I cut out one of those pictures and slid it under my pillow so I could see it at night. Greta would have disapproved, and Emmaline herself would have laughed fit to kill, but it was better than nothing. I decided I would ask her for a real picture when she came back. Perhaps she knew someone who could take a photograph for us, her at home and barefoot, pale hair bound in braids for sleep and a glass of red wine in her hand.

Without Emmaline and without Greta, I still went to the fires, walking between them with a kind of assurance that would eventually become the real thing. Sometimes I heard my name and turned away. Sometimes I stayed for a short time at Harry's fire, one of an adoring cadre. I looked at the knowing women there and the charming men, and I wondered, but didn't ask.

Once I walked through the darkness and found a gleaming platinum fire, and around it I could see men and women I didn't recognize. They were painted in silver and black, and though their mouths moved, they did not speak. They were ghosts, though I doubted they had ever been human in the first place, and I thought of the button-eyed silk dolls my mother had made.

I came home to Greta, who paced our apartment endlessly, only leaving it to step out onto the balcony in the orange-skied night. She slept in short bursts, coming awake at every noise, and more than anything else towards the end, she craved fish. I struck a deal with a grip whose brother worked on a commercial fishing boat. Every few days, he brought us gleaming cuts of halibut and yellowtail wrapped in paper and paid for from the money Greta never touched. She opened the paper with hands that shook from hunger, and with her hair tied back to keep it out of the way, she bit into the raw firm flesh with relish. She ate it, bones and scales and all, and when she did, she glowed with a kind of satisfied light.

It was easy to think that time never passed on the lots, but there was something different going into October. After a strangely arid August and September, October saw rain every day, even if it dried and was a memory by two in the afternoon. Walking down the dorm hallways, I saw some girls with altars set out to welcome their dead, small and private and ashamed in a place where the dead could rise up after a stabbing and where the only gods ruled at the Friday fires.

"I'm going with you," I told Greta one night.

She sighed, but there was a smile in it. She stroked her belly, by now unmistakable.

"I'll call her Luli if we all survive this, then," she said, and, startled, I began to laugh. I hadn't heard from my sister in months, though my mother sent me notes acknowledging the money I sent home.

"Good," I said, and sitting on the floor, I pressed my ear against her belly, getting a sharp kick to the cheek for my trouble.

"I'll be better to you," I whispered, and Greta's fingers combed through my hair.

Wolfe Studios was tense through the week leading up to Halloween. There was something fevered in the air, and we all felt it, from Oberlin Wolfe on down. I caught Brandt Hiller's name in the papers off and on, and his picture as well, smiling and hollow-eyed. He'd been seen sneaking out of Gloria West's house in Pomona, he was caught in a clinch with Dina Everwood at Del Ray.

"Poor boy," Greta said softly, touching a picture of him getting into Gloria West's limousine. "He's drowning."

As far as I know, she hadn't seen him since the night I had gone to get love-comes-home for Emmaline. Thankfully her anger had mellowed to something that she could live with, and the baby mellowed it further. She was almost human sometimes.

On Halloween night, Greta dressed for the first time in ages. She showered, scrubbing her hair until it was pure silver and sewing it up in a crown of braids around her head. She put on a long shapeless dress made of blue linen. I watched her twist and turn experimentally in it, ensuring she could move her arms fully, and then she slipped on a pair of lace-up workman's boots that I suspected she had stolen off someone on *The Belles of St. Desmond*. Iron was strictly regulated in the studio, no chance of getting any of that, but she slipped an ice pick into her pocket. It wasn't iron, but it could ruin just about anyone's day.

In a black cotton dress, I felt woefully unready, but I exchanged my heels for ballet flats. I didn't know what I would be able to do for Greta, but at least I would be able to do it without stumbling.

When it turned full dark, we made our way into the studio lot, dodging the fires that were built up higher than I had ever seen them. People counted their friends twice that night, making sure that all were accounted for. Greta and I only had to squeeze each other's hands to count, and we were all we needed.

The horns of the hunt were absent that night, as were the drums. Instead we went where the crowds thinned out, towards the darkest part of the lot, until we heard the rumble of engines. Once or twice, the darkness was torn by a short scream of laughter, and somehow, the laughter was stranger than fear might have been on another night.

Mrs. Wiley had told us Oberlin Wolfe's ride always ended at Lot 19, which was long and narrow, located as close to the back of the studio lot as it was possible to get without running off it entirely. Otherwise, the ride could run anywhere.

Greta picked up a number of nearby crates, piling them close to the road to give us some cover. I couldn't even push one, and simply sat at the top, staring hard into the night as she built.

"They're coming," I said, hopping down, and she nodded. She was sweating a little, her hair pushed back to reveal her wide forehead.

We took our place behind the crates as the rumble grew louder.

A pair of matched black Bugattis passed, narrow enough to ride two abreast on the road. I recognized Josephine Beaufort in one, her features silver and flickering and flowers in her black hair. She looked neither to the left or the right, and the black cars passed like ghosts in the night.

Peeking above the crate, Greta and I waited impatiently as a fleet of shining cars rumbled past. Some of them were faces we recognized; Irene Leonard rode in a smart Alfa Romeo, while Stanley Rye, serious for once, took a long pull from a flask before tucking it back into his signature loud paisley jacket. They were all this season's best and brightest, and then I saw Emmaline there, back from Gstaad perhaps just for Halloween night.

She looked terribly young for all that she was two years older than I was, her hair down and flowing. I saw her in stern profile, carved from shell, and as the rich brown Mercedes she rode in processed towards Lot 19 I couldn't tell if she was afraid or not.

There was a pause where nothing rolled by, and next to me, Greta tensed. Her body shifted next to mine, sleek and healthy, if unwieldy. Pregnancy made humans careful, but it seemed to make her kind reckless, possessed of a strength that went far beyond bending forged iron.

She saw better in the dark than I did. She hissed gently, and then I heard the purr of Oberlin Wolfe's Duesenberg Tourister. The car slipped down the road as if it came on tiger's paws, like a menace disguised in fog. It gleamed a dull pearl even in the dim light, and the top was down, letting Brandt Hiller perch on the back of the seat, feet braced against the dashboard, shirt open, and head tipped back to stare at the sky.

For almost a year, he had been the king-consort, offered the best of everything. On Halloween, the last night of his reign, he looked half-dead. The purple love bites on his chest were livid under the scanty light, and his eyes were dark and hopeless.

I caught this all in a moment, and then with a flash of blue and a barely audible growl, Greta had leaped up on top of the crate and jumped forward, down onto the car's narrow trunk. I hadn't expected her burst of energy or the leashed fury of her motion. I stumbled out from behind the crates just in time to see her throw her arms around Brandt Hiller's chest and then throw herself backwards, dragging him off the seat and onto the pavement. She twisted just in time to prevent his weight from crushing her against the ground, uttering a triumphant shout that carried through the night.

The cry went up from the cars ahead of us, doors slamming as people ran back to see what was the matter, Oberlin Wolfe hit the brakes and stood on the back of the Tourister, heedless of the marks his heels left on the pristine finish.

"Fucking goat girl," he snarled, face distorted with rage, and I shrank back against the shadows. Later, perhaps, I could try to rationalize it as staying hidden because there was nothing else I could do. Right then, I knew that it was cowardice.

"Mine," Greta snapped, levering herself up to her knees. Her arms were thrown around Brandt, who looked around like a drowning man suddenly and unexpectedly rescued.

"You think you want him?" growled Wolfe. "Let's find out."

A roaring erupted from thin air, and suddenly Greta's arms were linked around a golden lion. It was bigger than life, twice as big as the sad toothless creatures I had seen at the circus years ago. Her arms could barely meet around its maned neck, and it paced and shook her viciously, sending her feet up into the air as she hung on. I saw an enormous paw rise up to claw at her body, and she screamed, *Greta* screamed as the claws raked over her arm and her side. She hung on like grim death, and I saw her whispering into the beast's ear, quickly, urgently.

Oberlin Wolfe made a pass with his hands, and the lion disappeared, Greta's arms slipping closed as she cursed. I couldn't see what had happened for a moment but then Greta reached forward and grasped the tail of the dusty brown rattlesnake that was trying to slither away through the scraps of clothing Brandt Hiller had been wearing. It twisted faster than I could see, mouth open and hissing, but Greta only shut her eyes, turning her face away. It struck at her breasts trying to get at her throat, and pinpricks of blooming red appeared on her chest. I was frozen where I stood, and all around me, the riders stood as well, unable to take their eyes from the spectacle, the man on the car, the woman holding on to the beast below him.

When he saw that poison and pain would not move her, Oberlin Wolfe stood up straight, his face still except for the hate in his eyes. It made him look more like a man than passion had.

"All right, goat, you want him?"

Another pass of his hands and Greta fell under the weight. It wasn't a snake in her arms now. Instead it was a naked man, but it wasn't Brandt Hiller.

This boy was lanky and slightly unformed. His dirt-brown hair was shaggy around his ears, and there was a bloom of acne on his forehead and his shoulders. When he opened his mouth to cry out, he revealed crooked teeth, and he stuttered hard over her name. The eyes were the same, however, and for the first time, he looked utterly panicked.

"No," he moaned. "No-no-no . . ."

Greta was so startled she nearly let him go, but as he tried to scramble away, she took a tighter grasp on him. This wasn't a king-consort or an actor or anything like that, except it was, and he couldn't bear it. Tears ran down his face, and he turned away from Greta, the panic and shame coming out in his sobbing apologies.

"Oh, you're ridiculous!" Greta exploded. "Stop it!"

Brandt went still in her arms, and when she was sure he wasn't going to try to scratch her eyes or run away, she wrapped him in the blanket we brought from the dorms. Greta looked up at Oberlin Wolfe.

"Your tricks are beneath me, your court is a lie, and your movies are *terrible*," she said contemptuously, and for a moment, I genuinely thought the world was going to end. The thing that used Oberlin Wolfe as its face rumbled underneath us, and the man's eyes went as dark as ink, no life and no mercy there.

"The tithe must still be paid," Oberlin growled, and he reached down, not for Brandt, but for . . .

I stepped forward and wrapped my arms around Greta, staring up at Oberlin Wolfe and feeling like I was going to faint. I was somewhere behind myself again, above and behind and watching myself do this *stupid, stupid* thing.

Greta jumped a little when my arms were around her, but then I heard her delighted laugh. It was too joyous to belong to Halloween, but none of us did. She shifted to wrap an arm around me, Brandt to her left and me to her right. She cuddled us both as if we were kittens very dear to her, and Oberlin Wolfe mattered nothing to her, even if I was less confident.

I had no idea if I could hold her while Oberlin Wolfe turned her in my arms. I was stubborn, not strong, and I didn't know if stubbornness was enough.

It's been enough before, I heard Mrs. Wiley suggest, and I squared my shoulders and looked up at the king of Wolfe Studios.

Oberlin met my eyes, and hesitated. I don't know if he could feel his control slipping or if time was running out, or something else.

He shouted two names I didn't know, and a slender girl with a brush of flaming red hair stumbled out of the dark, followed by an older man dressed only in braces, trousers, and fine leather shoes. Their eyes were fixed on him, exalted, and I looked away. I heard them get into the car, heard the footsteps of the other riders leaving as well. The cars rumbled on their interrupted journey to Lot 19 and then we were alone.

I fell to my knees in relief, and the next thing I was aware of was Brandt apologizing.

"I'm sorry, I'm sorry, I'm so, so sorry," he kept saying, and Greta finally made an impatient snorting noise.

"Come on, stop that, stand up," she grumbled. She barely seemed to feel her wounds, for all that her dress was half tatters and soaked dark with blood.

Brandt stood up, wiping his eyes with one long hand. He wasn't bad looking, but I could see that he wasn't really Brandt Hiller, not anymore.

"Ah, good," Greta said. "Stop crying. What is your name?"

He hesitated for a moment, searching that corner of the mind that we all knew so well. What he found almost made him cry again, but his voice only trembled a little when he answered her.

"Lawrence Herman."

Greta hummed in consideration and then nodded.

"All right. Lawrence, you must stop crying because you are mine now."

He looked at her, and the love and nearly helpless adoration gave him a strange kind of beauty.

"What does that mean?" he asked.

"Ah, I do not know. I am very young, after all. But we shall find out."

X

The sun came up over Wolfe Studios on November first. I hadn't been sure it would. Greta and I sat on the balcony, Lawrence asleep in Greta's bed. Oberlin Wolfe and the riders were still somewhere in the fires, fighting and fucking and dancing to forget whatever price Oberlin paid to keep all this going. November second would come, though, and there would be no tithe or audience to hold back Oberlin's hand.

Greta held my hand gently in hers, watching the sky lighten with a peaceful look on her face. Her bandages were a fresh white, wounds already closed. I couldn't stop thinking about how she had held me so close just as I held her, how strong she was and how soft. Would Emmaline hold me like that? I didn't know.

"What happens now?" I wondered. I hadn't expected her to answer, but she turned to me with a smile. "Something new, something strange," she replied. "Good, eh?"

I wasn't sure. Greta had never wanted this, but I still did. *Return of the Siren* was wrapping up, and Whalen Mannheim had told me there was another role for me after that, something he and his brother had been working up for a while. Oberlin Wolfe had a long memory, and it wasn't like I could blend into the crowd of new actresses and work without notice in the studios. Elgin Aegis or John Everest might shelter me, but they were terrible themselves.

And there was Emmaline. She must have seen me wrap my arms around Greta, ready to face down Oberlin Wolfe for her sake. She must have seen Greta with her arm around me. She rode with them and had seen the tithe. Was I still welcome at her fire? I shut the questions away, too tired to deal with them. I squeezed Greta's hand.

"Good," I replied.

I struggled to remember that peace when November third came, and along with it, a summons to Oberlin Wolfe's office, Greta and I together.

"Not me?" asked Lawrence, who was still getting his feet underneath him. There was a frailness to him that irritated me, especially when set next to Greta's calm strength.

"You are dead to him," Greta said, not unkindly. "Wait for us here."

He looked pathetically relieved not to have to see Wolfe again, and I felt a sting of guilt over my impatience.

I dressed carefully in a green dress with my hair gathered at my nape with a faux gold clip. There were touches of gold at my collar and my throat, and I stepped into the highest heels I owned, because they were green snakeskin. I wanted to remind him of the siren movies, to make him think twice about whatever he might do, if it were possible to make a man like Wolfe think twice.

Greta dressed as if it were just another day, grabbing a shapeless lilac linen dress from the closet that made her look a little like a cafeteria worker. The lilac at least gave her some color in her cheeks, and she linked her arm into mine as we walked out.

It could have been a normal day, but just before we entered the offices, she turned to me.

"If he tries to hurt you or my baby, I will bend his spine into a wedding ring."

She said the words calmly, but there was a nerviness to her I hadn't sensed before. I squeezed her hand and let go. It felt like lightning was going to strike. On Halloween night, I had clung to Greta, defying Oberlin Wolfe to take her. She had clung to me in turn, and we had saved each other. Would I be as brave now, in the light of day? I already knew that being brave didn't mean anything unless you were willing to do it again.

It was the same receptionist I had met before, but this time she didn't make me wait. Instead she looked at me with eyes as hollow as empty tin cans and nodded.

"Mr. Wolfe is waiting."

The moment we were in, Greta and I dove to either side as a bottle of ink came sailing through the air to crash against the closed door behind us. The glass exploded like a gunshot and black ink sprayed out. For a moment I saw a screaming face in the spill, but then it was just black again.

I turned to the front of the office, where Oberlin Wolfe stood, utterly still except for the rage that lit his inhuman eyes.

"You fucking bitches," he snapped. "You fucking *children*."

Greta watched him with her eyes narrowed but otherwise entirely composed, and I kept as quiet as I could. If all he wanted to do was to shout and throw things at us, I was content to stay silent and dodge.

Wolfe shook his head. There was something stiff and pained about his movements. The last time I was in this office, I thought he was recovering from a hangover. This time, it looked like he was trying to shake off something much worse.

"You know how much it costs to run this place? It's money, and it's sacrifice, and it's blood . . ."

But never yours.

I didn't know I had said it until Wolfe's eyes locked on me. I wanted to cover my mouth with my hand, force those words back between my lips and swallow them. He stalked closer to me, and

I couldn't move, my weight pressing down into my painfully sharp heels.

"Oh it's mine sometimes, Luli. I started this fucking place with blood and sacrifice, long before money got involved, and at the beginning, it was *all* mine."

He got closer, and his hands came up. I wanted to move back, to run, but I couldn't, couldn't. He had given something up in those early days, whether he remembered it or not, but I could see the space it left in him, a hollowness where something else had come to live.

"*You're* mine," he said.

"Stop it. You do not want your price from her."

Wolfe turned his head towards Greta, his hands still too close to me. As I would in a nightmare, I noted calmly that his fingertips were red and bloody; the nails on his left hand were gone altogether.

"I want it from you too, so just wait, Caroline."

"No, I will not. I want to bargain."

Almost reluctantly, Wolfe turned fully towards her, and I could have cried for relief. I wasn't brave, and I knew that for sure now. All I could think was *better her than me.*

"What? What could you possibly have for . . ."

"I want to leave. I want to take my man with me. I want two tickets out of this place, and I want Luli clear of this mess."

"And what will you give me for that, Caroline? I own your name, I brought you from Sodermalm on a holy rope. What have you got left?"

Greta looked cold as ice, or maybe it was just as if every soft part of her had gone deep inside to hide. She didn't reach for her baby, but I saw with a twist of my stomach that she had a knife in her hand. Had she carried it all the way to the office without my noticing?

"I'll give you something no one else can have. I will give you every movie ever made by Caroline Carlsson. Her great beauty, you want that, but more, you want no one else to have it, yes?"

I remembered Mrs. Wiley's words, Mrs. Wiley's price, and I felt sick. I wanted to reach for Greta, but she was too far away, a river of ink between us. I wasn't in the room at all.

That had Wolfe's attention. He licked his lips, and licked them again. The thing that was using him as its face grew hungrier.

"Yes. Yes. Give it to me."

I couldn't watch. I covered my face as Greta's knife rose up and came down. She didn't make a sound. I imagine she hadn't made a sound either when they cut off her tail.

I thought I would faint, but then Wolfe turned to me.

"Take her out of here. I can't stand the sight of either of you."

I hesitated, and he sneered at the unspoken question in my eyes.

"Oh, someone else will take care of you. Now get the hell out."

The right side of Greta's face was raw meat. She had missed her eye, but it was not for a lack of ferocity. I put my arm around her, but she walked as steadily as I did, even if I was not walking particularly steadily. We went by the receptionist, who refused to look at us, and then we were out in the street again, under the bright, bright sun.

"Greta . . ."

She grimaced with pain, and then I realized she was smiling.

"Should have done it months ago," she said. "Should have done it then, but now I get a baby and a man out of it. That's good. That's a bargain."

To her it was, but that feeling of dread sat in my belly like a cut-glass ink bottle, holding something dark and screaming inside.

XI

Greta didn't let the sand shift underneath her shoes. She was on a flight back to Stockholm inside of a week, a boulder-like girl in a long blue coat with half her face bandaged up, obviously pregnant and cranky about the heat and her itchy healing wound. Lawrence followed her with their single bag clutched in his hand and a slightly stunned look on his face. Once or twice, when he looked at her, you could see the seed that Wolfe had used to grow the stunningly handsome Brandt Hiller. Besides that, however, no one who passed them recognized them as the stars of *The Belles of St. Desmond*, which was still playing to sold-out movie houses across the country.

A week after that, I hired a cab to take me to the Palisades late one night, where Emmaline lived. The rain had finally come to the coast after one of the driest summers on record, and as I got out of the car and walked up the long drive to Emmaline's hacienda-style bungalow, the earth opened up a thousand mouths to drink down the water.

At the door, Mari, Emmaline's girl, shook her head.

"Miss Sauvignon is not present. I will tell her that you have stopped by."

No invitation to come in and wait, no offer to call my cab back. I gritted my teeth.

"I know she's here. I want to see her."

Mari used to work for those actors that rotated through the historical dramas and mysteries and kept a stiff upper lip throughout. She gave me a beautifully cold look that would have gotten her an immediate spot on a Victorian drama if she weren't Black and Mexican, and shook her head.

"I am afraid that will not be possible."

"Her damn car is in the drive, you can tell her . . ."

"If you can see her car, *Miss Wei*, surely you can see the one next to it?"

I had been so focused on Emmaline's sleek little Nash coupe that I didn't see the custom forest-green Le Baron roadster just beyond it. That shut me up, because everyone knew that that car belonged to Cassidy Dutch.

I went silent, and Mari nodded. She changed Emmaline's sheets and cooked her meals; of course she knew about us, and in the end, she had no true interest in unkindness.

"I'll tell her you came by," she said, and she closed the door in my face.

There was a moment where I might have selected a handful of round stones from the graveled drive and slung them at those flashy cars until every window was as shattered as I felt, but I turned and walked away. I ended at the bottom of her drive, sitting on a boulder just inside the gate. I knew I needed to find a place to call for a cab to at least get out of the rain that was soaking me. I was wearing a light silk dress in deep blue, and it slicked to my skin, heavy and cloying.

I sat at the base of her drive until the rain let up and the acrid scent of water evaporating off of asphalt rose into the air. I had no real interest in calling for a cab or getting food or doing anything else at all. Helen Martel was rumored to have a garden full of cast-off lovers, all transformed to stone. That day, I learned that it wasn't a sudden strike of heartache that had done it; it was a slow petrifaction of things I no longer wanted because Emmaline refused to look at me.

Close to dawn, Emmaline came down from the house. The first light of sunrise turned her hair bronze, and she had a voluminous silk robe wrapped around her so thickly she looked mummified.

"I've called a cab for you. It should be here in twenty minutes or so."

"Did Cassidy Dutch tell you to do that?" I asked, and she gave me an impatient look.

"He don't—doesn't tell me anything. I tell him. And I'm telling you. Leave me alone, Luli."

"Just like that—"

"*Yes*, just like that, Christ. Do you know what you did? Did you know what you could have done? To me? To all of us?"

"I helped my friend! Greta needed help, she was all alone . . ."

Emmaline reached out to cup my face in her hands. When she had done it before, it was tender, but now I felt her urge to flex her fingers and to dig her perfect manicure into my face.

"I don't know how you failed to notice, Luli, but *we* are all alone! All of us. You, me, Harry, Helen Martel . . . We are all alone together."

"Because . . ."

"Because yes! You nearly brought the whole damn thing down on top of us. Wolfe doesn't forget, and maybe he knows how to forgive, but it isn't likely. We exist because Wolfe allows us to. We thrive because he turns a blind eye, and after Halloween, that eye is suddenly a little less blind, all because of you and *fucking* Caroline Carlsson."

It would have been better if she was just jealous. Jealous was a fight and a make-up, and a morning hiding the claw marks on each other's ribs and shoulders. There was a fury in her eyes fueled by a very real fear, and for the first time, I was sorry for what I had done, instead of simply being afraid of the consequences. I had been alone so long that I had never considered the risk to others like me, simply because for so long, there was no one even a little like me to consider.

"Emmaline . . ."

"No. You don't *think*, Luli, and that's going to cost you some fine day. And I refuse to let Wolfe or anyone see me as . . . just one more unfortunate part of your story. Don't come back here anymore."

She turned and walked away. I saw that she had been barefoot and the soles of her feet flashed whitely where they weren't dark with dirt.

Eventually, the cab came, and she must have told the company where to take me because he started to drive back to the studio lot. As we wound our way out of the Palisades, the rain started again, running down the glass just a few inches from my face, washing away everything that had come before.

XII

I spent November haunted by October. The room I'd shared with Greta was too empty, but no one ever came looking to share it with me, even when they were stacked three and four to a suite elsewhere. Caroline Carlsson was bad luck, or maybe I was. It didn't matter.

When I wasn't working, I stretched out on my unmade bed, smoking cigarettes I could never get a taste for, wondering how real people ever filled their days. The work never ended at the laundry, and the time before Halloween I remembered as being full of Greta and panic and fear. I should have been more afraid, especially after Wolfe's warning, but instead I was restless, bored, inclined to weeping and tired to the bone.

Two things happened in December. The first thing that happened was that *Return of the Siren* was released to raves. It was more popular than *Nemo's Revenge* had been, more daring, more dramatic, more dripping in pathos, gore, and plastic seaweed. Some of that was Scottie Mannheim's work, some of it was Harry's, but a lot of it was mine.

Suddenly the hall phone was ringing off the hook for me, and a thin and terribly upright man from the studio appeared to escort me to interviews and photo shoots, and also, I imagine, to pass reports of my behavior back to the studio. I never quite got his name, but he referred to himself as my assistant, helping me remember things about where I was from, what I liked, and how old I was.

That was when the story about me being the daughter of a Chinese spy and a Hungarian nobleman got around, where I learned English from a Bible left in the attic where I was kept until the age of ten. With my assistant's helpful guidance, I remembered the golden fields of Guangzhou, the cold castle in Budapest, the cruel stepmother that had driven me finally to the arms of Hollywood and Wolfe Studios.

("I heard they found you in Kansas."

"Kansas? I never heard that one."

"Yeah, a nice old farm couple who wanted to have a kid found you late one night after they heard a terrible crash."

"Jane—"

"Pulled you out of the wreckage of what could only have been an extraterrestrial craft, and soon they realized you were *no ordinary infant,* and in fact had great powers—"

"Remind me why I put up with you again?"

"You love me.")

Of course I couldn't come from Hungarian Hill. Even I didn't always quite believe that I had when I woke up at ten to be taken to a photo shoot where I would be dressed in silk and gold, turned and posed for the flash.

The second thing that happened was that meetings started for production on the third siren movie, tentatively named *Siren's Sea.* It was more Whalen's project than Scottie's, a risk given Whalen's artistic pretensions, but one they thought they could afford after two hits.

I showed up for what I thought would be a makeup test, only to have the door opened for me by Harvey Rose.

"Miss Wei," he said in his gravelly way, and I almost bolted. I had been waiting for the second shoe to drop for so long that I was exhausted. If I ran, I wouldn't have made it far, and so instead I made sure my step was steady and entered the room.

Whalen and Scottie Mannheim were both there, but neither of them would meet my gaze. Instead they sat behind their table as if it would protect them from Wolfe's right-hand man, busying themselves with the papers in front of them. There was no makeup team there, no one besides me, the Mannheims, and Harvey Rose, and when none of them would speak, finally I had to.

"Well?" I asked, glad it sounded more like arrogance than fear.

Before anyone could answer me, there were two knocks at the door, slow enough that it sounded as if the knocker wanted to think in between.

"Go get that," Harvey Rose said, and I didn't need to see behind his green-tinted glasses to know that he was relishing some small bit of cruelty I couldn't guess at.

With neither of the Mannheims looking at me and the shadow of October still hanging over us all, I crossed to the door and opened it to meet myself.

She was exactly my height with exactly my face, and her hair was done up in a chignon that my mother would have said was too old-fashioned to be borne. She wore gray silk in a shade I knew made me sallow but she hadn't figured out yet, and she smiled, showing all of her teeth.

"Hello," she said. "I'm Luli Wei."

My first instinct was to hit her out of shock and offense, but the moment my arm twitched, Harvey Rose stepped forward and I went still.

"No," I said instead. "You aren't."

I stepped back to allow her into the room. I felt as if I were shaking apart, but the dance teacher had taught me well, and I was as steady as a stone pillar on my tall heels.

My double came after me with a faltering gait, not tumbling

but as if every step could send her sprawling. It made me think of tender young creatures who were too slow and too clumsy to escape the things that would eat them. I had looked like that before I signed my contract; I never dared look like that after.

Whalen nearly toppled his water glass before he could right it. Scottie looked green, and he was the one who finally spoke to Harvey Rose.

"What's going on? Mr. Wolfe asked us here to do a test on Luli."

"And you are," Harvey said. "Here she is. Test her."

Whalen and Scottie shot me panicked looks as if I could save them, but I couldn't come up with anything. My thoughts whipped away in a high whistle of wind, lost in how wrong it was to watch myself stumble.

Finally, Whalen cleared his throat.

"Um. All right, Luli. Why don't you tell us about yourself?"

I decided I was going to remember how quickly Whalen had been willing to call a horror by my name. If I was allowed to remember what they did to me after this.

My double laughed and recited the story going around about learning English from the Bible. It wasn't how I would have told it. Her version was stiff and starchy and sweet, about her learning to be a real person from the good words, implying that of course she was a good American too. I never did. I hated that story. Mrs. Davis had told me to be sure of who I was, and she was right, because this was what would happen if I wasn't.

"Good, eh?" asked Harvey Rose with just a touch of menace, and to my dismay, the Mannheims shrugged uncomfortably.

"Give her a script page."

The words popped out of my mouth, and they turned to me, all four of them. My double was the closest to me, and her eyes went hard even as her mouth retained the small smile that so many of the interviews called mysterious.

"Hello, I'm Luli Wei," she said softly to me, and I wondered who she had been before this. There were a few stray stitches at her temple, and when I looked close, I saw the hint of blond hair underneath. Whoever she was, she had lost a lot to stand where she was now.

"Uh, yes. I have a few new script pages right here," said Scottie, fumbling with his papers. Whalen was still frozen, eyes darting back and forth as if he wanted to flee the room.

Scottie handed them to my double gingerly, and we all waited in silence as she read them over. When she read her face looked less like mine. In repose, her cheeks looked heavier, her chin more defined. When she was still, her face remembered even if she wanted to forget.

"All right. I would like to begin."

She took her place at the center of the room, and Harvey Rose stepped close to me, as close as he could get without touching.

"Afraid?" he asked curiously.

I lifted my chin.

"Not of that," I lied.

When she spoke the first few lines of the opening monologue for *Siren's Sea*, I started to breathe again. Her voice was as glassy as a department store window, flat as a pancake. She stumbled and paused, and she sped up when she realized how tinny she was. She started to sweat. Her hands clutched at the paper, and by the time she was through, she was shaking hard.

"I'm Luli Wei," she whined at the end, and I shook my head, laughing like the siren would.

"No, you aren't."

I pinned Whalen and Scottie with my gaze, reminding them of what had made *Return of the Siren* a hit. They looked at me, and they looked at each other, and it was Whalen who spoke first, turning to Harvey Rose.

"Come on, Rose. You can't be serious. She ain't no siren."

Harvey Rose's face was unreadable, and then he nodded, as if understanding that no, they did not have orange juice that morning.

"Thank you for your time, gentlemen. Miss Wei."

He nodded to me, and then he took my double by the arm, dragging her out. It sounds cruel, but there was no cruelty at all in his face. He was a man removing a piece of equipment that had failed to perform, but perhaps if he fixed it, perhaps if he had the experts look at it again, perhaps if it was taken apart piece by whining piece . . .

The next day, my assistant came to me with what he called amazing news.

"You know, of course, that Edward Parr is a great fan of Oriental antiquities. It only makes sense that you two would find each other of interest. So tonight, at the Knickerbocker—"

"Tonight, I will be staying in. Edward Parr can go out with his Oriental antiquities and leave me out of it."

My assistant sputtered and protested, but I turned away. They might have another Luli Wei, but they didn't have another siren, and that meant I wasn't going out to dinner with Edward Parr.

Three weeks later, we started filming on *Siren's Sea*. The days were long, but it was clear we had another hit on our hands. I shot during the day, I gave interviews at night, and I cultivated a reputation for Eastern solitude. Stars went out if they shone too bright, I said, and I said it mysteriously enough that no one ever asked me what it meant.

At night I dreamed of Wolfe's storage warehouses, triple locked and so deep some people said they never ended at all. I followed a thin voice I could barely hear, and when I moved aside a rack of sparkling gowns I found a nodder crouched down low, one that wore my face.

"My name is Luli Wei," she said, and I reached up to feel stitches at my temples. I spared only a single moment for horror before I started to scratch at them frantically, tearing them out with my suddenly sharp fingernails, desperate to uncover the jagged scales underneath.

ACT THREE

∾

I

"Cut!"

The entire scene froze for a moment, and then suddenly it was as if our wires had been sliced. Harry slumped against one of the foam-sculpted rocks, taking off his captain's hat to wipe at his brow with a ridiculous paisley silk handkerchief, and Annette Walker slipped her hands out of the aluminum manacles, loudly declaring that she needed a cigarette. As for me, I dropped my arms and hung limp in the harness that lifted me two heads above either of them, my toes in the rubber tail a good two feet off the floor, and the tail itself coiled underneath.

Whalen Mannheim shot Annette an irritated look because getting her back into the studio usually took twice as long as the break, but he came to me, scowling at the tail.

"Sorry about that, Lu, the wires for the fins weren't deploying at all. They were just flapping around."

"Seriously? You're making me miss the old tail," I grumbled.

The old tail was less flexible than this current iteration, so stiff that I used to just rest flat on my face when I wasn't actively shooting. The strain was bad enough that I spent most evenings with a hot water bottle balanced on my lower back, my mind a buzzing blank.

The new tail, pieced together by a brilliant girl in the costume shop, was twice as long but only half as heavy. A discreet series of latches were hidden under the frilled spine running along the back, letting the whole thing snap open and closed. No more Vaseline to grease me into the thing, and a clever system of wires helped the tail twitch convincingly along the ground. A dusting of mica gave it a bright shine that turned subtle in post-production, and after the first test photos came out, I was half in love with the way I looked in it. Red paint had been slopped over the rough surface of the rubber and then rubbed in with gold paint along the edges of the scales and fins. I felt more like a dragon than a snake or a siren, and every time I was strapped in, an elemental power rose up inside me.

Whalen and Braggo, the man who handled the prosthetics, decided that it would be more trouble than it was worth to pull me down out of the costume while they worked.

"Just hang around, huh, Lu?" said Whalen with a wink. He was too smart to give me an affectionate pat on the rear even through the rubber. The last time he tried, I threatened to bury a nearby prop harpoon in his foot. I heard him later on telling the gaffer that Oriental girls were very honor-bound and intent on preserving their virtue. I must have looked as if I were thinking about going over to do something really disastrous when Harry caught my eye.

"I tell them that in Catalonia, the afternoon siesta is a sacred tradition and required for excellent work," he had said quietly.

"Is it?"

"Oh who knows, but it does leave me feeling refreshed and well rested in the middle of a long shoot, doesn't it?"

Honor-bound or just plain murderous, either way, it meant that Whalen kept his hands to himself as he and Braggo fussed with the springs that mounted the fins. I was hardly needed for that, so I glanced over at Harry, who stared up at the rafters with wide-open eyes.

"Could you get Mr. Long a water and lime?"

The craft services girl running past nodded and pressed Harry's favorite on-set drink into his hand, rousing him to sit and give her a polite thank-you. Instead of drinking it immediately, he wiped the condensation off of the glass with his handkerchief and pressed it against his face. He briefly went boneless at the pleasure of the cold, and then, remembering he was in public, stood and straightened in one motion. He made his way over to where I hung and in another world all their own, Whalen and Braggo clucked over my fins.

"Thank you for the refreshment, Miss Wei," he said, saluting me with the glass. "I don't think I quite noticed how poorly I was doing."

"Long day, I suppose," I said, but I watched him carefully, ready to hear more if he wanted to say.

"Seems like they are all long days lately," he said. I wondered if he looked a little thin inside the bulk of the captain's jacket. Over the course of seven films, he had received a few costume changes as well, going from the exotic mariner Captain Nemo to the great captain's descendant, who accidentally freed his ancestor's dire enemy during the Great War. The grandeur of the first movies suited him better than the Navy uniform did now, and he knew it as well.

"I'm sorry to hear that," I said, wondering if I should say more, and Harry gave me a tired grin that still had some spark to it.

"Well, perhaps an old man can bore you all about it tonight. Dinner at my place?"

I smiled, aware that even as they flexed the marvelously webbed fins at my hips, Whalen and Braggo were listening closely to our conversation. Harry didn't press. He was good at that, moving the conversation to the creature features being done over at Aegis, the price of steak in the city, and other things. After the shoot was over, he smiled to find me sitting on the bumper of his Bentley.

"Is Whalen still giving you trouble?" he asked, and I shook my head.

"He doesn't dare. He's worried that my Oriental honor will skewer him straight through his privates."

Harry chuckled.

"I should remember that you are a girl who can take care of herself. Do I need to bring you home early tonight?"

I shook my head. I had moved out of the dorm two years ago. There hadn't been much point in staying after Greta left, and *Nemo's Revenge* impressed everyone enough that I could do as I liked. The apartment on Rexford Avenue was small and relatively ungracious, because most of my cash went home to my parents. My sister had moved out a year ago to live with some of her artist friends in San Francisco, and she hadn't been back since. I'd wanted the apartment because it felt like a thing that I should have wanted.

In a gloomy way, I liked the loneliness. Now it was a choice rather than something I felt in the empty dorm room or walking between the fires on Friday night. I still spent most of my time at the studio, returning to the apartment via streetcar. Sometimes, when the nights were still, I opened the window and rested my chin on the sill, listening to the growl of the automobiles grow louder day by day.

I was never the most voluble company, but I didn't have to talk at all. Harry kept up a stream of chatter from the studio all the way up to his house. He told me how hard it was to find a good man to look after the pool, he told me about the current feud between Brenda Marlow and Jean Livingston, he confided in me that Annette Walker was trying to sleep her way to the top, only to be stymied by the fact that she couldn't tell a caterer from a producer, leading to a rather scandalous mix-up at Robbie Duval's party . . .

As Harry talked faster and faster, he drove faster and faster as well. Finally, I reached over to touch his hand where it gripped the clutch. He was unexpectedly warm, almost feverish, but he glanced at me.

"You don't have to with me," I said, and he nodded once. He eased off the speed, and we made it to the house in Bel-Air in one piece. As he pulled into the garage, I noticed that there was something dark and almost foreboding about the house. When we entered, the lights were off, and the air inside was oddly stale, as if left unmoved for some time.

"Where's Teo?" I asked, looking around. I had seen him the last time Harry had asked me to come for dinner. I brought a bag of perfectly ripe, perfectly creamy avocados, and the three of us had eaten all of them, sprinkled with salt and lemon juice. I could almost taste the avocado now, a strange and ghostly sensation in Harry's suddenly unwelcoming house.

"Gone, I'm afraid," Harry said, gesturing expansively at nothing. "Gone and left an old man to putter in the kitchen as best he can. I can still do us up something, I imagine . . ."

He started talking again as he heated oil in the pan and browned a handful of hastily chopped red onions. Teo was a perfect angel, coming to rescue an old sinner who certainly did not deserve him, Teo was too pure to be sullied by the filthy world. He had never deserved Teo, never would, and of course, inevitably, Teo had come to see that. Yellow bell pepper, almost incandescently bright in his hand, was chopped and scattered in the pan as well, and when the onions were softened, he added bloody red tomato before turning back to me.

"It is the way of the world, I suppose," Harry said, smiling a faded smile. "The good move on, and the wicked remain."

I envied the kind of girl who could walk over and wrap her arms around him, but I wasn't that. I perched at the marble kitchen island, my chin in my hands, and watched him instead.

"The wicked is making me eggs," I observed. "I don't have any complaints."

He chuckled a little at least, and he cracked three large white eggs into the skillet. He salted them and peppered them, scrambling them as carefully as he tied his tie first thing on set. He never let the wardrobe girls do it. *Too hasty by half,* he always said.

He set two places at the table, and it seemed to me that there was already something lost and old about him, like a pensioner puttering around a house that was too large and too full of memories. The food was good at least, eggs served over leftover warmed rice, and we ate in silence, letting the clatter of real silver and real ceramic plates do the talking for us. Teo talked a great deal, and without him, we were two silent mirrors, reflecting nothing at all.

"I'm getting married next month," Harry said finally, pushing his plate away. I glanced up at him in surprise.

"I hadn't heard," I said cautiously, and he shook his head with bitterness.

"No, you wouldn't have. Wolfe decided it a week ago, but it took Harvey Rose a little while to find someone who would be suitable. Confirmed bachelors are out, it seems, and they would like to make a family man out of me."

Harry already had a family. There was Teo, of course, but there were others too. There was a sister and a mother still in Venezuela, and some changing number of nieces and nephews making their way through California. He sent money and kisses and loved them all from a stellar distance.

He came by Emmaline's fire sometimes to play indulgent uncle, but when he wasn't at home, he ventured deep into the night, taking a place at the still-roaring fire of the silvered Valetti, the silent king whose black death train was followed by no less than fifty thousand mourners as it ran from Los Angeles to New York, where his human part was finally buried. Valetti was as immortal as it was possible to be, and he cared nothing anymore for Wolfe or the moralities that would keep beautiful young men from sitting at his feet. Harry, who could have had a proper fire and a court all his own, said he felt more comfortable there, shadowed by the great.

I toyed with the last bit of my eggs, watching him. He felt thin. Somehow, he had lost a certain dimension, and I couldn't say when the light started to shine through him as if he were rice paper.

"Who is it?" I asked.

"Oh, did you happen to see that dull little pastoral that came through earlier this year? Something *Her Eyes*?"

"*Her Bright Eyes*?" I blinked. "You're marrying Lana Brooks?"

Lana Brooks was a studio changeling who had earned her name through her portrayal of urchin-ish scamps in comedic pieces, but *Her Bright Eyes* showed another side of her. She got the part through a neat piece of double-crossing that wiped another changeling from the studio entirely, name and record and all, and as the heroine with the bright eyes on the edge of the frontier, she was poised to launch.

"I am. We had dinner yesterday at the Knickerbocker."

"And how did it go?" He needed prodding, but he spoke readily enough.

"Oh, my girl, it was a *nightmare*. She nattered on about this and that, a house in La Jolla, vacations in Europe, with more than a few choice words about dirty Mexicans while letting on she thinks of the entire continent of South America as Mexico. Charming, I'm sure, if I lacked a brain and a soul."

I winced. I wore my difference, one of them, at least, on my face, and the strangeness was enough to excuse me from some things. At some point, Oberlin Wolfe might decide I needed a torrid love affair or a marriage, but it hadn't happened yet. Until then, at least people like Lana Brooks didn't think I was just like them.

"I'm sorry," I said, and he glanced at me, amused.

"You already think I'm going to go through with it."

"Aren't you?

Harry started in the silent pictures, but somehow he survived when that old magic died. His voice was deep and dark and smooth with a ringing tone that can still make me shiver when I remember it. He had been acting before I knew what a movie was, and the idea of him leaving it all behind was world-turning.

He sighed.

"It would be prudent, wouldn't it? Marry the girl, separate bedrooms after I do my duty for king and country, maybe even see a few little ones out of it. God, at least they'd be attractive."

"Marriage isn't forever," I said, as I knew Harvey Rose said so often to stars in Harry's position.

"What else are we doing here but looking for our little bit of forever? Otherwise, what's the *point*?"

On the final word, he slammed his hand onto the table, making me jump. He had always had flashes of temper and passion, but instead of apologizing, he stared at me.

"What about you?" he demanded. "What happens when the great and good Wolfe decides that his siren needs a mate? Or when he realizes that Emmaline is done playing the ingenue and needs a wedding ring before she can take on a more womanly role?"

I shifted a little, not meeting his eyes.

"Emmaline and I don't pass time much anymore," I muttered.

"They'll do it to her first, I imagine," Harry said, his voice cruel. "Maybe that boy who does all the damn Westerns, or Cortland Marsh. Cort comes to Valetti's fires too, and that wouldn't be so bad. Not that Wolfe cares—it might be someone who wants more than a sham, and . . ."

"Stop!" I snapped, coming to my feet. "Stop being horrible. Don't you know what you're talking about? Can't you see what that all means?"

Harry gave me a cold look.

"Of course I do, and he could do worse. If I were even a little less famous, a little less possessed of whatever glimmer of genius I have, I imagine he might have scraped me out and left a nodding shell in my place. Instead I grew up, got wise, became a king of all of *this*."

He opened his arms to encompass the empty house, the valley, perhaps his entire career and the length of his very life.

"None, *none* of this was enough to stop Wolfe from ordering Miss Brooks and me into bed together and having every expectation that we would breed him a family for the tabloids. None of it."

He sat back down as if all the force had gone out of him. He was pale and as fragile as crumpled newspaper. This time I did reach for him, stroking his fingers with my fingertips. He closed his hand over mine and held on tightly for a moment before letting go.

"I'm sorry," he said finally. "That was cruel of me."

"It was true," I said. "I knew it all before."

"Still. The world is ugly enough without my forcing more of it on you. Shall I call you a car, my dear? I find that I'm no longer fit for company, and I'm not sure I care to make the drive along the cliffs in my present mood."

I nodded, and when the cab honked from the curb, he escorted me to the door. I could almost see a fluttering dark veil drop over his features, and it sent a cold shiver along my spine.

"Harry . . . please take care of yourself." Even in my memory, it felt too little, heedless and uncaring. I meant it, but I also knew that he wouldn't listen.

"You are great, and you are good, my dear," he said, "and if Emmaline doesn't have the sense to see that, then that is her misfortune."

("I wish I could have known him," Jane said. "I wish I could have known both of you then."

"You would have loved him."

"I would have loved you both.")

The cabdriver was thankfully silent all the way back to Rexford Avenue, and I stared out at the passing lights. If I pressed my face to the cool glass, I could see the stars gleaming high above, constellations and novas that shone for Hollywood alone. I could recite their names as if they were saints, and they were larger than anyone who had come before.

That night, however, when I thought of Harry avoiding his bed because it was too empty, contemplating alcohol or small blue pills or something more dire, it hardly felt like enough.

Even the studios had to bend before the Santa Anas.

Every year, the katabatic winds raced down from the highlands, dry and sere, sweeping the chaparral ahead of them and bowing them low.

The winds brought madness, of course, adding to the not inconsiderable amount that already hovered over the studios, but more than that, they brought fire, sheets of flame that ate away at the landscape and left it black.

During the Santa Anas, Wolfe, Everest, and Aegis would go together up to the mountains, where the winds were kindled. They were propitiating the true gods of the land with blood, tobacco, and chocolate, hoping that their courts would be spared. It worked, mostly, even if they came back from the mountains and then weren't seen for several days after.

It was far too early for the Santa Anas. They should have been sleeping on the mountaintops still, and that was the only reason that Whalen Mannheim dragged us out to Santa Aidia to shoot.

Santa Aidia was already a ghost town, and before we went out there, Harvey Rose sent men to drive out the last stragglers. Homeless people, ghosts, and the odd coyote wearing a human skin were shooed out into the desert, and then the crew could come in to build up the remnants of a lost city over it all.

The desert town was meant to stand in for the ruin of Atlantis, the siren's ancestral home. It was there that Captain Nemo and the siren would have their final confrontation, over the bones of her people. We shot before dawn and at dusk, because the heat of the day could kill us. Whenever I unlatched my tail, my legs emerged soaked in sweat and clammy all at once. Our trailers were hopeless, and above and below the line, we lay as if dead under the shade sails that the crew set up.

"Just another few days, and we're back in town," I said hopefully, but except for his lines, Harry never seemed to speak at all. They had announced his marriage to Lana Brooks, and out of some morbid fascination, I read the story in *Variety*. Supposedly they had met at the racetrack in La Jolla, Harry seeing to the racehorse he owned and Lana dragged along by overeager friends. She had bet on his horse. He had made her come collect her winnings personally, and then asked her to dinner.

It was terrible, as was the picture of them in the paper together. Lana looked as bright and brittle as glass, and on Harry, bare tolerance and panic was made to pass for casual European dissolution. Tongues were already wagging about the age difference, as Oberlin Wolfe surely meant for them to do, and there were bets made and taken about who would end up ruined. From the gleam in Lana Brooks's eyes, I could tell she didn't mean for it to be her.

My tail seemed to weigh a hundred pounds that day, and I could have cried when the wardrobe girls helped me buckle it on. At least it wasn't heels, I told myself. I told myself that a lot. The harness dug into my skin, an itchy meridian around my ribs, but I lofted into the air as gracefully as a bird, hovering over Harry as Annette Walker clung to him, looking over her shoulder fearfully at me.

"I am weary to death of this," the captain said, and every line of his last half century stood out in stark relief. "Fighting, running, killing . . . it destroys a man from the inside out."

I twisted an esoteric pattern in the dust, my face implacable and cruel.

"What does that mean to me?" I asked. "My kind were born for viciousness, for the hunt and the kill. I have sworn to chase you forever, and so I will as long as you and I both live."

I rose tall and proud, balanced perfectly on my tail. The trident in my hand glinted gold in the sun, a weapon that had been used by my ancestors to end lives. They were gone, but the trident and I remained.

The captain's hand tightened on the archaic sword at his side. It had belonged to his ancestor, a man with whom he shared both a name and a face. For a moment, that warrior's resolve tensed. It seemed as if battle must be joined. The ghosts behind us seemed to call for it, and then they went silent in shock.

The sword hit the sand with a soft thump.

"No," said the captain. "This will not continue. This is over. I kill you, you kill me, it all comes out to the same thing in the end, doesn't it?"

He gently unwound the shivering girl's arms from around his neck, giving her a long and regretful look. She was as fresh as a bouquet of waxy white flowers. The promise of a new life was perhaps the most difficult thing to pull away from, but he did it.

"Promise me you will not harm her," the captain said. "Promise me that you will not seek your terrible revenge on her or any children she may bear."

"And why would I promise such a thing?" I asked, tracing circles in the dirt.

"Because I surrender. I give myself to you, and when you spill my blood over the stones of your ancestral home, it will finally be over."

"No . . ." whispered the girl, but neither monster nor man paid her any heed.

"I give you my word as a Knight of the Blood that she will not be harmed so long as she does not offer harm to me," I said with gravity, and the captain nodded.

"Go from this place," he said to the girl. "Go. Live a long and happy life, and know that I went to my death thinking of you fondly."

The girl fell to her knees instead, but neither of us stopped to look at her. I reached for the captain, and with his head bowed, he came to me.

It was a risky scene for Whalen, but he had always been the more daring of the brothers, the one most inclined to tell the strange stories that only he could tell in flickers of color and light. People had followed the captain into story after story, and what he was doing here was a kind of murder. If it played out well, it would be the kind of murder that Harry would rise from like a phoenix, shedding sparks to light the way. Otherwise, ignominy, defeat, darkness, and a name that Oberlin Wolfe wouldn't spit on, let alone bank.

As Harry stared me down, I could feel the brush of a dark and whispering wing across my face. My body tightened as if drawn on wires. It was like what I had felt when I saw Josephine Beaufort that day in the Comique, spilling her blood for a Romeo who would never rise again, not like she did. His eyes met mine steadily, and for the first time, the siren looked away.

He crossed the desert ground towards me, and I moved restlessly, almost afraid. His sword was still on the ground, but there was something subtly more dangerous about him now. As he came towards me, he lifted his arms, palms entreating the sky. *Christlike*, the theses and analyses written afterwards said. They love a puzzle that will never be solved, and *Siren Queen*, the way that Whalen envisioned it, would never come to pass. None of us knew it in that moment, but Whalen's film was breathing its very last.

"All right, monster," Harry said softly. "Come at me, then."

I reared back, the wire rig pulling me up even higher, and five feet above any other cast or crew member, I saw the rolling smoke. For a frozen moment, my brain tried to tell me it was a solid mass of black rock that was rolling down the hill, but then I smelled the air and knew the truth.

"Fire!" I shouted instead of my line. "Fire!"

The production moved like a large animal composed of many small parts, each person rushing to secure their own responsibilities and nothing else, but all moving slow, too slow. I turned my head towards the man operating my crane only to see the last of him as he ducked into the crowd. I looked around wildly at the people rushing below me, and then again at the rolling black smoke. Now I could see the vivid orange of hungry flames as well, and the wind blew the harsh smell of singeing wood towards me.

With three years of vocal training, I should have screamed my head off. I could make them turn their heads and look at me just as much for a wildfire as I did for the death throes of a monster, but after my first cry of *fire*, my voice curled in my throat and refused to come. Instead, I twisted about, grasping for the wires attached to my harness and slicing my fingers on their taut strands. Something in my side tore, spilling dull agony to my hip as I spun slowly, so slowly in the air, trying to reach the harness that was buckled at my back.

"The latches!"

I looked down to see a girl from wardrobe, her arms draped over with heavy costumes dangling from their hangers. She must have worked with Harry or Annette because I didn't recognize her at all.

"Not the wires, the latches!" she shouted again, gesturing at her thigh, and then someone shouted her name—Aguila—and she ran for the trucks.

It took me a moment to understand her words, and then grimly, I bent my body as much as I could, bringing the latches that lined the side of my tail up to my reaching fingers. My tail was lighter than it had been, but it still took two girls to move comfortably. My frantic fingers undid two out of the five before the tail dragged my legs down again, and I took a deep breath to steady my hands before trying again.

The third latch opened and the tail dropped again, but on the fourth, with a loud, unwilling squelch, the rubber peeled from my kicking legs by its own weight, falling dead to the sand underneath.

My teeth were clenched so tight my jaw ached and there was a tearing pain in my side, but I couldn't stop. Instead, freed of the weight of the tail, I could work on the harness. I jerked the end of the belt so hard I gave myself bruises around my ribs, but then—so suddenly it wrenched my wrist—my weight tumbled free, sending me flailing to the ground. The distance was not so great, but I still might have shattered an ankle or worse if Harry hadn't been there to catch me on the way down.

I blinked at him in surprise, and he smiled at me briefly.

"I would have cut you down sooner, but Annette managed to have hysterics and a fainting fit all at once."

"How . . ."

"I don't know, and it became someone else's problem when I pushed her into Whalen's car. Can you walk?"

I hung on to him like grim death until I learned the answer was yes, and then I stood away. I was barefoot and my sweaty legs were already studded with grit and grime, but I could walk.

"Good." Harry reached in his pocket and handed me the keys to his Bentley. "Fill up the car and get going."

I stared at him, the keys almost unnervingly heavy in my hands. There was a smudge of cinder caught in his hair, giving him a roguish and dashing look, and it felt all wrong. Harry was a man who loved grapefruit in the morning, a dinner of cold salmon and tennis every Saturday. This was real life, not another final confrontation between the siren and the captain. Death in the Santa Ana fires was something that happened to the migrant workers, to the unlucky, to the foolish, not to us.

"Don't," I said. "Don't."

He gave me a bright grin, the kind of charm he never really got to show in the siren movies.

"I won't," he promised. "Not like you're afraid of, anyway. But go."

He turned away, striding into the worst of the crew tangles. The cameras were monsters then, slow to move, precious beyond all measure and protected fiercely by the men who worked them. I didn't trust Harry, but there was nothing I could do for him now.

I knew where he had parked, in the shade of what had been Saint Aidia's general store, and on my way there, I grabbed a lost light technician who was supporting a girl from craft services. There was room for one more, but everyone else was occupied with securing gear or making their own escape. The pair huddled in the back seat as I eased the Bentley out of the shade and towards the road. Harry had taught me to drive the Bentley a year ago, and though it never liked me as well as it liked him, it went willingly enough.

I had just pulled onto the tarmac when I saw a figure standing by the side of the road, boxes in her arms and a wayward gait that told me she didn't know what she was meant to be doing.

"Get in," I shouted, pulling up next to her, and, boxes still in her arms, she piled into the front seat next to me.

I paused for a moment, looking at the smoke that was coming closer and closer, and then shaking my head, I followed the convoy heading towards town. Everything felt faded except my hands clenched on the wheel and my unblinking eyes. I followed the bumper of the truck in front of me all the way back to the studio, and when the houses and buildings grew up on either side of the road, I became aware of a small hand on top of my own on the clutch.

"It's okay," said the girl who had told me to undo my latches first. "We're okay."

I stared at her, and then abruptly pulled over by the side of the road. I was back where fire was a beast carefully controlled by the pyrotechnicians, and where the smoke came from the cars and from dry ice and not the burning desert. I took my hand carefully from the clutch. I had been hanging on to it so hard that the first two nails on my hand were shattered.

"We left my tail in Santa Aidia," I said, my voice echoing and distant, and I started to laugh, tears rolling down my face.

III

For want of direction, the cast and crew of *Siren Queen* met back at Lot 12, where we had all started from that morning. Whalen Mannheim strode from group to group, trying to keep order while dealing with runners from Oberlin Wolfe himself, demanding to know what was going on.

People gathered with their own, counting heads and tallying losses, but it was far too early to see what those might be. Annette Walker sprawled with a cigarette in her fingers in the director's chair, a pair of wardrobe girls fluttering around her and repairing her hair and makeup. The tech and the craft services girl I had hauled back in the Bentley had disappeared into their respective clans.

Time seemed stuck where it wasn't flowing too fast, and it took me an hour or more of sitting in a dark corner behind the flatted sets to realize that I needed pants. I was still wearing the artful drape of fishnet and shells with nothing but a pair of cotton shorts on underneath. I had at least cleaned off my legs with a hose and a dirty rag, but otherwise, I felt like a cinder blown off the mountain.

When I stood up, every part of me ached. My actual clothes were somewhere back in the desert, but before I had gone more than a dozen paces, the girl from the side of the road waved me down.

"Here," she said, handing me a pile of clothing.

She guarded the door while I changed in a janitor's closet. The smell of chemical cleaners dragged me farther out of my daze, and I finally noticed that I was dressing in men's clothes. The shirt was too long for me, and the trousers had to be cinched tight around my waist, but at least I was covered.

"Sorry," said the girl when I gave her a questioning look. "I don't know where the truck with your proper clothes ended up. Those belong to Jalisco. He keeps a spare set in his locker."

"Tell Jalisco thank you for me," I said. "No shoes?"

"Sorry, can't have everything," she said, and I smiled a little at her brisk manner.

"Guess not. Where's Harry?"

There was no need to ask which. Even if there had been another, there wasn't one that was more important on this set. The girl's brow furrowed.

"That was his car, wasn't it? I don't know. I know Ms. Walker made it back, but I didn't see him . . ."

I thanked her and promised that I would get Jalisco's clothes back to him when I found some of my own. She gave me an oblique look that I didn't have time to read, and I went to scout the groups of people who were standing around.

No Harry with the makeup girls, the stunt men or the lighting technicians. No Harry in with the extras, craft services, or Oberlin Wolfe's runners. Everyone I asked had seen him right before they got the hell out of Santa Aidia, and the fear that was seeded when I saw him last started to bloom.

The hours passed and the cast and crew slowly drifted away into the early evening. I haunted Lot 12 until Whalen gruffly told me to go home. No Harry yet, and with every moment that passed where he didn't emerge, brilliant and triumphant or burned and gasping with smoke inhalation, the odds grew ever slimmer.

I walked off of the lot in Jalisco's clothes, the keys to Harry's car still clutched in my hand. My body had given up screaming because I had demonstrated that I wasn't going to give it what it wanted, but I knew that I would barely be able to move tomorrow.

I stepped out onto the parking lot, and I stood still under the smoky blue sky. I didn't want to go back to Rexford Avenue, and I couldn't go to Harry's house in Bel-Air. Couldn't go back to the dorms, couldn't go back to the laundry, couldn't go to find Emmaline, who was probably in Nice or Cairo at the moment with Cassidy Dutch.

I had no reason to take a step forward or back, and that stunned me.

"Hey, Ms. Wei."

The girl who had given me my clothes was smoking in the shadow of one of the big convoy trucks. I remembered her name, Aguila, and watched with nothing but mild curiosity as she walked up to me.

"You don't look much like a movie star like that," she said candidly, and I looked down at the men's clothes I wore. I had found some shoes finally, a pair of cheap red flats that had been abandoned and unwanted in wardrobe for who knew how long.

"Are you going to tell *Variety*?" I asked, and she laughed.

"Nah, I ain't, and I wasn't trying to tease you either. I was going to say, you look a lot like the girls at the Pipeline."

She put a peculiar weight on the last word, as if it was meant to grab my notice. After a moment, my sluggish brain caught up. I had heard Teo mention the Pipeline once, a dance and then a raid that made him shrug philosophically.

Fun until you get caught, he said, and I blinked at Aguila. She watched me patiently, and I decided that I wasn't too worried about getting caught that night, even if I wasn't sure about the fun.

"Lucky me," I said. "I've never looked much like anyone else before."

She smiled a little at that, shrugging diffidently and swinging her clutch lightly from one hand.

"You wanna go? Plenty of girls there that dress worse than that."

"You'll have to give me directions," I said, and I didn't start crying because whatever the hell the Pipeline was, it was better than being alone.

The Bentley was less out of place than I thought it would be in the dirt parking lot outside of the roadhouse. It might have been the most blue-blooded ride there, but it wasn't as flashy as some of the others, the Tourister or the brand-new Ford coupe.

Aguila made me stop at her apartment so she could change, and now she came out of the car in a cherry-red dress and her lips painted to match. She had been doing hair and makeup since she was little, she told me on the drive over, and that's what she wanted to do eventually. Wardrobe wasn't all that much fun, but it was a place to start.

The glow from the Pipeline was discreet and guarded. Only the barest traces of light escaped the windows to light up the weedy yard in front. Years later, I would find the Cendrillon in New York, C-Street in Chicago, and someday, Jane would take me to the Sphinx in Seattle where she'd kissed a parade of girls on her eighteenth birthday, but the Pipeline that night was still magic, even if it was a ragged and dusty kind. The door swung open, and a short Black man with his hair buzzed tight glared at us briefly before letting us in. As we passed, I saw that despite the suspenders and heavy black shoes, it was a woman at the door. The club was filled with women, only women, and I felt a little dizzy. It was nothing like Emmaline's fire, all shadowy and dim and gorgeous. These were flesh-and-blood women, in trousers, in dresses, smoking and drinking and so open I didn't understand how they could stop from crying their names and their natures to all the world.

"You gonna run out on me now?" Aguila asked, and I shook my head. I knew what I must look like in Jalisco's clothes, a dull imitation of the sharply dressed woman at the door and the ones that were slung up at the bar, their arms around women in dresses or lazily eyeing the room as if they were lions in their very own preserve.

Aguila called hellos to a few people she knew, but she didn't stop walking until she came to the bar, throwing a mischievous glance at me.

"You're buying, right? I sure as heck haven't gotten paid yet."

I had found my alligator clutch at least, and feeling more real than I had since I had shouted *fire* in my harness, I gestured at the bartender. She was tall and dark-skinned with a thick scar running along her jaw and large liquid eyes that took in me and Aguila in a single glance.

"Two Mary Carlisles," I said, and she raised a perfectly etched eyebrow at me.

"This ain't the Knick, kiki," she said, and Aguila frowned.

"She's not a kiki, Lita. Lay off. Let's say two Chicago fizzes, and maybe go easy on the water for once in your life."

"Whatever you say." Lita shrugged. "Though you know Alice don't like you stepping out."

"Huh, Alice," Aguila snorted. "I don't care what she thinks."

"If you get me punched, I will leave you here," I said. "I can't even kick in these shoes."

She led me back to a cracked leatherette booth at the rear of the roadhouse. Though I could feel people regarding me over the tops of their drinks, it was a relief to put my back to the wall and to sip at what turned out to be a fairly good Chicago fizz. It was cold and lemony, and the gin wasn't even so bad. I carefully didn't think of the stuff that Harry kept locked in a walnut cabinet, pure juniper and shivery ice.

"Oh just ignore Lita," Aguila said with a wave of her hand. "She's always nervous about folks unless they've been coming for a while."

"What's a kiki, anyway?"

"You know," Aguila said, tilting her hand back and forth like a seesaw.

"I don't."

"I thought . . . you and Emmaline Sauvignon and Caroline Carlsson . . ."

"No. And Caroline Carlsson's gone back to Sweden."

Greta wrote to me haphazardly from their homestead north of the Ume River. She and her pale-haired daughter sounded as if they were thriving; Lawrence was still adjusting to the long nights and thin days. She wondered to me, brooding, if he had left something vital in Los Angeles, but it didn't matter. It wasn't as if they could come back and get it. A heart of Norrland ash wood would have to suffice for a crown of stars, and only time would tell how well he could bear it.

Caroline Carlsson missed the snow too much to ever work again, was what the studio put out, and that was true enough.

"Well, a kiki's a girl who's not all . . ." She pointed at herself in shocking red. "Or all . . ."

She pointed towards a tall, lean woman in a slightly dated brown suit, fedora pushed back on her dark head. She didn't have the close-cropped hair some of the other women sported, but instead slicked it to one side in an Eton crop, already a little out of date. She saw Aguila's nod and lifted her drink to us with a slight smile.

"Neither fish nor fowl," I said. It was a position I knew well enough.

"Well, more like a narc," she said. "She'll get over it. Especially if you come often. Thursdays are the only time it's all women, but the men ain't so bad. Little safer, too, if a raid comes up and you can switch partners fast."

"Would you like it if I came often?" I asked, trying a smile.

Aguila started to say something, but then her eyes lit up and she flew out of the booth to a powerfully built Black woman in a pinstripe suit. I stared, and when their kiss got past conciliatory, I tilted my head back against the cushioned booth and shut my eyes. My mind, when I tried to focus on anything that wasn't right in front of me, was the buzz of a dead channel over the radio.

"This seat taken?"

I opened my eyes without moving my head. It was the woman with the Eton crop, and now I could see the broad set of her shoulders and the serious set of her face. She didn't look like someone who laughed easily, and that suited me just fine at the moment.

"Not at all. If you want to take her drink, too, go ahead. It doesn't look like she's got much need for it."

The woman smiled slightly and took Aguila's fizz. I watched as she rolled the glass between her long fingers before bringing it to her lips. When she joined me in the booth, she sat on my side rather than across from me.

"You've never come here before," she said, a statement and not a question.

"No. I didn't know places like this existed."

She tilted her head, watching me like I was an interesting bird or insect that had rolled into her backyard.

"Most people who make it here are a little happier than that."

"I'm not sure I'm a happy person," I said, and when that sounded a little too much like a line Scottie Mannheim would write, I added, "Aguila brought me here. I needed to be away for a little while."

"Well, dear, this is *away* all right. I'll say thank you for Aguila's drink and move on if you want to be away and alone . . ."

I surprised myself by reaching for her hand, pressing it down to the table under mine. She was cool to the touch, but then I realized that that was because I was warm. It was as if the Santa Anas had blown a curl of fire into me, and now it was eating me carefully from the inside. She glanced at the white bandages that I had wrapped around my palms at the studio, covering the wounds the wires had given me, but she said nothing.

"No, stay. I'm not going to talk much right now, but stay."

I sounded imperious, and she snorted a little, but nodded and leaned back against the seat. One arm came out to drape over the booth behind my head, not around my shoulders, but corralling me close nonetheless.

She sent one of the rare waitresses for a vodka on the rocks, and she sipped it with one foot slung up on the seat across from us. She seemed as inclined to quiet as I was, and as I watched her, she watched the room, the groups of women gathered at the shadowed edges, the couples that didn't so much dance as rock slowly in each other's arms. There was a record on, and Joey Fletcher's sweet, soulful voice floated over us, telling us she'd never lie to us, make us cry, or deny us.

The entire place was veiled with something less tangible than smoke. I watched it all as if I was both in my body and floating above, the one connected to the other only by a tenuous string. I sat perfectly still because I did not know what would happen if that string snapped. I was quietly in love with each and every woman in the place, and when I turned to watch my companion, I saw an edge of gold all around her, a dull gleam that warmed me and allowed me to climb back into my body.

"What's your name?" I asked her after making a study of her face for a half dozen years. There was a cragginess to her features, her strong nose and her sharp jaw. It would crash ships rather than launch them, but I never knew a woman who didn't want to crash at least a few ships.

She glanced at me as if I were some animal that might be frightened off by eye contact.

"Tara Lubowski," she said. "Pleased to meet you. What should I call you?"

I hesitated, and she laughed.

"That's fine if you don't want to," she said. "Shall I name you?"

"You don't have to call me anything at all," I said, disliking the idea of names. I could tell somehow instinctively that Tara Lubowski was her own name. It grew from her like a tree from good soil, roots reaching deep and breaking through to something gleaming beneath.

She nodded easily, and I noticed for the first time a dark mole right above her upper lip. It was too dark and large to be called a beauty mark, but it gave her face an irregular kind of elegance that made me very much want to kiss her.

"I guess if there's only one of you, you don't need a name," she said, so gravely I wasn't sure if she was flirting at all.

"One of me? There's another Chinese girl over by the bar." There was. She had glanced at me with interest when I came in with Aguila before turning to whisper something in the ear of the adorably chubby Latino girl on her arm.

"I meant girls as beautiful as you," she said even more seriously, inviting me to lean in or laugh and push her away. I did neither, and instead ran the tip of my finger along her long hands. She wasn't beautiful, but there was a vitality to her, something living and breathing every moment of her life. I made a humming sound, and because she did not need me to think of how to answer, I didn't.

Slowly, like a gravity I couldn't deny, I ended up leaned against her, her arm closing around me. I realized that smoke clung to my hair and even my skin, acrid and unpleasant, but Tara didn't push me away. As I watched the dancers from under her arm, I felt a little closer to it all, more in my body and present.

"The next time I come here, I'll wear a dress, something nice," I said suddenly.

We were breaking some kind of code, I could tell. Girls went with girls, but trousers went with skirts at the Pipeline. Aguila and her pinstriped lover and the other Chinese girl and her sweetheart in a plain and pretty floral dress were the rule. Tara and I were the only exceptions, and I could hear Lita calling me a kiki again.

"Wear whatever you like," Tara said with a shrug. "It doesn't bother me."

She sounded as if she meant it, and I glanced at her curiously.

"But would you like it?"

She looked at me with one dark brow raised and a quirk to her thin lips. Tara would have been twenty-four or twenty-five then, and I could see she found me funny.

"I'll like what you do," she declared. "Wouldn't say no to something bright on you, but I don't think I'll be saying no to you a lot."

"Who writes your lines? You have a lot of them," I said a little caustically, and she smiled.

"I can safely say I write them all."

I talked in starts and stops like a faulty faucet. I hadn't really talked to another woman since Greta left and Emmaline put me in a cab. Sometimes my apartment on Rexford Avenue felt like walls made of silence, which I liked more than I didn't, but I was out of practice.

Tara didn't seem to mind, not even when she walked me out to my car just a few minutes past two. Aguila had gone home with Alice, all forgiven, and I was on my own.

"I'm not going to ask to come home with you," Tara said easily. "I don't think you would like that."

Maybe I would have, but I could already tell what a relief it would be to be alone.

"You're good company," I said, protesting by form, and she picked up my bandaged hand, bringing it to her lips in a courtly gesture that wasn't as ridiculous as it sounds when I relate it now.

"I know I am, but I think right now, dear, you don't want to be asked or have to answer. I come to the Pipeline all the time, though, and you know your way here now, don't you?"

"I do," I said. She nodded and headed towards the people she had come with, a band of girls who hooted and cheered for her as she walked away from me.

I guided Harry's car back to the road, and as I drove into the city, I found myself glancing up at the stars in the sky, cold and white and alone in the inkling blue.

IV

Every morning, I got a runner from Whalen Mannheim that told me there was no shooting that day, but I went in anyway. It was the most idle I had been since I had come to Wolfe Studios, and I spent my time haunting the small café close to Lot 12, sipping the weak iced tea and nibbling on the stale toast. The idleness suited me in a way I found strangely distasteful. It was so easy to simply sit and listen, a newspaper in front of me and my tea melting to water beside me.

For a solid week, the papers were full of the disappearance of Harry Long. The first reports were spurious and sensational, declaring he had perished fighting the fire like a hero, or that he had gone back to save a wardrobe girl who was cut off from the rest of the crew. Though we had all felt the heat from the fire, I knew that no one had tried to fight it, and the cast and crew did their own headcounts to find no one missing.

One story said that he had been terribly hurt in the dash back to safe ground and that he was dying in a private hospital in La Jolla, Lana Brooks dressed in black and mourning by his side. Another claimed that Harry had heroically saved Annette Walker from the flames and spirited her away to a secret love nest in Baja. Annette Walker put these rumors to rest quickly when she checked into an exclusive convalescent home, giving interviews from a bay window in her rose dressing gown.

Another story which got a little more play suggested that Whalen Mannheim was hiding him, readying him for a triumphant return when *Siren Queen* premiered. I knew that wasn't true because I saw Whalen Mannheim talking with Harvey Rose at the café just a few days after the fire. Whalen knocked his tea off the table, sending the tumbler bouncing off the tile below. Miraculously, it didn't break, but neither man noticed. Whalen covered his face with his hand, and I realized he was crying. Harvey Rose's face was serious, even sympathetic, as he reached out to clasp Whalen's shoulder, but he didn't let go of it. Instead, they both stood, and with his hand remaining on Whalen Mannheim's shoulder, he forced the still-weeping man out the door. I rose from my seat to watch them get into a sleek black car waiting outside. Right before he got in, Whalen looked wildly up at the sky, the most desperate look I've ever seen on a man, and then he was gone.

Harvey Rose paused a moment after he shut the door, looking back with a sphinx's calm over the rest of us watching from the café. From where I sat, his green-tinted glasses looked like eyes themselves, and I shivered when I thought of what those eyes had seen. We were all problems that Oberlin Wolfe might need fixed one day, whether we needed to disappear, to have a new face or to have every bit of light scraped out of our heads and to be set to nodding, and he seemed to promise us that when the time came, he would be there.

No one ever saw Whalen Mannheim again. Scottie Mannheim went on to some lasting fame in war propaganda films, but that there was ever a second Mannheim brother, no trace remained. He survives, in some small way, in footnotes and in unexplained mentions of two Mannheims and not one. Once I thought I saw him feeding birds at Holmby Park, but then I got closer, and it was someone else instead. It was enough that I remembered him for a moment. It might have bought him another handful of days, wherever he was, to be remembered by something like me. Immortality is a tricky business.

Two weeks after the fire, I knew it was all over when Dottie Wendt's piece came out. THE LEGACY AND LOYALTIES OF HARRY LONG took up the entire front page while Harry's publicity shot from *Love of the Sun*, his first big hit, stared out below. There was a subtle shock in seeing Harry so young, and I felt the thing that had awakened in me when I saw Josephine Beaufort's immortal Juliet again.

Dorothy Wendt declared Harry dead on the mountain, burned up like a harvest king of old. Lana Brooks was devastated, taken to her bed and cared for by grave doctors, and those who knew him best sank into mourning.

"A star has been extinguished, and all the world is darker for it," Oberlin Wolfe was quoted as saying, and that was what made me cry, hiding behind the paper and trying not to put my fingers straight through it. If Oberlin Wolfe said it, it was true even if it wasn't, and I knew Harry was gone.

The stories started up almost immediately. Lennie Washington, the man who beat the devil on the trumpet in Abilene, said he had been hitching along Route 66 and Harry Long appeared in his midnight blue Bentley, taking him from Tulsa to Santa Fe. A young housewife from San Diego swore up and down she saw him buying sandwiches at her bodega, while firefighters from San Dimas saw a figure in coat and tails walking through the flames on a mountaintop inferno four years later.

"Like he was in his own house," said the fire chief.

I'll tell you what I saw. Some eight years ago, the Majestic on Third was doing a classic film festival. They were showing two of the siren movies, but in glasses, scarf, and a long coat, I went to see *Love of the Sun* instead. It was well attended: grave filmmakers, young hopefuls, girls and boys in love with ghosts, and auteurs of all kinds filled the velvet seats. The first shot of the movie was Harry gazing out over the dim passageways of Barcelona, his body lean, young and lovely in silver.

Believe me when I say it was *horrible*.

Love of the Sun was well loved in its time—brilliant, even—but the acting, the light work, the dialogue, even for a silent film, was terrible. It came out when I was only two, and if I had seen it at seven instead of *Romeo and Juliet*, I imagine I would have fallen just as in love. Today, it's ridiculous, a lumbering slab of black-and-white kitsch that barely manages to hold on because of Harry's young beauty and the incandescent loveliness of his co-star, Elsa Bergeron. The entire theater watched it with grave rapture, but I had to hold my hand over my mouth, lowering my face so that I wouldn't laugh out loud at the worst lines.

Someone else in the theater didn't hold back, however, and he started snickering from the very beginning, when Harry wrapped his arms around the neck of a nervy palomino, the silver text telling us the horse was his only friend in the world. It wasn't until the climactic scene where Harry and Elsa fall into a very Los Angeles swimming pool standing in for a silent Spanish grotto that a loud peal of laughter rocked the theater. I sat straight up, because I knew that laugh, twisting around in my seat to see two ushers gesture for the offender, an old man and his somewhat younger companion, to leave. They stood and left in high good spirits, but my breath caught in my chest.

Muttering apologies, I pushed my way to the end of the row. I dashed to the front of the theater only to find the lobby empty of everything except the smell of popcorn and a hint of smoky cologne.

∽

I got the call to be back on set the third Monday after the fire, and when I arrived, I could tell that no one knew what was going on any more than I did. We milled around, waiting for someone to come and give us direction, and when Jacko Dewalt appeared, I felt something freeze over.

It had been three years since I had seen him, and at first, he looked just the same. It took me a few minutes to notice the way his hair thinned at the temples, how much rounder his shoulders were, and how he lumbered when he walked. As if he could feel my eyes on him, he turned to me. He must have been expecting it because he was utterly expressionless. There was something dire at the back of that gaze, but then someone else needed his attention and he looked away.

A door had opened in the center of me, and now everything was threatening to fall out through it. I was drawing back again, watching myself and the other people on the set as if we were puppets on a stage. Then I saw Tara striding up in her brown suit, and the sight was so strange that I had to return, my fingers and my eyes and my lips and my tongue suddenly my own again.

I watched as she walked up to Jacko, a thick sheaf of papers in one hand and a black marker in the other. They talked briefly, checked something on the papers, talked more, and then Tara nodded, walking away. I lost sight of her to the crowd, and I was so startled to see her at all that I was completely myself when Jacko called everyone together.

He was blunt and to the point. Whalen Mannheim was out, he was in, and Oberlin Wolfe wanted the picture done inside of three weeks. With both lead actor and screenwriter out of the equation, there had been hefty rewrites from some new studio talent. It was to be business as usual, and on the set, at least, Harry and Whalen weren't to be mentioned, let alone mourned. Jacko would be in meetings with tech this morning, the script would be out in a matter of hours, and we would be getting ready to shoot at one sharp.

There were some grumbles, but overall, people were relieved.

Business as usual, but I was falling, hands looking for something, anything that would slow me.

Harry gone, Greta in Sweden, and Emmaline untouchable in her house in the Palisades, there was no one left to talk with me. I was alone, but as I stood in the eye of my own private hurricane, untouched by any of the people around me, I wondered if I had ever been anything but.

I wanted badly to leave, to go at least to the café so that some assistant would be sent to find me when I was needed, but that was how stars acted. Instead, I found a hard folding chair set back from the crowd, and I sat there instead. Not for the first time, I wished that I had taken better to smoking, but I could never tolerate the taste or the smell of it so close. Instead I cultivated the stillness that so many said made the siren such a fearsome and alien presence. The reviews were full of awe for my menace and my reptilian silence. I could have told them that it wasn't menace but fear, and that instead of fighting or fleeing, some things simply froze. Of course no one asked me, and so I waited.

"Ms. Wei, the director wants to see you now."

Of course he did, and it was the opposite of a request. I nodded and rose easily to my feet. The entire way to Jacko's trailer at the back of the lot, my tall heels clacked a military beat. They still pained me, but I had learned years ago that there were things more important than pain.

I learned, I reminded myself. *I don't have a patron, but I'm not helpless. I never was.*

Jacko sat behind a desk piled high with paper, and even from where I stood, I could see red slashes through the text, edits and revisions that would likely be made even as we filmed. He would pull it together though. That had always been his reputation, that and a terrible eye for young women. He turned that eye towards me, and I simply looked at him. I could wait longer than he could when I was a child, and that hadn't changed.

Finally, Jacko chuckled as if he had won some sort of bet with himself, shaking his head.

"Same dull old CK," he said. "Still as cold as the Atlantic, aren't you?"

He came around the desk towards me, but he didn't advance, only looking me over with a kind of detached interest.

"Well, well. I knew I saw something in you. Didn't expect it to be a monster, but hell, can't always call 'em, can I?"

I bristled at the idea that he had made me anything.

"No maids, no funny talking, no fainting flowers," I said. "That's the deal I struck with Wolfe, and so I guess monster was what was left."

He shrugged, rolling those shoulders like barrels.

"You'd be a star sooner if you were willing to bat those damn eyes and swoon a little. You think you're better than Su Tong Lin? Now you got a rubber tail glued to your ass, and Harry Long killing you in six features."

If he thought that would rile me, he was mistaken. All I cared about was that he came no closer and that he didn't kick me off the picture. It should have been ridiculous, but directors had done more foolish things for pride and spite, even ones as competent as Jacko. He looked me over again before shaking his head and snorting with disgust.

"Goddamn you, you're just the same, ain't you? I would have made you a queen."

"I don't care." I wasn't Greta, who turned her lack of care into a bludgeon, but that was the truth. Whatever happened to me, it happened in spite of Jacko, never because of him.

He bared his teeth, and they looked long and yellow to me. I would have said that whatever demon lived in Jacko Dewalt was becoming more overt, less subtle, but of course there was no demon at all, only the man and his hungers and grudges.

"I couldn't believe that you really burned those pictures. Those were the real ashes you sent me in that goddamn bottle. I checked, you know. Down in Pescadero, old Ma and Pa must have kicked up their heels when their precious Baby Jenny could walk and talk and dance and sing again."

I had. A voice like Hezibah Wiley's told me to keep those pictures close and dear. They might have prevented what was happening now at the very least, but I couldn't. I didn't know what would happen when I burned them, but I knew it would be an ending of some kind.

He laughed, shaking his head at my idiocy.

"All right. You say you don't care about that. Well, CK, you better fucking care about this. You fuck me over on this picture, and I'll have Wolfe send you to the loony bin. Tell him you were shacking up with Harry Long and lost your mind. He'd do it too, because he remembers that stunt you and Caroline Carlsson pulled two years ago, believe me."

I did. None of the studio heads were known for a short memory.

He glared at me, but when I made no response, he decided I was cowed, or he decided to believe I was, anyway.

"Whalen Mannheim is gone now. He liked you a lot, you know, and even if he was an asshole who thought your pussy opened sideways, it wasn't nothing. Harry Long's gone too. Yesterday he stood for you, and today he's bones in the desert."

Jacko watched my face for a flinch, and when I refused to give it to him, he bared his teeth at me again.

"You had some heavy hitters in your corner, and when they realized they couldn't just give a white girl from Detroit your face, maybe you were untouchable for a while. You're not. You're a monster, and eventually, CK, monsters go down. I want to make this movie and I want the payoff more than I want you ground back down into Hungarian Hill trash, but only a little more, you get me?"

I was as still as a statue, but in my purse, I knew I had a small knife. I had liberated it from the craft services table. I resisted the urge to reach for it . . .

"So we're going to finish this picture. And maybe I want to see you humiliated a little too, enough so that I smile when I go see this godawful shit in the theater. And then we're done."

Jacko slapped a script against my breasts, hard enough the skin stung.

"Get your ass out of here. Read the script, I'm addressing the crew in an hour, and we're going to start filming two hours after that."

I was steady walking out of his trailer, even through the lot, but my skin was burning. When I finally locked myself in the tiny women's bathroom, I pressed my forehead against the wooden stall door, forcing myself to breathe. I would have been ill if there was anything in my stomach. Finally, I ran water as cold as it could go out of the faucet and let it flow over my hands. They were almost completely numb before I drew them away and dried them.

My fear drew itself into a small ball at the center of my belly, but I knew it wasn't dead or even dormant. My hands were steady, however, and that was all I needed for the moment. I took the script back to my chair and started to read.

They would be able to use at least some of Harry's footage, though Annette's was a lost cause. She was gone to a convalescent home, ostensibly treating her grief over Harry's absence and incidentally her growing dependence on benzodiazepines. Instead, in a scene shot with a man in shadow and imitating Harry's distinctive voice, the torch would be passed to his daughter, described in the script as a virtuous maiden, one who had no idea of the terrible burden her profligate father had inflicted upon her.

It was a surprisingly daring take for Wolfe Studios, and I read on, intrigued. My first major scene would be a confrontation where the siren menaced the daughter, Olivia Nemo, telling her she would never be as mighty as her father, and that I would relish getting the chance to slaughter the last of the Nemo dynasty. Then

I disappeared, and Olivia fought her way past a bevy of the siren's minions, aided by a handsome soldier who seemed brought on specifically to act as a vehicle for some young star or other. He barely had a name, and I could tell that Olivia was the real centerpiece of the story—the hero, not the heroine.

For the first time in a while, I found myself envying the actress who got to play Olivia. After the first rush of heartbreaks at being passed over for such roles, I had given up wanting to play any of the shrinking violet lead actresses in the siren movies. I never quite got over envying Harry, but that was its own impossibility, not something I paid much mind after a while.

I read with interest, almost forgetting Jacko and Harry as I did. Then on page 110, I found Jacko's revenge. No maids or funny accents, but it was there all the same.

⌒﹏⌒

Olivia stood bowed but far from beaten, her father's sword fallen from her numb fingers. The siren, monstrous and strange even in her death throes, hung on to a spar of rock, maintaining consciousness only by some animal instinct.

"It's over," Olivia said, her voice tremulous but strong. "You are beaten, and your people will never rise again."

"We will always rise," the siren protested, but its voice was finally as weak as it truly was. No more illusions, no more tricks; it was, after all, only a monster, and monsters were made to be beaten.

"No, you will not," said Olivia almost gently.

The siren tried to protest, talking about the spires of Atlantis and her dead kin, but Olivia was undeniable. Step by step, she walked towards the siren, who slid farther down her rock until she writhed in the dirt, a worm and not a dragon after all. She was beaten once and for all, and everyone, Olivia, the silent soldier by her side, the audience watching in the dark theater, knew this.

"No," the siren moaned at last. "Stay away, stay away . . ."

She begged for her life, promised to leave and crawl away on her belly if that's what Olivia wanted. She pulled herself away from the advancing angel on her hands, her magnificent tail cut in half behind, dragging dark blood. She abased herself, begging for her unworthy life until she was huddled against a boulder, unable to go any farther. Still unwilling to face her death with dignity, she pleaded and begged until finally Olivia silenced her with a sharp gesture.

The innocent girl had become a hero in her own right, a woman grown who dispensed justice on the end of a blade. She was not the rage of her errant father or the blind mercy of the convent nuns who raised her, but some impossible mix of the two.

First, she kissed the siren, mercy and absolution, and then, when the siren looked up, cravenly hoping for forgiveness for the unforgivable, a small dagger appeared in Olivia's hand, and she stabbed the monster through the heart.

There were a few pages after that. I skimmed them quickly, seeing that Olivia went off to live happily ever after with her hero, the siren dead on the beach behind them. The end that Whalen Mannheim had envisioned was still execution for the siren, but it wasn't this.

Jacko's warning echoed in my ear, and I clenched my fists until I could breathe normally again. For some reason, I thought of my grandfather, crushed under rock and lulled to sleep every night by the lonely trains that ran through Colorado. I reached for some of the cold that lived in his bones, a ghost of the iron that ran in my mother's blood, and I could stand.

Jacko called everyone together again. It was past noon, late to start shooting, but he had gotten his pictures in under deadline and under budget before by knowing just how far he could push production, that is to say, to its knees and not into the ground. No one was surprised by his instructions—it was going to be the first of many long nights.

"And before I let you go, two introductions," he said, champing indolently on a toothpick. "First, this is Tara Lubowski, who's doing all our scripts, but it's Mr. Moore if anyone asks."

He pointed towards Tara, who waved to the crowd. She looked as serious as she had at the Pipeline, if less confident. I froze, and I was still half-convinced she wasn't real when Jacko spoke again.

"And stepping up as our Olivia Nemo, Miss Emmaline Sauvignon."

As if someone had flipped on a spotlight, Emmaline—who had been standing off to the side, in the shadows of the sound stage—turned so we could see her, and the crowd sighed. She smiled, and you could sense the thing that had made her a star, the ability in her slender hands to reach into your chest, close, and *pull*.

Her eyes skipped over me, and her smile was pure and still.

"You must know that I didn't. Know, I mean."

I sipped at my fizz, giving myself time to think before I replied. Tara slid into the booth across from me without asking, taking her hat off to rest it on the table between us.

"Does it matter? You still wrote it."

"Yes, but I didn't write it for you," she said in frustration. "I didn't know you were the siren."

"But someone was."

It was a strange place to plant a flag, I knew. It was safer to protect the siren. I had acted the part for more than two years now. No one else had. Fan letters came to Wolfe Studios in the armloads for Harry, and mixed in, like scanty flecks of pepper in a drift of salt, were always a few dozen for me, or more appropriately, for the siren. Some were disgusting, some were worshipful, and some were girls from Ord Street, from the Chinese American enclaves in New York and San Francisco and from the lonely outposts in between. They saw different things, from glamour to fame to fear that for once they might wield, but most importantly, they *saw*. Now, thanks to Tara Lubowski, they were going to see humiliation, and while I didn't have the words to protect myself, I had plenty to protect the siren.

"It's a good scene," she said, jutting out her jaw stubbornly. "I know it is. It shows Olivia being strong and merciful, it shows how she's grown."

"It's a good scene for *Emmaline*," I said, taking another cold sip of my fizz. "Not for anyone else. Not even for you, Mr. Moore."

That was the name on the script, Lester Moore. They didn't want Tara Lubowski any more than they wanted me, perhaps even less.

"It's my first big script," she said. "First time for a piece this big, first time it wasn't just scenes that were too sloppy or where the actual writer was dead drunk and couldn't sit up at his typewriter. It's the best I've ever done."

"Do better," I snapped, downing the rest of the fizz. Without Aguila to order for me, it was mostly water, and when I stood up from the table, I didn't have any kind of satisfying waver in my vision or my step. I didn't know why I had come.

I started to leave, but Tara laid her hand over mine. It sent a shiver through me. *Real,* my brain noted. Not the real of the Friday fires or Harry's big house in Bel-Air, but real at the Pipeline nonetheless.

"Don't go," Tara said. "Please."

"I'm too angry to speak with you," I said honestly, and her lips quirked in a small smile.

"Want to dance instead?"

There was a hint of vulnerability in her dark brown eyes, longing and sadness that didn't have words, even if she was a writer. She wrote all her own lines. Maybe someday she would write about this too, in some secret journal that she would hide or burn.

I had come in a lilac dress this time, sewn over with a shimmer of icy glass beads, turning heads as I walked in and stirring a murmur of recognition. People were starting to look our way, and I glared at her.

"Why would I want to do that?"

"Because you don't want to talk, and you don't want to leave. And because I think you want to."

She was right. I did. By the bar, the elderly coin-operated pho-
nograph hummed to life, and something sweet and soft started
playing. I sighed, and allowed her to guide me out onto the dance
floor.

Tara was light on her feet, but she led with a tentative touch,
as if I were something she was afraid to rattle. At this point, after
all my time with Mme Benoit, I could dance through hell on high
heels, and I took the lead almost absently. She was tall enough that
I didn't bother trying to meet her eyes, but by the end of the dance,
we were closer than we had been. She smelled a bit like whiskey,
a bit like pomade and soap, and I knew she could smell my own
perfume, something warm and floral floating over my skin and my
hair.

"I'm sorry," she said when the music ended, and I sighed.

"I'm not going to thank you for that," I told her, and she smiled.

"All right. But I will try to do better."

I nodded, and allowed her to bring me back to the booth. It was
the same one that we had sat at a few weeks ago, giving us a sense
of ownership over the space.

"You should tell me about yourself," she said. "All I know about
you is what Dottie Wendt says, and she thinks that you're the
daughter of a mandarin and a silk spinner, or maybe a spy and his
secret French mistress."

"You first," I said, and she shrugged.

Her stories were like pebbles from the beach, small and smooth,
easy to hold in my hand. Her parents were Jewish communists
from Poland, fiery and occupied with their own lives, leaving their
only child, Tara, to live and dream out her own way in a narrow
and drafty house in Chicago.

"I wanted to be warmer, so I came west," she said, smiling a
little. "Being a writer is an inherently unlikely and rebellious thing.
My parents approve, to some extent."

And as to her first girlfriend, her time at the Pipeline, and the group apartment she shared with an anarchist and a pair of union agitators?

Tara shrugged.

"I like to think if they knew, they would approve. Jewish and communist, remember? They can appreciate the need for a certain kind of secrecy."

She leveled a look at me, considering and somehow understanding.

"Tell me something you want to tell me. True would be nice, but I don't think either of us are really in the business of truth."

I paused, and she gave me all the room I wanted to think over her question, only breaking the silence to call for a cucumber water for me and some bourbon for her. I sipped at the cool drink and watched how her eyes were never still, flickering to the door, to the girls seated at the bar singly and in couples and corteges, to the rows of polished bottles behind the bar and the high-strung and supercilious gray cat that perched on one of the bar stools.

"Three years ago, after my sister and I tricked Jacko Dewalt, I stole her name."

Tara looked at me curiously, and I told her the rest of it, how Oberlin Wolfe had struck off name after name and how my tongue had grown thick in my mouth, dry and stupid. I had never told this story to Greta or to Harry, but when I told it now, I wondered if it was the fact that it was a real name, used and loved, that drew Wolfe's attention where none of the others had.

"I thought for sure that Luli Wei was your real name," she mused. I shrugged.

"It's real enough, even if it's not mine."

I had wondered if I would feel lighter after telling her, but instead I felt possessed of a strange and restless energy. I thought of my sister, who had moved up to San Francisco the year before. I got news of her once in a while through my mother, terse and vague things, whether because my mother didn't understand them or because she thought I might disapprove. I wondered what would happen if I sneaked away to the house my sister shared with her artist roommates. Would she welcome me? Would she turn me away from the door? I would accept the latter, but the former made something in my chest flutter. Hope, I decided. It lingered, and even though I put it from my mind for the moment, I knew it would stay with me.

"Thank you for telling me that," Tara said gravely, and for some reason, that made me blush.

"I don't know why I did," I confessed, and she smiled.

"Because you wanted to? Because you liked that I wanted you to?"

She was right, and I took a sip of my drink, hiding my face from her too-knowing glance.

VI

When Tara offered me her arm as we approached the fires that Friday night, I had a strange moment of déjà vu. She was as different from Greta as it was possible to get, and no matter what I might have idly fantasized about late at night in my bed, Greta had never given me that slow and lingering look, sliding like a drop of warm water down my body.

"Red suits you," she said, and I smiled as I looped my arm through hers.

"Suits and fedoras suit you," I said. "Did you wear them back in Chicago as well?"

"Nope. In Chicago, it was all frocks, chignons, and cloches. I didn't mind them, or at least, that's what I told myself until I didn't have to wear them anymore. Two days after I made it to LA, when I was living in this disgusting apartment with six other people, I bought a suit from a pawn shop and sold every dress I had with me, as well as my hair. Guess I minded more than I thought I did."

"You must have been happy."

She puffed a soft breath between her lips, shrugged.

"I was free. That's better than happy. Happy came later. Are you?"

"I will be," I said firmly. "Both."

She didn't ask me how I expected to achieve that, and there was a bone-weariness in my spine that made the idea of going back on set with Jacko Dewalt seem like a trek across the Mojave Desert. Emmaline kept a cool distance between us, and it surprised me how little I thought of her.

"You'd rather be proud than happy," Tara said, squeezing my hand. When I looked slightly offended at her words, she reached up to tuck a stray lock of hair behind my ear. "It's part of you. I don't think you would fight it if you could."

She was perhaps right, but then we had come to the edge of the fires, the small ones lit by people without names, by ghosts and by the scavengers. To my surprise, Tara moved closer to me, and she watched all around with a wary stare.

"They tell stories about the fires," she muttered. "They say that they go on as long as they need to go on, and that you can walk in and never walk out."

"I can take you back to the gate," I offered, but she shook her head.

"No, I want to see. I think I might need to see."

"If I can do it, you can?" I guessed, and she did laugh at that, shaking her head.

"I don't have your pride, I'm afraid," she said. "I'm curious, though, and my father said that if I could be curious instead of afraid, things would probably work out some kind of right."

The fires were carefully tended that night. The early arrival of the Santa Anas made everyone nervous, and it was terrifying what an uncontrolled blaze might do to the studio, let alone the fragile people gathered there. It was strange when the studios were so much a world apart to be so touched by the outside world.

Over the last year, I had grown unafraid in the fires. I might not be able to find Emmaline's any longer, but I was always welcome wherever Harry roamed, and unexpectedly, Helen Martel, Harry's friend and Emmaline's first mentor at Wolfe Studios, took me into her circle as well. Otherwise, I had learned to walk as I wished through the long night, hearing my name from every direction and knowing to ignore most of them.

Tara didn't gape like the occasional townie brought past the wolves at the gate, but neither was she pleased to weave between the fires. When a pack of studio changelings ran by, their laughter sweet and high and close to terror, she swore before apologizing.

"Writers don't have anything like this," she said with a pallid smile. "It's much lonelier when it's just you and your typewriter, I suppose."

"This is the loneliest place in the world," I found myself saying, and when she would have asked me more, I pulled her forward.

To comfort Tara, I sat for a while at a quiet fire tended by some girls from the dorms. They weren't the ones I had known, because those girls had moved on or blown away, but they were like them, and they were happy to let us stay for a while. I caught them sneaking speculative glances at me, wondering what had let me rise, whether it was just my skin and my eyes instead of something they could achieve for themselves.

"They're jealous of you," Tara said when we started walking again.

"Of course they are. I was jealous enough when I was in their place."

"You weren't there long," Tara remarked, and I frowned at her.

"No one can be there long," I explained. "There's a window. You bloom brightly for a moment, and that's when you can rise. If you don't . . ." I shrugged. Failure hovered at the edge of my vision, but I learned that you never allowed it in, never brought it home to sit like some honored guest.

"No such thing for writers. We rise when we rise, and it doesn't matter if we're young or pretty," she said, sounding completely sure of herself. She hadn't written either of her great novels yet, or even the pulp that gained her a second life of fame from the strange children who craved all things odd and grotesque. I didn't know if what she said was true or not; of course I had nothing to do with writers.

"I think you're pretty," I offered, and she gave me an impatient look.

"I don't want to be pretty," she said with a jerk of her head, "and it's a damn good thing I know that because I never have been."

She shook her head almost sadly.

"There are things that are more important than being pretty, you know," she said, and anger rushed over me at her condescension. I dropped her hand and stood away from her, my fingers curling convulsively into claws.

"Don't you think I know that?" I snapped. "Do you think we're just little dolls made out of silk and hair? We work here, Tara, we bleed, and we suffer, and we cry all so that we can be seen . . ."

"What's so great about being seen?" Tara demanded. "What's so important about that?"

She might have had the words for it, but I didn't. They locked up in my throat, about being invisible, about being alien and foreign and strange even in the place where I was born, and about the immortality that wove through my parents' lives but ultimately would fail them. Their immortality belonged to other people, and I hated that. I couldn't say that, so instead I simply struck.

"Don't ask me that when you want to be seen so much yourself," I said. "Did you know when you came west that you would be Lester Moore?"

Her head rocked back as if I had slapped her, and before she could respond, I spun away from her and stalked into the night. She followed me, because lost in the fires that could go on forever, what choice did she have? I didn't make it easier for her, and I wove around the wayward ones who danced from fire to fire and the darker ones who didn't dare enter into any kind of light at all.

"Dammit, wait," Tara called from behind me, but I didn't. Instead I walked so fast I was nearly running, kicking off my shoes and letting the asphalt turn my stockings to shreds. I barely felt it.

I wasn't just running away from Tara as I dodged the lights and slid through the darkness between them. I was running away from my sister and what I had done to her, from Harry and how I couldn't save him, even my mother, who I had left so very far behind without a real good-bye.

Running, I was reckless, especially with no safe haven I knew I could dash to if something dark and monstrous found me. Tara was even more vulnerable, though I knew in a vicious, vindictive way that nothing wanted her. That was wrong, I came to learn years later, but that night, I knew she had a kind of safety I lacked, even if it was coupled with something unfair and ugly.

I ducked around a silent cabal of sound engineers, conversing in the booms of bass drums, and I skirted Stephen Caine's fire, which was roaring its last as he died of syphilis, no last great role to save him. Tara wrote a poem about seeing him that night, a ghastly, grave and dying splendor, but that was years in the future yet.

The problem with running is that eventually, either you stop or are stopped. In the weird magic and terrible logic of the fires, I might have run forever without seeing the same place twice, dragging Tara along behind me, but there was certainly a humor to it all. Eventually, I ran into the person I wanted to see the least.

I turned to see if Tara was gaining on me, and suddenly gravity slowed me to a stop, wrapping me in soft arms and the scent of aloewood. I didn't quite crash into her, but my speed carried me forward and her back for a few paces before she steadied us both.

Emmaline was dressed all in white that night, a shimmering soft billow of silk that called to mind royal bedrooms and women who drowned weighted down by fabric. She didn't sit in state reigning over her silvery fire, but by herself at a small brazier that smelled of burning cedar twigs, a half circle of stubby white candles around it.

"There you are," she said tenderly, and when she brushed a lock of errant hair off my forehead, it felt as if no time had passed at all. Tara stumbled up just in time to see that, and she stood awkwardly on the borders of Emmaline's fire, uncertain and cautious. Emmaline's sweetness pulled at me like a sludge of tea and sugar, and it would have been so easy to fall back into her arms. She would have held me and kissed me, and that was the thought that pushed me back. The idea of kissing her frightened me, and I stepped away.

"I haven't found your fire in two years," I said stiffly. "Is this why? Did you stop holding court?"

She glanced at her single flame with a touch of amusement, shaking her head.

"No, not at all. Tonight I just wanted to be alone. Like Caroline, I suppose."

"Greta," I corrected, because at the very least, Emmaline should have known. She knew Greta even before I did, but she only shrugged, *have it your own way.*

"Will you come and sit with me?" Emmaline asked, gesturing to a small pile of cushions beyond the candles. Her gaze shut out Tara entirely, and even if I had been running away from Tara in a fit of temper, I bridled at that.

"Not if you want to be alone," I said, mimicking her mimicking the excuse that Greta and I had made, and she frowned. She was less beautiful when she showed anything beyond a wistful sadness; perversely in that moment, it made me like her better.

"You're being childish," she declared, and then Tara stepped forward.

"I feel like I should introduce myself if no one's going to bother," she said with an ironic nod towards me. "I'm Tara Lubowski, pleased to meet you, Miss Sauvignon. I know you from set."

Emmaline took Tara's hand after a brief moment, insulting but not overly so. Tara's look towards her was cool as well. She would have known what to do if Emmaline was wearing trousers, I think, but lovely girls in shimmering white silk still left her defenseless then.

"Oh, Lester Moore," Emmaline said. "The girl doing the script for *The Ghost of the Siren*."

"Just Lester Moore on the script," Tara said gamely, and she allowed Emmaline to look her up and down in a mixture of dismay and amusement.

"You need to rein yourself in," Emmaline said, turning to me and dismissing Tara completely. "You're on thin ice as it is with Dewalt, and after Whalen, Harvey Rose is still around."

"I'm not sure you have anything to tell me," I said shortly, but she tilted her head to one side.

"Are you certain?"

I started to say yes, but when I hesitated, she smiled.

"Come sit with me."

I might have said no, but Tara moved past me, making me jump. "Tara . . ."

"I can tell when I'm not welcome, and I'll save Miss Sauvignon the trouble of pretending I am," she said with a faint smile. "I'll just have myself a smoke around that corner, shall I?"

Emmaline's fire was built against the side of one of the sound stages. With the iron it contained, the structure was as good a touchstone as anyone was likely to get, and I nodded.

"Don't . . . don't stray, all right? It gets nasty around here on Friday."

"I'd believe it," Tara said with a nod at Emmaline. She disappeared around the corner, and Emmaline and I were alone.

I thought to demand she say what she wanted to say, but she took my hand, drawing me to sit down on the cushions by the candles. I balked when she wanted to draw her wispy shawl over my shoulders, and she sighed.

"I missed you so much," she said, her eyes searching my face by firelight.

"You knew where I was," I said shortly. "In the dorms, in the fires, on Rexford Avenue. You always knew. If you wanted me to find you, I would have found you."

"I missed you," she repeated. "That . . . doesn't mean it was good for us to come together like we were."

"You decided that, not me. I'm not going to have the same fight we had before."

"I don't want to fight at all. I want to be . . . well. Friends again."

I studied her, watching the silver fires flicker across her face, washing out the ruddiness and enhancing her romantic pallor.

"We were never friends, Emmaline," I said, realizing that that was true. We couldn't be. She was something I wanted for myself, and then she was something I wanted to consume me like a fire. In the end, I wanted Greta safe more than I wanted her, and that was enough to end us.

If Emmaline was shocked by my blunt words, she did not flinch.

"Does that mean we can't be friends now?"

"I . . . I don't know."

She could still make me feel like a tongue-tied girl from Hungarian Hill, and I couldn't blame her for liking it.

"Be my friend," she said, leaning her shoulder against mine. "I wasn't lying when I said I missed you."

"Are you going to be Tara's friend too, or are you going to scratch her eyes out?"

Emmaline wrinkled her nose in distaste, looking more like a displeased cat than she could have intended.

"She's bad news, sweetheart. You know that, don't you?"

I shrugged, enjoying her disapproval in some strange way.

"I'm bad news, and you still want to be friends with me."

"Not like she is!"

She said it loud enough that Tara must have heard, but Tara had probably heard worse in her time.

"Just like she is," I insisted. "Like Harry Long, Helen Martel . . ."

"Stop baiting me," Emmaline said sharply. "There's a difference between Helen Martel, and . . . Lester Moore."

"She's not any more Lester Moore than you are Emmaline Sauvignon," I snapped, but that was the difficulty, I saw right away.

"Of course I am," Emmaline said, almost shocked. "And you're Luli Wei. And she's . . . obvious. There's the trousers, and there are all sorts of rumors about her running around with communists and Jews and who knows what."

Emmaline suddenly looked very sad, and when she put her arm around me, I let her.

"The world lets you get away with some things. Oberlin Wolfe does too. But darling, she's too much, and you know it, don't you?"

Too much, too strange, and I knew right away that she had a truth between her teeth. Like I knew earlier that pretty was a painted target that Tara lacked, I knew this too.

Instead of it making me sink back into Emmaline's arms, however, I pulled away, standing up and shaking out my royal blue skirt.

"I was too much and too strange long before I came here, Emmaline." I said it gently because in her own way, she was looking out for me. She was trying to keep me safe, even if incidentally it kept me hers and not Tara's. "And after all, you decided I was too risky two years ago."

Emmaline sprang to her feet, hands clenched. I stepped back in surprise.

"Stop it! I'm not some kind of villain!"

"No, you're not. You're the heroine. I read the script same as you."

She took a deep breath, letting her face smooth out to its normal loveliness. It was a shame that the studio would never tolerate

Emmaline's face screwed up in rage or pain; it could take the heart right out of you. I was almost relieved when she put it away because her real face could still hurt me so.

"All right," she said. "So we can't be lovers, and we can't be friends. What should we be instead?"

"You'll be the heroine, of course. And I'll be the monster. And it'll be a hit."

She still looked hurt, but that wasn't my concern any longer. I thought about kissing her, and then I walked around the building to find Tara.

The Avalons she smoked were rich and harsh, but it hadn't stopped a cocky stray dog from wandering up in search of a meal. Her hat pushed back on her head, Tara scratched the dog behind the ears as he pressed ecstatically against her hand. She stood, wiping her hands on her trousers.

"So?" she asked.

"Let's get out of here," I said. "Come home with me instead."

She smiled at that, bright and gleaming as a star, and my heart quieted at the beauty of it.

"I'd like that a lot," she said, and I took her offered arm, limping back to the gate on sore feet and shredding stockings.

VII

My apartment on Rexford Avenue was furnished, and if it wasn't I would likely still be setting my tea on an apple crate and sleeping on a mattress that I bought without realizing I had to buy a frame as well. After I took her coat, Tara inspected the place like a cat, stepping lightly through the rooms, flicking the lights as if amused by their cleverness.

"This is all yours?" she asked, and I understood why.

She lived with three other girls in half as much space. My family had fit the four of us and a business into a building not much larger. The apartment, empty as it was, was a luxury even as it was a burden to fill up.

"It is. Do you like it?"

"I like you," she said, and after I latched the door, she took my hand and pulled me close.

We both had some experience with kissing. I tasted tobacco on her, strong enough that it competed with the taste of her mouth, but I sought until I found her, tracing my tongue along hers, her sharp eyeteeth, the inner sleekness of her lip. She sat down on the only chair in the room, and without asking, I came to straddle her lap, tipping her hat back so that it fell to the floor behind her. She laughed at me as I fumbled with her tie.

"I don't have much experience with clothes like this," I protested, and she undid it for me, unbuttoning her shirt as well. I pressed my face against her worn white undershirt, breathing in Avalon tobacco, her sweat and the trace of perfume she wore. Her hand came up to grasp the back of my head for a moment before pulling out the pins that held my hair. She wove her fingers through my hair, tugging a little until it fell dark and shining around my shoulders.

She didn't say that I was pretty. Instead, she looked up at me with something that was more awe than worship, and it had nothing at all to do with the fact that I might be painted thirty feet high on a screen in front of hundreds.

"What do you like?" she asked. I jumped because it was what I had said to Emmaline years ago. That echo didn't hurt, but instead it made me feel as light as a balloon floating over Hungarian Hill.

"I like you," I said honestly, and she grinned. It made her look younger; maybe that was why she didn't do it so often.

"Good," she said, approving, and she reached for the silver buttons that held my dress closed.

I let her undress me, only compulsively checking that the curtains were closed once or twice. After she pulled the dress and slip over my head, she ran her hands over the cups of my bra and the girdle below, which clipped firmly to the stockings that I had ruined on my run through the fires.

"I don't miss these. At all. But damned if you're not pretty in them."

I stood up from her and did the rather unflattering dance to squirm out of them and the plain drawers I wore underneath. I could have wished for a screen that I emerged from with a robe trimmed in marabou over my nudity, but I had no screen, no robe, and her eyes followed each inch of bared flesh so hard that I needn't have worried about any awkwardness.

"Now you . . ."

She undressed with the casual grace of a woman who was used

to little privacy, and without thinking, she laid her shirt and trousers over the arm of the chair. I couldn't wait until she was done, however, and when she bent to remove her drawers, I wrapped my arms around her, burying my face in her back.

"You smell gorgeous," I murmured, and she laughed.

"I smell like smoke and cigarettes," she said, "but whatever works for you, darling."

I led her back to the bedroom. It was dim and therefore lost at least some of the starkness of the living room. The bed was a crisp white field that I had never shared with anyone else, and Tara and I dragged each other down on it. There was a moment, our heads on my single pillow, where we watched each other, irresistible smiles on our lips. She tucked my hand under her face, and I kissed her calloused fingertips. Her hands themselves were fair and white, but the fingertips were hard, apt to catch soft fabric and snag.

We kissed again, hands moving shyly at first before becoming bolder. I found a space under the tip of her chin that made her gasp when I kissed it, and when she raked her nails lightly down my back, I sighed with need for her. I slid one leg over her to press my weight on her hips. To get purchase, I set my hands against her shoulders, pushing her down.

"Oh, so that's the way it is?" she said, but there was a blush that told me how much she liked it.

"I think it might be," I retorted, and I leaned down to bite her shoulder. Light nibbles at first, but encouraged by her moans, I bit harder. She was squirming underneath me as I bit her lips red, but she never pushed me away.

I could kiss her for a thousand years, I thought faintly. Her mouth on mine, after the initial shock of being that close to someone else, dazed me, and I pressed my weight against her for more of it.

I think perhaps our kissing did do something strange to the way time flowed in the space occupied by our two bodies. Underneath me, she was perfectly open and sweet, content to be kissed and ravished. It couldn't have lasted as long as I thought it did—long enough to build monuments that crumbled to marble ruins, long enough that the entire city of Los Angeles fell into the fault line and was rebuilt on its own corpse—but when I looked up, I felt oddly sphinx-like, other and strange.

"What is this doing to me?" I found myself asking her, and in the dimness of my bedroom, Tara's breath came slower and she smiled.

"What sex does," she replied. "It tells you something about yourself or the person you're doing it with. Sometimes it changes you."

Perhaps it should have bothered me. I had changed so much over the past few years, I should have balked at yet another one. Instead, I leaned down to kiss her, wild for it and ready in a way that I had not been ready for anything else.

Our bodies slid against each other. I could feel the grit that clung to us from walking in the fires, and I thought of snakes shedding their skin.

I slithered down her body, kissing my way between her small breasts and taking soft, flickering licks at her brown nipples. Absently, I pressed my face under her arm, breathing in her smell there as well before angling down over her hips and the slight hang of her belly. Her hair underneath was a wild thicket, lighter than the hair on her head, and when I nuzzled it, she laughed, reaching down to pet my head and my shoulders.

It was another way of losing myself. I was nothing but motion, friction and spit searching for the very center of her, and when I found it, I couldn't keep my mouth away from her. I lapped at her, learning her taste and her textures, how I could make her gasp with surprise and how with the right touch she stiffened up like a wire run through with electricity.

I was lost in her when she slid her fingers through my hair and tugged, hard enough to send a spike of pleasure through my center and make me look up.

"Come this way," she said, patting me and shoving me into position so that we were pressed against each other, me half on top of her and my legs spread for her eager fingers.

It was messy and awkward and sloppy; whatever magic we were making was different from what I had done with Emmaline in the light of the fires, but it was real as well.

She worked at me with her strong fingers even as her body rippled and convulsed beneath me. Her climax only paused her for a handful of breaths, and then with a growl, she was after me again, pushing me farther and faster out of my body.

I dug my fingernails into her firm thighs, not caring that I was leaving red crescents that darkened with blood right under her pale thin skin. I made a deep guttural noise as my back arched and my body released all that tension at once. It was as inevitable as falling, but I never landed. Instead I rolled over and floated in the pleasure of what we had done.

After a while, I was distantly aware of Tara turning around to rest close to me, our feet towards the head of the bed. I rolled her over on her back so that I could rest on her arm.

"Well that was . . ." Tara laughed, shaping her hands in the air like flying birds.

"It doesn't need words, Miss Writer," I said, resting my hand flat against her belly.

"Maybe not," she conceded.

VIII

I had spent my life up until that point doing reckless things, but I never considered myself a reckless person. What I would and wouldn't risk were always things that had set me apart, but now, as production rolled forward, I was standing on some narrow, windswept ledge; at any moment, I might realize that I could fly.

I was lucky I had to wear the tail. Otherwise I might have spent even more time sneaking off with Tara, to the storage warehouses where the flats were kept, behind the wardrobe girls' door, even once up on the catwalk while Jacko Dewalt fought things out with the crew below.

Things were going badly, and Jacko grew more and more irritated. He had inherited the crew from Whalen Mannheim, and it showed. When he pulled, they pushed, and even if they had wanted to obey, there was no common language between them. Time seemed to stretch on set as scenes were delayed, shot poorly or replaced completely.

Tara was delighted by my boldness, even if it shocked her sometimes.

"I never made it with a monster before," she said one day, keeping lookout while I rearranged the fishnet clotted with shells and rubber seaweed that had been draped so carefully before we had gotten to it. We had found twenty minutes in a crevice between large rolls of canvas. It wasn't a great deal of room, but it was enough for us.

"Good, isn't it?" I asked, giving her a kiss.

I had thought that we were done, but the kiss stretched until it became two kisses and then three. She planted her hands on the wall over my head to keep from disheveling my costume further, but I had no problem with twisting my hands in her jacket and pulling hard.

"Moore isn't back here, Jacko," Emmaline said calmly.

The words made us freeze. They had come from too close by, far too close, and Tara pushed away from me, her face panicked and guilty. Mine probably wasn't any better.

"I saw her talking with the lighting guys though," she continued. "Maybe try over there?"

The growl, unmistakably Jacko's, rose up like a gathering thunderstorm, but after a long minute when no one burst around the corner, we let out deep breaths of relief.

"Button your shirt all the way up," I whispered to Tara. "I bit you too hard."

While she hurried to tend to her clothes, I crept out of the canvas rolls to see Emmaline striding away. Olivia wore white until the final confrontation with the siren. She held her long skirts out of the dust of the studio floor, her white kid boots making a brisk tapping sound as she went.

"Emmaline, wait . . ."

She paused but instead of turning, she just kept walking. I cursed under my breath and picked up my pace. We hadn't talked since that Friday. I hadn't been back, didn't know whether I could find her fire there or not.

"Dammit, wait . . ."

Finally, close to the rear exit at the back of the sound stage, I hooked my hand around her elbow, pulling her back. She spun fast enough that I nearly stumbled, and she shook my hand off of her viciously.

"What?" she asked. "What the hell could you possibly want from me?"

"I wanted to say thank you," I said unsteadily, and her eyes narrowed.

"You can thank me by learning just a little discretion! Goddamnit, Luli, why can't you just take her home and do it with the blinds shut?"

"Because I don't want to," I said sullenly. "Because it's fun. What do you care, anyway?"

There was still a farm girl somewhere inside all that gleaming white cotton. She grabbed my fishnet and dragged me forward, so strong that I couldn't do anything but follow.

"Do you think I want to watch after you on set like you're a baby I can't leave alone? If I wanted a baby, I would have stayed in fucking Waverly."

I knocked her hand away and stepped back, glaring at her. "No one asked you to look after me like that. You made it clear at the fires that we were done, so let's be done, Emmaline. What were you even doing following me back there? What the hell did you want?"

Emmaline looked as if she wanted to take great handfuls of her hair or maybe mine and rip it out. She was red and blotchy and angry, furious like she only ever seemed to get with me.

She doesn't get like this with Cassidy Dutch, I thought, and that still pleased me a little.

"Be careful! Just that. We're all in this together, why don't you understand that? You, me, all the ones who came before us and will come after. We survive because we're not seen, and you . . . you go to the Pipeline. You go dancing with the girl from makeup, and you kiss the screenwriter who don't know enough not to wear pants!"

I narrowed my eyes, because I heard something in her voice that wasn't worried about safety. Oh, she was worried that I would bring the whole world down on us, but I knew that. There was something else there too.

"Are you jealous?"

Her eyes flashed, and if she could have struck me down in that moment, she might have done it.

"Of course I am," she said bitterly. "You go dancing, and I sit at home kissing Cassidy Dutch. What do you think?"

"But—"

She slapped her hand down over my mouth like I imagined her slapping the lid on a pot boiling over.

"I can't come with you. Maybe you're so foreign and strange that you can get away with it, but not me."

I saw it then, or rather I saw Emmaline Sauvignon. Emmaline Sauvignon was the woman all the little girls should want to be, the one all the boys should want to fuck. She got top billing, and she earned it by being their perfect, untouchable dream. I got to be the monster, and I earned it by being a monster: foreign, foreboding, and poisonous.

Emmaline took a deep breath, the red fading from her cheeks slowly.

"There's no amount of strange or foreign or valuable either that will cover up them finding you with your knickers down for Lester Moore," she said coldly. "You think it hasn't happened before? It has, and Helen Martel told me their names, because you can't even type them anymore, not in any place Oberlin Wolfe can reach. Every one that went took another two or three with them, and by God, Luli, I have worked too hard to suffer for your shipwreck."

In the silence between us, I heard someone on set shouting for some more sand to cover the concrete.

"I won't let that happen to you," I said, and Emmaline stepped closer to me.

"Why? Because you'll protect me?" she asked.

I could tell she meant to say it scornfully, but there was something deep inside her that was still soft for me too. She was a star, and for just a moment, I would have promised her the whole world just to make her shine a little brighter.

She was so close to me, and it awoke every memory of kissing her throat, of touching her skin and feeling our arms and legs twist together until there was nothing in the world that could tear us apart . . .

"Hey, what the hell is going on here?"

Jacko's voice was like a hammer bludgeoning the scene to pieces. Emmaline let go of me as if I had burned her. We didn't have the leisure of freezing. Jacko stomped in, an assistant and of course Tara on his heels.

Absently, I noticed that Tara looked as if she had scrubbed in cold water. She looked clean and patently virtuous, her collar buttoned all the way up in the heat. I avoided meeting her eyes because that was all we needed, and I turned to Jacko instead.

"It's nothing, there's nothing . . ." I started, and we might have gone on as we were except that Emmaline made a choked sound and ran.

I started to go after her, instinct or a derelict affection or both, but Jacko's large hand clamped around my wrist, nearly jerking me off my feet as he held me in place. Tara's protest was lost in my yelp, and I turned to look at him.

"No, stay," he growled. "You've done enough, from the looks of it."

He pushed me to one side like he would shove a prop hat rack out of his way, and he stalked after Emmaline. Tara looked between us for a moment, obviously torn, and I really couldn't think of anything worse than giving ourselves away if Emmaline didn't.

"I'm going to get some tea," I announced somewhat nonsensically, and with a nod to show she understood, she trotted after Jacko.

I did go to get some tea, perched on a tall rickety chair with my toes hooked through the legs. I felt oddly calm as I waited, and I watched the crew move around me like tides pulled by a dozen moons.

Jacko came looking for me, and with relief, I saw that Tara wasn't with him, but Harvey Rose was. A prickle of fear ran up my spine, quickly drowned in rage, and I gave them both a long and cold look. Jacko's face was red with irritation, but Harvey Rose was as calm as stagnant water. I had never been this close to him before, but I still couldn't see his eyes behind the green shades. It occurred to me that perhaps he didn't have anything behind them, and it shook me less than I would have thought.

"Care to tell me what the beef is between you and Emmaline Sauvignon?" Jacko asked. "She don't got a history of starting shit with her co-stars."

"Neither do I," I pointed out sullenly, and he looked as if he would have very much liked to slap me.

"What the hell did you do to her?"

I narrowed my eyes. I wasn't very good at faking indignation. All I had was the truth.

"It's personal," I said mulishly. "We're going to be fine on set."

He looked at me angrily, and I could tell that he wanted to see if he could force me to talk. The answer was of course he could. Harvey Rose could have taken me to the old women who haunted the edge of the studios, their fingers long and bone-white, especially shocking if they happened to be dark-skinned. If you were held still enough, they could reach their fingers into your brain and hook out whatever a director wanted to see. Of course they couldn't always put what they had stirred back to rights, and it wasn't a risk any good director took lightly.

Jacko looked like he was considering it for a long moment, and I tensed to fight. Instead he shook his head with disgust and stabbed his forefinger twice against the center of my forehead, so hard it rocked me back a step.

"I told you," he said. "I warned you, don't pretend I didn't. This is the last siren movie. Your contract is up in a month. Don't *fuck* with me."

He turned and stalked away, but Harvey Rose remained, watching me with those green-tinted shades.

"Mr. Wolfe has taken a personal interest in this picture, Miss Wei." Harvey Rose's voice was soft, and higher than you would expect. There was nothing in it besides a flat courtesy, but it made me flinch. "He has been watching you for some time, and so have I."

He dropped something lightly in my lap, and as he followed Jacko, I picked it up to see that it was a crumpled matchbook. I tugged it open to show the runny ink that spelled out *Pipeline* and I started to shake.

My cheeks burned with humiliation and rage, because both were better than fear, and suddenly I was a child again, too small to fight a world that could do whatever it wanted with me. I closed my eyes and swallowed until the feeling of nausea passed, and then I stalked to wardrobe.

"Get this shit off of me," I said, and Aguila blinked. There must have been something terrible in my eyes because she hesitated.

"The schedule says that we might get to your scenes tonight."

"Get it off me, or I'll take them off."

My voice spiraled high to the edge of hysteria, and bless her, she didn't pause. She and another girl that I didn't know worked fast, stripping me to the skin and laying out the fishnet so that it would be something better than a tangled mess when I came back to it. If I came back to it.

My head was a pile of hay and Jacko and Harvey Rose had thrown a match on it. I blazed so fiercely that no one questioned me as I made my way back to the parking lot. That, or perhaps they had heard about Jacko's blowup and they didn't want to be standing too close in case he needed someone more expendable to bear his anger.

I sat in the Bentley for several long moments. I could smell cold cream on my face, scraps of it on my clothes as well as the peculiar dusty smell of a sound stage and the scent of rubber that flavored everything when I was shooting the siren.

The fire in me faltered briefly. I experimented with the thought of going back and making Aguila haul my costume over my head again. Jacko would probably never know that I was gone, not when he was dealing with whatever Emmaline had to say, holed up in her star's dressing room. The moment the thought occurred, I thought I was going to throw up, and a hysterical laugh nearly escaped my lips. At least if I said that I was sick, it would be the truth.

I started the Bentley, and I could tell from its uncertain growl that it was becoming more restive. It didn't know where Harry was, and I couldn't explain that Harry was gone. He wasn't coming back for it.

"Put up with me for a while," I murmured. "I'll take care of you . . ."

"I might stay longer than that if you ask me nice," Tara said as she opened the door and slid into the passenger seat. I stared at her. My brain told me she was a cut-out from some other life placed in whatever life I was in now. I could only marvel at how little sense she made here.

"You can't be here," I started, and she shrugged.

"Of course I can. I left Jacko with a dozen script changes, all of the ones he wanted and a few that he hasn't come up with yet. He only needs me when he thinks of it, and if I'm not showing my mug around, it might be a while before he thinks of it."

She leveled a steady look at me.

"You, he's going to miss. What are you doing?"

"He can miss me all he likes," I retorted. "I'm not staying today."

"All right," she said, settling into the passenger seat and passing her hat to the back. "Where are we going, then?"

I almost told her to get out of the car. I didn't need her there, but I realized uneasily I did want her. Was that enough?

"To my place first. I need to call my mother. And then up to San Francisco."

In those days, it was easily seven hours between Los Angeles and San Francisco. If all went well for us, it might be ten by the time we got there, and even if we turned around immediately, the odds were against us driving all the way back before Jacko opened another day of shooting.

Of course I cared. For the first time, though, I didn't care enough.

IX

When I drove north to San Francisco in a dead man's car, the Pacific Coast Road was California's dream turned flesh, the way Illinois dreamed of Chicago. There was finally a way to race along the coast from Los Angeles to San Francisco, and I guided the Bentley up the ramp onto the hot ribbon of black.

I don't remember very much of the ride up. I drove fast as the sun set into the ocean on my left hand and the dark mountains rose up on my right. Tara counted the cars that kept pace with us at first, but as they dropped off in Santa Barbara and Santa Maria, she grew silent. She had hitched most of the way between Chicago and Los Angeles, and she told me about some of it now, getting picked up by a man who insisted she pray through most of Arkansas and the trucker who stopped in the deep desert to howl at the moon.

The sun set, and the sky turned towards indigo. We were out from under the hand of the studio. Their influence wore off sooner than I would have thought, and the glamour that sat like a fug of cigarette smoke over the city was blown away by the winds from the ocean. I took a breath of surprise.

Tara was content to let me drive, but she insisted on deciding when and where we stopped. We relieved ourselves in wooded copses by the road, and when we needed food, she stayed in the car, slouched down until I came back.

"I don't even know which bathrooms you should use," she said as we came on one small town just after sunset.

"Why, the white bathrooms, of course," I said, shocked it was even a question. "At least . . . I always have."

She nodded uncertainly, and it occurred to me that things would be very different outside of Los Angeles. I decided to evade the question altogether, and when we could, we simply kept driving.

Soon after it hit full dark, we could both see on either side of the road the ghosts of the prison gangs that had built the freeway, moving silently and carting gravel and buckets of tar. Their eyes burned through the darkness, and I checked the Bentley's gas gauge over and over again. We weren't the ones that had forced them to build the road, but I had a feeling that they wouldn't be too particular about their hunger if we were to stop so close to their uneasy rest.

"The ghosts of Chicago are a lot like this," Tara said softly. "They walk in flame, and if they put their hands on you, they won't let go."

The ghosts of Los Angeles were usually painted in silver, and I felt very lucky.

Once or twice, the Bentley wanted to pull off the road. The forests of Big Sur called to it, and I wondered what it would become if I let it loose there to wander in the live oak and the Douglas fir. The thought was not a comforting one, but the car was loyal to Harry. It pulled at my hand slightly when the forests were their thickest, but otherwise it drove smoothly.

I was exhausted by the time San Francisco rose up around us. The worn little towns appeared, and then they flowed together and grew higher until we were surrounded. That late at night, the Bentley could roll freely down the streets, but we were hardly alone. Next to me Tara stared out the window, eyes bright and sharp.

When she saw the Golden Gate Bridge next year, she would be lost and San Francisco would be her home. Even now, though, she could sense something about the place simply made sense to her in a way that Los Angeles never would.

We pulled over to puzzle at the map that my mother had handed to me. She admonished me to take good care of it, or at least to make a copy to bring back to her. She had never been out of Los Angeles, but having directions that would take her to her youngest daughter comforted her. As we sorted out the streets and made sure that the bay was on the right side, I ran my fingers along the velvet-soft creases that divided Grant Avenue and Stockton Street. My mother must have touched the paper often, wearing away the loose graphite from the lines. Did she have any token of me she touched the same way? Did she even need one when I was just on Rexford Avenue? I hadn't come to Hungarian Hill in more than two years.

We left the car on the street and walked down a narrow alley behind a row of dark theaters. There was a group of roughly dressed men and women enjoying the late night seated on a collection of milk crates and upturned buckets, and when we walked up, they looked at us, curious but not unfriendly.

This was where the map led, and I stepped forward into the only illumination, an orange lamp hung over the backstage door. I opened my mouth to ask for my sister, but I was interrupted by a low whistle.

"Holy shit, it's Luli Wei."

Suddenly I was surrounded by men and women who looked like me, something that hadn't happened in years. They wanted to know what I was doing in the city, what it took to get into costume as the siren, if I was really related to Su Tong Lin, if it was true that I was born in Guangzhou.

I'd never had an interview like that one, where every question was edged with a kind of hunger and possession. It fed me even as it frightened me, and I answered as best I could, smiling automatically and unable to focus on any one face. Tara had faded to the background, a skill that had always served her well. I was actually signing a scrap of paper (*With Love, Luli W*), when my sister finally appeared in front of me.

"Ma said you were coming to see me, not to conquer San Francisco's Chinatown," she said with a small smile, and the people around us fell back, murmuring in interest.

My sister sighed. She was dressed in a man's shirt, trousers and braces, a boy's cap cocked on her head. She was taller than me now, and her forearms, bare beneath her rolled-up shirtsleeves, were sleek with muscle. Despite her men's clothes, her hair was braided long and straight down her back. She would have been popular at the Pipeline.

"Okay," she said, and it took me a moment to realize that she was speaking to the avid crowd around her. "I'm heading out, and I'm taking the Star of All the East with me. She's my sister, we haven't spoken in years, and that's all you're getting, all right? Talk among yourselves."

A tall and handsome man with a narrow face dressed much as my sister was stepped up to her, whispering something in her ear.

"Well, you'll get the rest of it. Maybe. If you're good." As casually as she might brush back her hair, she reached up to plant a kiss on his lips, and then she turned to me.

"All right," she said, the smile falling off her face. "Let's go."

I fell into step beside her, slightly envious of her sturdy boots. I was just as fast on heels these days, and I kept pace with her while Tara trotted behind.

"Where are we going?" I asked, more pettishly than I wanted to, and she gave me an indifferent look.

"We're grabbing some food. I'm starving, and then I promised Hai I'd go watch his act at the Silver Moon."

"I came all this way—" I protested, but my sister only rolled her eyes.

"If you wanted me to roll out the red carpet, you should have given me some notice. I don't entertain many *movie stars*."

I bit back my first retort, which was that I wasn't asking to be entertained, but the truth was that I didn't know why I was in San Francisco except for the fact that I couldn't be in Los Angeles right then. My sister watched to see if I would argue, but when I didn't, she gave a short nod, as if satisfied.

"Wait a minute."

She ducked into a narrow restaurant that was still busy this time of night, and when she came out a minute later, she had something steaming wrapped in newsprint, already bleeding grease through the gray paper.

"You want some?" she asked nonchalantly, and held the packet out to us.

At first, tired as I was, I thought she had offered us worms, thick and red and laid out in bundles in her hand. A second look revealed not worms, but fried chicken feet. They were thickly drenched in sauce, the skin puffy and crisp from the oil. The nails hadn't been clipped, which made them seem cruel, and I frowned.

"Ma never let us eat this kind of stuff from the restaurants. She said it was dirty."

"Ma's not here," my sister said. It wasn't a fight, but it wasn't *not* a fight either.

"I'd like to try one," Tara said cautiously, and my sister turned to her in surprise, as if she'd forgotten her. Whatever point she was trying to make dissolved as she held the packet out to Tara, ready to be defiant and defensive.

"Watch out for the claws, they'll scratch you if you're not careful," I said, plucking out one of the feet for myself. It was sweet and spicy, more sauce than meat, and I stripped the fried skin with my teeth. It was good, very good, and as I reached for another, my sister watched me.

"You want to know it's me," I said softly. "It is."

My sister's face closed, and she expertly spat the tiny bones into her hand.

"Of course I know it's you. I can see your face at the Balboa every Sunday I have off."

"You've seen the siren movies?" I asked, oddly touched. It had never occurred to me she would.

"Everyone has," she said shortly. "Come on."

The Silver Moon had a beaten tin sign over the door, a crescent of cheap glinting metal that was the only indication that it was anything at all.

"Looks like a speakeasy," Tara commented, and my sister grinned, opening the door as if she belonged there.

"It was. They used to deal hash out of here too, and girls, sometimes."

The basement club was deep and narrow like so much of San Francisco seemed to be, and my sister waved to some people she knew but led us to a booth at the back.

"Middle of the week, no one cares who's here," she said, slouching against the vinyl as Tara and I squeezed in opposite. "As a matter of fact, shouldn't you be at work? I heard about the fire and stuff."

I was saved answering when the curtains over the tiny stage came up to reveal a thick-set young man with his hair slicked and shiny with water and dressed in what I could now tell immediately was a hand-me-down suit. He stood, I thought with remarkably little stage presence, seeming to gaze over our heads as the woman in the announcer's stand, dressed in a sheath of vibrant green silk, tapped the mic.

"Ladies and gentlemen, the Silver Moon welcomes back Hai Thuan Vu, the Ronald Wright of Chinatown!"

I had been to see Ronald Wright's show a few times in LA. He was a lean and sepulchral man with deep shadows under his eyes, and when he wasn't on stage, he mostly preferred to be called Andor.

"Well, Hungarians aren't in fashion," he said to me one night after a show, and if Hungarians weren't, then Vietnamese certainly weren't.

Still, as the music started, my sister's friend was composed, doing the kind of nothing that is surprisingly hard to do when people are watching you. There was a tiny skip in the record playing, something that buzzed in my ear with every revolution, but then Hai Thuan Vu opened his mouth and sang, and I did not care about anything else.

It was fair to call him Chinatown's Ronald Wright—like Andor, he had a rich and rolling voice with the kind of power behind it that could stop hearts. He filled up every corner of the room with the song, something French and soaring and joyful. It was like being drowned, and my mouth dropped open as I listened.

He sang and sang, and then on the high crescendo, he turned so that his side was to the audience and we could see his profile, his snub nose in line with his chin, the rise of his wise forehead and the cliff of dark hair oiled into place above.

As we watched, he reached into his mouth, still singing, his long fingers disappearing without stopping the torrent of melody. He was pulling something out, and when it came, it unfolded from his fingertips into a vast red shape, translucent and pulsing like my own pulse at my throat or—

"His heart," Tara whispered, as enthralled as I was. "Fuck, but it's his heart."

Hai Thuan Vu turned to face us again, throwing his hands open so that the shape of his heart, pure red light, hovered over his head, and then, as if his voice pierced it with its final rise, it was gone and so was his song.

He was only a sturdy Vietnamese man standing on the stage,

looking around diffidently at the scanty crowd. He had lost something, or dropped it, but it was gone. There was a scatter of clapping—I didn't, I was much too stunned—and he took a brief bow before walking off the stage.

"He needs to stop doing that," my sister sighed. "He loses the audience when he's not singing, and he shouldn't, not after something like that."

"It was his heart," Tara murmured, and she fumbled for her handkerchief, handing it to me so that I could wipe the tears from my face.

"How did he do that?" I demanded, and my sister raised her eyebrows.

"With skill and training and because, after all, it's his heart. Why shouldn't he?" She snorted. "There's lots just as good on the chop suey circuit. Not that you would know that, would you?"

I bridled at her caustic words, handing the damp handkerchief back to Tara.

"No, I wouldn't," I shot back. "We don't have anything like that back in Los Angeles."

"Wrong again. But if you want, I can hook you up with Hai, or maybe the Yang sisters, and Doreen Ng, and lots of others."

There was a kind of tension to her voice. She wasn't asking. She couldn't, and she wouldn't, but this was one bridge I could cross for us at least.

"Yes, I would like that," I said. "You can write them down for me, or you can send the list on later. But I would very much like to have it."

My sister looked at me a fraction too long, but she shrugged.

"Sure. Sounds good. Now I need to go make sure that Hai's not losing his dinner in back after a performance like that. Come on. You can meet him now if you want to."

We met Hai, who turned out to be as shy as any ingenue despite the power of his voice. I couldn't stop staring at him, but it turned out that when it came to actually talking, I was as shy as he was. My sister filled in the gaps for us, all but wrestling his card out of his pocket to give to me, and I nodded my thanks, hoping he knew how much I meant it when I said how skilled he was, how beautiful his heart was to see.

"You can relax, you know," my sister said, exasperated, as we left. "Dottie Wendt isn't here to expose the fact that you're Chinese to the world."

"I know," I said, scowling, but I realized that maybe I hadn't before that.

We made our way back to the car, Tara tactfully asking my sister more about the chop suey circuit and the performers who were making their way in it. They sounded like me, American born, most of them, eager to show the world how they could sing and dance and juggle, and I did my best to remember as many names as I could. My sister didn't want to be me, but I suspect that there were few who wouldn't have minded.

My sister cocked an eyebrow at the Bentley, but she climbed into the front seat next to me. She directed us to a sheltered spot behind her apartment building, and then she led us up the dirty stairs to the very top, where we traded our shoes for slippers like I hadn't done in years. There was a girl sleeping on the tattered couch, a thick book over her chest, but my sister ignored her as she took us to a bedroom at the back. The door shut behind us with a click, and my sister indicated the wing chair in the corner, just big enough for two, while she took the unmade bed.

She lit a cigarette without offering one to either of us, and she pierced me with a sharp glance.

"Well?"

"'Well?'" I echoed, and she laughed.

"You drove up the coast for a reason. What is it?"

I had put off thinking about this moment the entire ride up and throughout Hai's act. I had watched out for the chain gangs of ghosts by the side of the road, kept a wary eye for the highway patrol that would ask too many questions that Tara and I didn't want to answer, and the whole time, I had never put myself here in San Francisco itself, in my sister's small apartment as she watched me with unimpressed eyes.

"I wanted to say that I'm sorry," I began experimentally, but she cut me off with a sharp gesture, making the smoke from her cigarette rise in surprise.

"Would you do it again? If you knew then what you know now, would you have done it anyway?"

I didn't know the answer to that. Tara sat very still, and I was strangely and masochistically glad she had slipped into the car. This wasn't something I could tell her about, so instead, she would have to see it.

My silence stretched out, and my sister laughed softly, shaking her head.

"Then you're not sorry, are you? Did you just want to come say the words? What did you expect, sissy?"

The old nickname made us both flinch, and I could see her resolving not to use it again. It reminded us of a very brief period when she had looked to me for everything, translator and protector and custodian, and that time sat terribly on us now.

"I don't know what I expected," I said, folding my hands in front of me. The toe of my sister's embroidered slipper bounced as she waited. "This morning, I was on set, and someone made me angry because she said some very true things about me."

"And what were they?" my sister asked. Her tone was exaggerated patience, but she deserved it.

I hesitated. Tara tensed next to me, but I could tell she wouldn't stop me. That made me think for perhaps the first time that I loved her. The thought of love dazed me, so I pushed it aside, and took a deep breath.

"Among other things, she kept calling me Luli Wei," I said at last. "And that's not me. That's you."

My sister's denial was as swift as a rapier cut.

"No, sis, that's *you*. It's not me that's playing at the Plaza, that's Luli Wei. She was born in Shanghai, the daughter of a Chinese spy and a Hungarian nobleman, or she was a foundling on the doorsteps of a Beijing acting troop, or—"

"Stop it," I said sharply, the same tone I used when she was being a tiresome little girl. Now she only laughed, shaking her head.

"Sis, you became Luli Wei, and now you don't want it anymore? What, you want to take it all back, go live at the laundry again? Those dolls Ma made are mean. They used to pull my hair when I was trying to sleep, and they're probably worse now."

"You lived alone with them after I left," I realized, a sickening feeling in my stomach. I knew of course she had, but the weight of the laundry, those dolls, the loneliness, pulled me down for the first time. I had never been troubled by loneliness, but my sister, always.

Her face trembled like disturbed water. She hunched in on herself sullenly.

"You can leave if you want," she said ungraciously. "I forgive you for the name thing, whatever."

"It must have been so quiet," I said, and Tara stirred with a certain recognition as well. Children troubled by loneliness share a common space, some plain-walled room that is dark too long and too often.

"It was," my sister said, picking at a loose thread on her quilt. "Ma was never one for talking, but Dad talked with those fucking dolls. All the time."

She coughed, and I realized that no one else in all the world knew what the second floor of the laundry was like, knew the pattering of doll feet or the way the steam of the laundry made the walls breathe on particularly restless days. We had the same dull scars on our forearms from being careless with the heavy irons, the same memory of huddling under a patchwork quilt made from our maternal grandmother's old clothes.

"I'm sorry I left you alone," I said carefully. The words came out flat, nothing graceful or pained about them. I think that was the only reason she believed me.

"What are you going to do, stay in San Francisco? You want to move in with me and Yun, see if you can show some leg and tit over at the Forbidden Palace?"

For one brief and dizzying moment, I actually considered it. In San Francisco, my bonds to the studio felt less, like things that could be broken instead of immutable truths that must be obeyed. There was no Jacko Dewalt in San Francisco, and no Harvey Rose either, and they would both be waiting for me when I came back.

But there was no fire either, no silent burning stars, and even if it left me nodding around the back lots, I knew I had to go back, to finish the siren queen's story wherever it ended.

"No," I said. "But . . . maybe I could write? And you wouldn't need to answer unless you wanted. But I could write to you here."

She was perfectly still, the only sign of life on her the trickle of smoke from her spent cigarette.

"I might not write back right away," she said, not looking at me. "I'm bad at it, and there's no phone here either. We take calls at the restaurant downstairs."

"But I could have your address?" I pressed. "The building and apartment number, at least?"

Her friends at the theater must have called her something, but what that name was, she didn't tell me then. I didn't think she was a Mary anymore.

"You can," she said finally. "I don't mind."

It was barely more than a whisper of hope. The past rose up

around us, jagged stones that would bloody our feet if we took a
step wrong. The only way was forward, and I knew as she shrugged
and asked us if we wanted to go downstairs for some dumplings
that we had at least taken the first step.

◦✕✦◦

We did have to sleep eventually. My sister didn't have to go back
to work until the next evening, and by that point, Tara and I had
been up for more than twenty-four hours. Tara said that she would
do very well in the wing chair in the corner, her jacket rolled up
to pillow her head and her feet propped on a fruit crate, and my
sister and I curled up together on her thin mattress. It was new and
familiar all at once, but I was too exhausted to be troubled by it.
We fell asleep back to back, her breathing matched to mine, and
my mind filled with steam and lye.

I woke to my sister and Tara speaking companionably in the
living room, the roommate gone out to earn a living. For a bleary
fifteen minutes, I lay in bed and wondered at how alien the idea
of living with people already was. I listened as my sister described
designing scenery in stage shows and the murals she had painted
around Chinatown. In the bathroom down the hall, my reflection
had a greenish tint, as if everything was underwater. If I was going
to be in San Francisco, I thought sleepily, I would need to learn to
breathe all over again.

When we were dressed and had been fed again at the restaurant
downstairs, it was past noon. It wasn't enough sleep for any of us,
but Los Angeles wasn't getting any closer to the bay. I didn't tell
her that I would write, because she didn't need to believe anything
I said just then, but when I offered my hand for a shake, she pulled
me in for an awkward angular hug.

"Be careful on the road," she said. "Call Ma, and she'll call me
when you make it."

"All right. I will. Thank you for seeing us."

She ignored that, but nodded slightly.

"If you take Stockton Street south, you'll see one of my murals. Green and gold tigers. If you want."

Of course I did. The street was already crowded, and I had to drive carefully, but twenty minutes later, emblazoned on the side of a dry goods store, there were a trio of tigers chasing each other over a field of green leaves and gold flowers. I wanted to pull over and stand in front of the mural and to find my sister's name, signed somewhere hidden, but I kept driving.

"Your sister's nice," Tara said, somewhere on the road.

I considered. She was more than nice. She was clever and determined. I could see it in her tigers, in the life she had built so far away from everything either of us had ever known. I needed a silver screen to give me a dream, but she had painted her own out of nothing at all.

"She's forgiving. Good for me, I suppose."

Tara laughed.

"Yeah, forgiving's good. My folks forgave me for lighting out west pretty quickly. They want me to come back to Chicago sometime soon. Don't know what they're going to think of the suit and the hair."

"They'll think it's very handsome," I said loyally, and she squeezed my hand where it rested on the gearshift.

"Well, if the Star of All the East says so . . ."

"Oh, stop that!"

She only laughed when I punched her lightly on the arm, and when she spoke next, her voice was casual in the way that told me she cared very much.

"You could come tell them that if you wanted. It wouldn't just be dinner with my parents. I could take you dancing in the biggest gin joint you've ever seen. I could get you a real pickle."

"I've had pickles before."

"No, you haven't. Not a real one. Los Angeles doesn't have real pickles."

"I do like pickles," I said finally. Chicago with its sea that pretended to be a lake and its tall towers that didn't care how they looked on camera was as alien to me as the surface of Mars, but for the first time, I could see the appeal as well.

It wasn't until Tara had fallen asleep, snoring slightly with her hat pulled over her eyes and slumped against the door, that I realized she had offered me Chicago, some awkward future date with her parents at a Polish restaurant, dancing in a gin joint, and apparently pickles. I had taken Los Angeles for myself, and maybe someday, I would come to share San Francisco with my sister, but Chicago would be a gift from Tara.

I swallowed hard and wiped a few errant tears out of my eyes as I drove south, matching Tara's soft breathing to my own.

X

There was, of course, hell to pay.

I had missed a full day of shooting, and after all of the driving, I was as stiff as if I had slept strapped to a wooden board. I found someone who gave me both a painkiller and something that would give me at least a bit of energy before I went in to see Jacko. He was waiting for me in his office, and Harvey Rose stood by the door, silent and always watching. To talk to Jacko, I had to put my back to Harvey Rose, and his eyes measured me, seeing some esoteric list of numbers and values that suggested what might be done to me, what could be gotten away with, and what should be recommended.

Jacko slammed a stack of receipts down in front of me so quickly that I assumed he had had them banded together for the purpose.

"That's how much money your damn fool stunt cost us," he hissed, "and you better believe it when I tell you it's coming out of your pay."

"Fine," I said with a shrug, and he snorted.

"Fine, fine," he mimicked. "You think you're so goddamn irreplaceable? We could have walked over to a noodle joint on Ord Street to find another girl to put on the damn rubber tail."

"So why didn't you?" I asked. I could feel myself drifting, wanting to step back from everything, but I refused to let it happen. I wanted to be here for this, as ridiculous or unpleasant as it might be.

Jacko's jaw dropped and the toothpick clenched between his teeth wavered tremulously on his lip before he bit down on it again.

"What the hell did you say?" It almost sounded like a favor, as if he was letting me take back the words I had just uttered.

"Why didn't you?" I repeated obediently. "I've been nothing but trouble to you since the day we met, right? To Oberlin Wolfe too, especially after that Halloween. So . . . why not? There are a dozen girls prettier than me walking down Ord Street every day."

In the back of my head, Hezibah Wiley cackled with delight.

Jacko raised his hand, palm up, but then like Emmaline, he thought the better of it. Words like *reconstructive surgery, scandal,* and *more money lost* ran in front of his eyes, and he settled for slamming his hand down on the desk instead.

"Get to wardrobe," he snapped. "This isn't over."

I left, and as I did, Harvey Rose stepped forward, and I heard him say in his high, soft voice, "You must consider . . ." before the door closed.

There are dozens of ways that a director can make things hell for an actress, especially one who is strung up on wires and only able to reliably move the top half of her body. I made sure I was never alone with him. However, he was more afraid of Oberlin Wolfe than he was angry at me, and that helped. *Siren Queen* was meant to be one of the big moneymakers of the year, and Jacko couldn't go too far. He didn't force me to piss myself in the tail, he didn't work me until I fainted, and I decided that short of those things, I was just going to keep my head down. I would keep moving forward, even if Harvey Rose haunted the set, even if Jacko muttered about my contract being up soon.

"What are you going to do after this is all over?" Tara asked, sitting on the edge of my tub. No one had figured out that she had disappeared with me. Well, Emmaline did, but she had retreated inside herself, a pale and beautiful shell left to play her part so she could hide. If things were difficult for her or easy, I couldn't tell.

Like the siren itself, I had started to crave water when I wasn't shooting. I soaked in baths scented with Egyptian musk and rose oil, draining out the cool and replacing it with hot whenever it got the least bit uncomfortable.

"When this is all over . . . then I'll decide what I'm going to do next," I told her, sinking into the water.

In the final days of shooting *Siren Queen,* I felt as if my thoughts had turned to the fine white sand they used on the lot, running through my fingers whenever I tried to take a tight grasp on them. My dreams were haunted by the smell of Jacko's cigar, by the musty smell of the warehouses where nearly anything could be stored until it became useful and obedient again.

I went to see Mrs. Wiley, and she only watched me over her bouquet of pink roses, shaking her head.

"You want too many things, Miss Ambitious," she said. "You want the fame, and you want to be safe. You can't have both. You never can."

She wouldn't even take five years off the end of my life for more, and that told me how bad my trouble was.

Harvey Rose popped up at odd places, at the deli where I liked to get my sandwiches, lurking around the door after I had creamed the makeup off my face. Once he showed up in the parking lot of the Pipeline, just as I was arriving. He drove off with a cordial nod, and I was left with clenched fists and shaking in the moonlight.

Tara had suggested we go home, but I shook my head. We danced instead, because if I couldn't do that, then what the hell was all of this for?

"You should let me write down your life story," Tara said in the dark one night.

"Why would you do that?" I asked, amused. "Unless you want to tell all the world that the Star of All the East knows how to get blood and shit out of cotton."

"No, not for anyone to read. But . . . so this is something I learned from this pulp writer back in Chicago. He wrote out his life, and he hid it in a lock box that he dropped into the river. He said that after that, there were no ghosts that could haunt him, and no one who could take his life away."

I turned on the light, taking in the tightness around her eyes and the unhappy curve of her mouth.

"Which life would I be saving?" I asked. "I never wanted to be a Shanghai foundling with a Hungarian nobleman for a father, but I will be damned if I let them push me back into the laundry."

"That's the hell of it. You could be damned. You get that, don't you?"

I did.

The end of *Siren Queen* was coming. My contract was almost up.

Was I big enough to disappear and hold the whole damn thing hostage for some leverage? Was I desperate enough to go to the crossroads and pledge myself to something worse than Wolfe? Everest and Aegis lurked at the edges of my vision. My contract kept me from being able to open my mouth or my eyes in the presence of their agents, but after, if I moved fast enough, if I was sly enough, if I survived, they could protect me.

The days stretched out, and my sleep grew as thin as paper.

⁓⁓

"All right, and beg!"

That was Jacko, exacting a bit of revenge from a spot just beyond the camera's eye. If I turned my head just a little, I could see his blockish face set in something like amusement and satisfaction. Behind him as always was Harvey Rose, calm to Jacko's smug. It was disgusting how little it took to satisfy him, which should have comforted me, but instead it scraped me raw like ground glass.

"Please, by great Poseidon's mercy, please . . ." I clung to the fabricated rock as if it could grant me some protection. The vast length of my tail lay some yards away, and I couldn't look at the tarry stump that was left to me. It was a burning pain that was only shut out by my fear and panic as the descendant of the great killer of my kind advanced slowly towards me. Her face shone, too bright and beautiful to look at, and I shut my eyes tight.

"Please, let me go. Let me go, I swear, I will hide under a rock for a thousand years. I will eat seaweed and mud at the bottom of the ocean, and never lay eyes on a man again . . ."

Nemo's daughter wavered for a moment, something foreign on her face. It was a quality my kind lacked. Before I would have said that it was weakness, but now I knew that the weakness was inside myself, something ugly that brought me low to crawl on my belly like a serpent.

My numbing fingers lost their grasp on the rock behind me, and with a graceless slither, I sprawled on the ground. I tasted sand and blood between my lips when I licked them, and I dragged myself backwards.

"Please, please. I will go away. I will never return."

"Cut!"

He had waited until I was on the ground to call a halt to the scene. The half tail was less flexible than the full one, and there were no wires or hidden poles to maneuver it around me. It dragged behind me like the shorn appendage it was meant to be. My whole body ached, my shoulders and hands from hanging on to the rock, my lower back from trying to support it, and my abdominal muscles from rearing up in spite of it all.

I flopped to the ground, taking the tension off my upper body, but then I tensed to haul myself back up at least into a sitting position, watching Jacko's approaching stride with exhaustion. It was the twelfth take, when he was famous for one and done.

He stood over me, shaking his head.

"CK, come on, you're holding everything up, you sound like you got a stick up your ass. This girl is coming to kill you. She's going to wipe you out. The siren's terrified out of its mind. It's fucking crazy with terror. *You* sound like you're ordering something off a menu. Come on. Sell us on it."

"I think it looks good," said Tara from close by. I didn't have the energy to turn my head and look at her, but I heard the tension in her voice. It sounded like she was ready to fight, but it wasn't even a question as far as Jacko was concerned.

"Yeah, when I want your opinion, I'll ask for it," Jacko said, not even looking at her. "I'm talking to CK right now."

I could feel the crew watching us, the ones that weren't busying themselves with the set or the cameras. I didn't think that I was imagining their sympathy for me, but I knew that that wouldn't go very far either. They wanted to go home and rest, and right now, as Jacko was making quite plain, the fact that they couldn't was my fault.

"Fix it," Jacko said, revealed by only a small curl of satisfaction twitching at the corner of his mouth. "We'll be here all night if we have to."

He turned away to tend to something with the camera, and I nearly let myself flop face-first into the sand. Tara looked like she wanted to come closer, but I shook my head just a fraction at her, and unsmiling, she backed off. Instead it was Emmaline that came to me, sitting back on her heels so that we were nearly eye to eye.

"Want me to pitch a fit?"

I blinked.

"What?"

She smiled a little.

"I could, you know. Too cold, too hot, not enough salad on the craft services table, too much this, too little that. Jacko thinks I hate you, and it would get us all off set for at least a little while."

"You don't hate me?" I asked, and it came out smaller than I would have liked, almost meek. She looked surprised.

"I think you're a hard person to like, honey, but I don't hate you. Never could."

That little bit of a Minnesota drawl in her voice made me believe it, and she started to draw back. Before she could, I reached for her, laying a fingertip on her wrist. I was so filthy with grit and sticky fake blood that I didn't dare touch her more than that.

"Thank you."

She sighed.

"Can't help being yourself, can you?" Emmaline asked, almost unwillingly fond.

No, I couldn't.

She returned to her mark, and two crewmen came forward to hoist me up on the rock again. Soon enough, Jacko was back next to the camera, he shouted, and the girl with the clapboard set it all in motion again.

I drifted from myself, watching with interest as the siren clung to the rock and begged for her life. She was desperate, but it wasn't just her end she feared. It was the end of everything she was and of the people she had come from. They were already mostly gone when she was young, and this was their final death knell. The girl who had slain her watched with dispassion as she begged.

No, not dispassion.

Nemo's daughter held a light in her, pure and silvery, and it was not fueled on hate. It burned steadily in her heart, so strong that surely it would never go out, never be extinguished, and the siren could feel herself reach for that.

Beautiful but not pure, my mind whispered while I begged. Nothing we had done in the shadows of the Friday fires was pure.

It was better than that. It was true. It was everything I was and everything I could be—was meant to be—if only I dared. It twisted inside me, hungry and vicious and clever.

It was worth dying for, it was worth living for, and now Nemo's daughter was walking towards me as I writhed in the sand.

I pulled myself up painfully to rest with my back against the rock. I didn't look at my precious tail any longer, not because it was so terrible to look at but because Nemo's daughter filled my world. I thought of a boy on a stage far away who pulled out his heart for everyone to see, and then I could only see the shining woman in front of me.

She had a saint's sternness as she approached me. Of course I saw the sliver of steel in her hand, what predator would not? It didn't matter. My mouth opened slightly as if she was something good I could eat. She came to kneel in front of me, the blood and sand not marring an inch of her white silk dress.

"Good-bye, monster," she said, and one hand came up to cup the side of my face. It felt so familiar, as if she had done that same motion before in some other life, but of course she hadn't. No one had ever touched me like that before.

She leaned in. In that moment, it wasn't fear or dread that I felt. Instead it was awe, and I gave myself to her entirely. My arms came up, and I pulled her to me, and her mouth came over mine as if this was what we had been destined to do from the first, not bleed, not war, but kiss.

Her mouth was warm and growing warmer. It fed me, burned me with her brilliance and made me live again. She was giving me something instead of taking it away, and underneath all of it was her desire, her need, her fear and her pride rising to meet their match in me.

My heartbeat filled my ears as we both pulled back, but the air went up in cold fire. I could see shadows around us, rocks, cameras, people shouting with fear and confusion, the clatter of steel on concrete, and then it was too brilliant to see anything at all. The din beyond the light fell away to an incessant ringing, or perhaps, a distant tolling that did not cease.

I couldn't feel Emmaline any longer, but in some other distant and primal way, I was aware of her. I could feel how the blood coursed through her veins, the way steel pins pulled at her hair, how the silk sat on her skin and was grateful for her warmth.

"Emmaline," I whispered, or at least, I thought I did.

Well, you've done it now.

I wasn't sure if I had imagined those words or if she had actually spoken them. I was fully in my body, fully in my own mind, it felt, for the first time in my life, and the reality of it pierced me with sharp delight and power. I was bursting from my own skin. At any moment, I might spin out into the sky and be lost.

The glow faded, and my body was cold because for a few moments, it had been lit up with fireworks. I slumped back against the rock, Emmaline sat back on her heels, and we looked around at a changed world.

The ground around us was scorched black, a few of the rocks close by reduced to singed scaffolding. The cameras stood, glass and steel bastions, and so did the men behind them, because they were trained for this very eventuality, prayed for it, as a matter of fact. Still, I could see some of them reaching for the iron icons sewn into their hidden pockets, and a deep thrill coursed through me.

Tara was on her knees, hands pressed to her mouth. She would lose the awe sooner than you might think, but for now, her eyes shone with the love of the acolyte, a talent for worship that I had as well. *I do love her,* I thought absently.

Jacko sat flat on the concrete, his legs straight out in front of him. His face was closed, but unwilling tears dribbled from his eyes as his hands opened and closed. I realized belatedly that he was as much a worshiper as I was, as Tara was, as Harry or Emmaline were. None of us would be here if we weren't.

All eyes were on me. Emmaline was a monster they knew, and in a way, so was I, but today, I was something they had never seen before. A monster, a miracle.

A star.

I stood up, my tail burned away to scraps of rubber that still sizzled on the ground. I was still hung with seaweed drag, but I didn't even mind that. Under Emmaline's careful and faintly amused eye, I took a few steps, shaky as a newborn lamb. A phosphor glow was fading from my skin, and I held my hands up to watch it go. When it was gone, and I was just flesh again, I started to laugh.

XI

There were a few more scenes to film, but they didn't need me, and the moment I was cool enough to touch again, Harvey Rose appeared and told me I had an appointment with Oberlin Wolfe.

"I'm going to get dressed first," I said, and I knew how much had changed because he only nodded and stood back to wait.

I dressed hurriedly, and when Tara came to find me in my dressing room, I pulled her into a hard kiss. She hissed because I must have tasted of acetate and heat, but she clung to me.

"What happens now?" she asked, and I smiled at her.

"Now I go and talk with Oberlin Wolfe," I said. After a moment of hesitation, I passed her my keys. "Wait for me at home."

"How long?"

"Until I come back."

She grinned at that.

"All right."

I was mostly human, mostly just tired, when Harvey Rose escorted me up to Oberlin Wolfe's office, going right by Janet, who stared at me with a kind of empty loathing and open envy.

Wolfe sat at his desk, and he watched me with eyes filled with the opposite of worship. He looked like an animal who could see a meal but knew it had been laced with poison.

"So it's true. You rose."

"I did. And my contract is up in a month."

I could feel the edge of it even now. Wolfe and I had agreed on three years, and they were almost up. Over at Everest, they had been haunting Ord Street for their own flower of the East, while Aegis had gone farther afield, only to be tricked by fox girls in Beijing and swindled by snake girls in Guangzhou. If I walked in like I was, glowing and with the siren queen's smile on my face, they'd give me whatever I wanted.

Oberlin Wolfe held my gaze, and then he looked away. He had been planning to scrape me out. I might have spent the rest of my life nodding away in some forgotten corner studio, trotted out to give a scene a bit of exoticism and Oriental wonder. Now he couldn't touch me, and I drifted closer until it was only the desk that separated us. There was some narrow animal part of him that was frightened by me, by the light that still clung to my body.

"What do you want?" he asked, his voice dry and papery.

Everything, I could have said, but I only smiled.

"Let's start with what you're never, ever going to do to me."

No maids, no accents, no sham marriage, no more attempts to replace me with imitations, and then I paused.

Su Tong Lin had never gotten to ride off in the sunset with a handsome hero, and now that I had the chance, I wasn't sure I wanted to.

"Monsters, however, are just fine," I said finally. "I'd like to see more monsters."

EPILOGUE

So you've probably seen *Siren Queen*, or at least the last two minutes of it. Somehow, the cameras caught it all, my wonder, my fear and awe, and then of course, the kiss that obliterated everything else. We could have burned straight through the film, but instead it caught us.

There was another minute of Emmaline and the hero talking seriously about monsters, and how in the end they will always be defeated, but no one remembers it. What they remember is the kiss, wild and gorgeous and the very first of its kind made everlasting in silver.

A few months later, I met Emmaline on a Friday night, all alone at her fire and ready for me to find her as I had so many times before. I sat in her chair with her, and my body remembered all the curves of hers. I also remembered the flash of her white feet in the November mud, leaving me and shutting me out, so eventually I rose, and went to tend my own fire.

My own fire. I had thought before that I understood what it meant to have a fire of my own, but I didn't, not until I looked around the flickering silver glow and saw faces like mine. There weren't many at first, just Paley Hong, who came six months after I earned my star, and Carmen Hensen, who held hands so tightly with Lauren Main that it must have hurt. I made sure that the ones who needed to find us did. When necessary, Tara dropped a message into the hand of that girl or boy, telling them to come, it was as safe as it could be, as safe as I could make it, and they would be welcome. Later, Jane came as well, and though we never sat in the same chair, she watched me from across the flames, her eyes alive with something that could never be caged.

Tara came sometimes, too, but she never cared for the fires. I thought for a while that we could live like that, split with my heart in the flames and hers on the page, but we couldn't. There were five years where we were good to each other, a year where we weren't, and then she moved to San Francisco to join the dreamers in the fog.

After I became a star, I worked with Scottie Mannheim, and after the war, after she walked out of Manzanar with a fire that wouldn't be quelled in her heart, with Jane Takamura. I don't know what deal Jane struck with Oberlin Wolfe, but it won her seven pictures with her pick of the stars, and I was in four of them.

I met Jane one morning when I was sipping tea at the commissary. She came up to me with a bright grin and a half dozen scripts in her arms, and sat down all uninvited.

"So I hear you're the famous monster of Wolfe Studios," she said, and suddenly, all I could think about was kissing the single dimple on her chin.

Jane didn't make me a monster. I was a grieving young widow in *The Rubies,* and in *One Parisian Night,* we worked on getting my Cantonese back so I could play the spy. Her movies are more famous because of her name than mine, but it was a fame I didn't mind sharing, not with her. Stars dim and flare. After almost thirty years of quiet obscurity, where I mostly slept and watched the diamond cities with a calm and agate eye, *Siren Queen* played to a whole new generation, and the girls went wild over me. They dug up Tara's *Starlight Requiem,* where she's less kind to me than she could be, and *The Demons of Big Sur,* where she does a little better. They talked in intrigued whispers about how close Greta and I were, and it pleased me that decades after Oberlin Wolfe died in that mysterious fire, they called her Greta. They realized that I must be the L that Jane talks about in her autobiography, her star, her darling, her grief, and sometimes her wife.

These digital days, when a single kiss can be played over and over again, I may do as I like. Many of my compatriots do not descend, finding earth too strange, their beauty rendered odd and dim by better cameras, more damning eyes and the noise of over-loaded freeways. Emmaline will not come down at all, content to sit in silent splendor. She says less every year, but her smile is a thing of celestial charm, enduring even as the rest drifts away. Our names are linked together in books now, though they never get it quite right. They make one or the other of us the villain or the se-ductress, they talk about who she loved and who I loved as if there were words big enough and grand enough for it. She said she didn't mind, and we let them believe some wonderful stories about us. For myself, I have never been more comfortable on earth or more tempted by the fun of it. My best dresses are fashionable again for those who don't care about fashion, and my favorite thing to do is to walk the sidewalks along the movie theaters before buying my ticket on a silver-plated black credit card and going in to see the show.

Last night, as I waited for a showing of something ghastly, grim, and elegant, I saw two women on the corner. They were chattering happily about something, arms around each other's waists. One was thin and elfin, the other sturdy and with thick hands adorned by beautiful gold rings. They hugged each other as if there was too much light and love in their own bodies, and they could only survive by passing that light between them.

They laughed, the sturdy one whispering something into her companion's ear to make her throw up her hands in mock dismay.

"Well, shall we?" the smaller woman asked, and her partner nodded.

They walked arm in arm to the ticket window, where a woman with eyes lit up with neon and her hair in intricate knots sold them two tickets and then sold me mine.

"Have a good show," she said with a wide smile, and I told her I would.

ACKNOWLEDGMENTS

I started *Siren Queen* in the summer of 2017. Though it's not my first novel published, it's the first novel I ever wrote and completed. There's something incredible and more than a little unlikely about it turning into a real book that I can hold in my hands today.

The first finished version of *Siren Queen* was completed in November of 2017, but that's not the version you've got now. First it had to recover from being three novellas in a trench coat, and then I had to learn about things like stakes and consequences.

This novel as it is, better, bolder, brighter, and more ambitious than what I came up with in 2017, would not exist without the passion and patience of Ruoxi Chen, my editor at Tordotcom, and Diana Fox, my agent. Thank you both, so very much.

Thank you as well to the Tordotcom team who have championed this work since the beginning, including Irene Gallo, Sanaa Ali-Virani, Lauren Anesta, Alexis Saarela, Anna Merz, Isa Caban, Eileen Lawrence, Michael Dudding, Angie Rao, Amanda Melfi, Lauren Hougen, Christina MacDonald, Christine Foltzer, Juliana Lee, and Jess Kiley.

Thank you to Cris Chingwa, Victoria Coy, Leah Kolman, Amy Lepke, and Meredy Shipp—you guys know what you did.

As for Shane Hochstetler, Carolyn Mulroney, and Grace Palmer,

I actually never know what you guys are going to do, but thank you so much for doing it!

Life's only getting weirder from here, so let's have some fun, okay?

PUBLISHER CREDITS

EDITORIAL
Ruoxi Chen, Editor
Sanaa Ali-Virani
Irene Gallo
Devi Pillai

MARKETING & PUBLICITY
Alexis Saarela, Lead Publicist
Michael Dudding, Lead Marketer
Megan Barnard
Isa Caban
Alex Cameron
Ariana Carpentieri
Samantha Friedlander
Eileen Lawrence
Khadija Lokhandwala
Anneliese Merz
Angie Rao
Sarah Reidy
Lucille Rettino
Amy Sefton
Stephanie Sirabian
Yvonne Ye
Rebecca Yeager

ART
Christine Foltzer, Art Director
Julianna Lee, Jacket Designer
Jess Kiley

PRODUCTION
Steven Bucsok, Production Manager
Lauren Hougen, Production Editor & Managing Editor
Heather Saunders, Designer
Christina MacDonald, Copyeditor
Jaime Herbeck, Proofreader
Jeremy Pink, Cold Reader

AUDIO
Natalie Naudus, Audiobook Reader
Claire Beyette
Amber Cortes
Steve Wagner

ACCOUNTING
Louise Chen
Nellie Rodriguez

CONTRACTS
Melissa Golding

DIGITAL PRODUCTION
Caitlin Buckley
Ashley Burdin
Chris Gonzalez
Maya Kaczor
Victoria Wallis

OPERATIONS
Constance Cochran
Michelle Foytek
Rebecca Naimon
Edwin Rivera

And a huge thank you to the entire Macmillan sales team, the buyers, and the booksellers who have supported this book.